RECEIVED

NO LONGER PROPERTY OF
SEATTLE PUBLIC LIBRARY

What Ales The
EARL

NO LONGER PROPERTY OF
SEATTLE PUBLIC LIBRARY

Also by Sally MacKenzie

What Ales The
EARL

SALLY
MacKENZIE

ZEBRA BOOKS
KENSINGTON PUBLISHING CORP.
http://www.kensingtonbooks.com

ZEBRA BOOKS are published by

Kensington Publishing Corp.
119 West 40th Street
New York, NY 10018

Copyright © 2018 by Sally MacKenzie

All rights reserved. No part of this book may be reproduced in any form or by any means without the prior written consent of the Publisher, excepting brief quotes used in reviews.

To the extent that the image or images on the cover of this book depict a person or persons, such person or persons are merely models, and are not intended to portray any character or characters featured in the book.

If you purchased this book without a cover you should be aware that this book is stolen property. It was reported as "unsold and destroyed" to the Publisher and neither the Author nor the Publisher has received any payment for this "stripped book."

All Kensington titles, imprints, and distributed lines are available at special quantity discounts for bulk purchases for sales promotion, premiums, fund-raising, educational, or institutional use.

Special book excerpts or customized printings can also be created to fit specific needs. For details, write or phone the office of the Kensington Sales Manager: Attn.: Sales Department. Kensington Publishing Corp., 119 West 40th Street, New York, NY 10018. Phone: 1-800-221-2647.

Zebra and the Z logo Reg. U.S. Pat. & TM Off.

First Printing: August 2018
ISBN-13: 978-1-4201-4671-4
ISBN-10: 1-4201-4671-8

eISBN-13: 978-1-4201-4674-5
eISBN-10: 1-4201-4674-2

10 9 8 7 6 5 4 3 2 1

Printed in the United States of America

For friend and fellow Regency writer Caroline Linden,
thanks for listening to my plot over dinner
at RWA in Orlando and suggesting the character
that became Lady Susan.

For Harker—Welcome!

And, as always, for Kevin, who keeps telling me
to just write the damn book.

Chapter One

A Friday evening in August, Duke of Grainger's estate

She's very beautiful.

Harry Graham, Earl of Darrow, stood in the Duke of Grainger's music room and listened to Lady Susan Palmer, the Earl of Langley's daughter, talk about . . . something. Ah. A dress she'd seen at someone's ball—Lady Norton's?— during the Season.

She had a very English sort of beauty that he'd missed in his years on the Continent. Porcelain skin. Blond hair. Blue eyes.

Dark blue, not the light, clear blue of Pen's . . .

"And then I asked Lady Sackley for the name of her mantua-maker though I already knew the answer. I was just trying to make conversation. And she said . . ."

How *was* Pen? She must be married and a mother several times over by now.

He'd hoped to see her when he'd come home to England— just as old friends, of course—but he'd discovered she'd left Darrow not long after he had.

He hadn't asked any more questions. It might have looked odd for the new earl to be inquiring about a tenant farmer's daughter. Someone might remember how much time they'd spent together that summer before he'd left to fight Napoleon.

Not that there'd been anything particularly scandalous about their affair. His brother, Walter, had certainly sown his share of wild oats among the local maidens, many of which had taken root. He'd had so many bastards, people had given them a name—"Walter's whelps." It was easy to pick them out—they all had the distinctive Graham streak, a blaze of gray hair among otherwise dark locks.

He frowned. He didn't like to compare himself to Walter on any front, but particularly this one. He wasn't a monk, but he hoped he treated his paramours with more respect than Walter had. At the very least, he was careful not to gift them with a child.

Walter hadn't been the only one frequenting the maidens'— and matrons'—beds. Felix, the blacksmith's son, had given him stiff—ha!—competition. It had been so bad that far too often, no one, including the mother, knew which man was a new baby's father until the Graham streak showed up, if it did.

It had been better for all concerned when Felix was the father. Then, if there was a husband involved, the man might never realize he'd been cuckolded. Harry still remembered all too vividly the time one of the tenants had come, pitchfork in hand, to find his older brother. Usually, the Graham streak appeared by the time a child was two or three years old, but this man's firstborn son's hair hadn't shown its silver blaze until his tenth birthday.

"Exactly! I'm so glad you agree with me, Lord Darrow."

His attention snapped back to Lady Susan. Good Lord, he had no idea what she'd been rattling on about. He was losing his touch. He'd never been so unaware of his surroundings when he'd been working for the Crown.

He had to keep his mind focused on matters at hand. He'd

promised Mama he'd propose to the woman, after all. He was planning to pop the question tonight.

Lady Susan laughed. "To tell you the truth, I was amazed Madame Merchant—"

"Marchand," he said, correcting her and giving the name its French pronunciation. Apparently, she was still droning on about dresses.

If I take her into the shrubbery, at least she'll stop talking.

Though, on second thought, he wouldn't bet on that. Even if he attempted a kiss, he'd likely not slow her verbal torrent. "Madame Marchand. She has her shop just off Bond Street."

"Oh, yes. I suppose you are correct." Lady Susan sniffed. "As I was saying . . ."

He kept one ear on Lady Susan's monologue while his thoughts drifted off again, this time to the French dressmaker. He'd visited Bernandine a few times when he was in London. He liked to practice his French—and other skills— with her. But once he married . . .

There was no need for any of his habits to change when he married, especially not if his wife was Lady Susan. She'd likely thank him to take his male lust somewhere beside their marital bed.

And he *was* going to marry Lady Susan—if she would let him edge a word in. He'd never met a woman who could talk so fluently about nothing.

Do I really want to wed such a jabberer?

No, he didn't, but he didn't have much of an alternative. She was the best of a bad lot.

His mother had laid the matter out quite clearly the moment he'd set a foot back in Darrow Hall after almost ten years abroad. He had to marry and get an heir as soon as possible.

He'd been in Paris when he'd got word that Walter had broken his neck going over a jump. Zeus, he'd never forget how he'd felt when he'd read that letter. It had been as if someone had administered a flush hit to his breadbasket and followed it by dumping a load of bricks on his head.

I never expected to be earl. I never wanted *to be.*

He'd liked the life he'd built for himself. He'd spent the last decade in Portugal, Spain, France, Austria, living by his wits, dealing in ideas, in stratagems and politics, *not* in crops and drainage ditches and leaky roofs.

But he *was* the earl now and with that came the duty to continue the succession. And Walter's death had proved all too conclusively that no one was guaranteed another day on this earth.

Which Mama had pointed out most emphatically. He needed an heir, she'd said bluntly. There was no time to delay. Walter had been only thirty-five, and here he was, dead. And, as Walter had also illustrated all too well, Harry couldn't be assured of having a son on his first attempt. Or his second. Or third. His sister-in-law, Letitia, had produced a baby a year: Adrianna, Bianca, Cassandra. Likely she and Walter would have carried on through the alphabet until they'd got a boy if she'd been able, but she'd lost the last three pregnancies and then, if rumor was to be believed, had refused to let Walter back into her bed.

So, Mama had handed Harry a list she'd made of eligible women, young females with the proper pedigree *and* several brothers. All he needed to do was choose one, marry, and get down to swiving his brains out.

Well, Mama hadn't said that last part, at least not in so many words. But her message had been painfully clear: the sooner he got an heir and a spare, the better.

She'd wanted him to make his selection on the spot, picking a name off the list, but he'd insisted on meeting the women first. They'd all still been in the schoolroom when he'd left England. So, they'd compromised. Mama had agreed to let him take a Season to shop the Marriage Mart without constantly badgering him. And he'd agreed to make his choice once the Season was over.

The Season had ended in June. He hadn't encountered a single woman who made his heart—or even his baser organ—long for a closer relationship, but he'd given his word. He had to choose one.

Lady Susan would do as well as any other. Better, perhaps. At least she was in her early twenties, older than most of the others on the list. Mama would have preferred he choose a debutante—she'd argued that he'd get more breeding years from a girl in her late teens—but he couldn't stomach the thought of taking what to him felt like a child to bed. And since, as far as he could discern, Lady Susan harbored no tender feelings for him, she wouldn't be offended by his inability to feel any affection for her.

He only hoped he didn't go deaf from her constant chatter.

At least she was pleasant to look at. And Darrow Hall was a big place. It wouldn't be hard to avoid her there, and when he was in London, he'd spend all his time at his clubs. Except for the obligatory swiving. With luck, he'd get her with child on their wedding night, and their first two children would be male.

Lady Susan's fashion commentary showed no sign of abating, but time was marching on. He could feel his mother's and his sister-in-law's eyes boring a hole in his back. It was the last day of the house party. He was supposed to invite the woman for a stroll in the vegetation where he would perhaps steal a kiss and discover if she was agreeable to him asking her father for her hand in marriage.

Of course, she was agreeable. She wouldn't be at this infernal party if she wasn't. Her father was likely sitting in a room somewhere, waiting for him to make his appearance.

His stomach twisted, and he took a settling swallow of brandy. He'd faced worse assignments during the war. At least he wouldn't die from their trip to the garden—unless he drowned in her never-ending stream of words.

The sooner he married and got a son, the sooner he could reclaim his life. He wasn't looking for a love match, after all. Hell, he wouldn't know love if it bit him on the arse.

What I'd had with Pen had felt very much like love. . . .

Ha. He'd been eighteen. What had he known of love? Nothing. His feelings had been lust, pure—very pure—and simple.

This union with Lady Susan would be a typical marriage of convenience. A business arrangement: a title, prestige, and wealth in exchange for a son or two. It was a very common sort of thing among the *ton*. Once his wife—once Lady Susan—completed her side of the bargain, she'd be free to go her own way as long as she took sensible precautions.

He just hoped he'd be more efficient than Walter at getting an heir.

He stiffened his spine, metaphorically speaking. There was no point in delaying the inevitable. He opened his mouth to utter the words that would seal his fate—

And then a bolt of lightning lit the room, followed by a great crack of thunder and a torrential downpour.

God had saved him. There would be no stroll in the garden tonight.

The Lord had even managed to stop Lady Susan's chatter. Briefly.

"My, that was a surprise. I don't like storms. Why, last summer I was caught in a terrible one."

Was he now doomed to listen to an accounting of every raindrop that had ever hit Lady Susan's lovely head?

No. The Duke of Grainger came over to finish what the Almighty had begun.

"Good evening, Lady Susan," the duke said into the silence he'd created by his appearance. "I hope you don't mind me stealing Darrow away, but I'm afraid it's getting late and I have an urgent matter I must take up with him in private."

Harry glanced around, surprised to see that almost everyone else—except his mother and sister-in-law and old Lord Pembleton, sipping his sherry in a corner by the potted palm—had left.

"Oh?" Lady Susan looked uncertainly at Harry. "But I thought . . . That is, I expected . . ." She frowned. "Lord Darrow, I was given to understand we had something of particular interest to discuss."

Then why did you drone on about dresses?

Harry opened his mouth, not entirely certain what words would come out, but Grainger clapped him on the back and spoke before he could.

"Well, there's always the morning, isn't there? I'm sure it will keep. Unfortunately, my issue will not. Please excuse us."

And with that he hauled Harry away.

Harry had never been one to allow himself to be led anywhere, but he also wasn't an idiot. He could see salvation when it was dangled before him. He went meekly—and quickly—along until they were in Grainger's study with the door firmly closed.

"Zounds!" Harry collapsed into one of the leather chairs by the hearth.

Grainger laughed and went over to a cut-glass decanter. "Can I offer you some more brandy?" He grinned. "It's even better than what you have there."

Harry tossed off the last drops in his glass and then held it out for Grainger to refill. "I should have finished my conversation with Lady Susan, you know."

Grainger chuckled as he took the chair across from Harry and put the decanter on the table between them. "Good luck at finishing any conversation with that woman." He cocked a brow. "You weren't about to suggest what I think you were, were you?"

"If you mean was I going to offer for her, yes, I was."

Grainger shook his head, a mixture of disgust and sympathy on his face. "Offer for that magpie? You'd be deaf before the ceremony was over." He snorted. "I wager you'd have to gag the woman so you could say your vows."

Possibly. "She's very beautiful."

"Then commission a painting of her and hang it in your study. Paintings don't talk."

If only that would solve the problem. "I promised my mother I would find a wife this Season."

Grainger's nose wrinkled in distaste. "And you picked Lady Susan?"

Harry shrugged a shoulder as he took another swallow of brandy and stared into the fire. "I wasn't going to marry a child just out of the schoolroom. Lady Susan will do."

"For what? To drive you mad? She'll manage that in short order, I assure you." Grainger pulled a face. "I've had the misfortune to be seated next to her at more than one meal. The lips move and words come out. They even make sense most of the time, but they are so soul-sucking boring, you want to pick up your knife and stab her to make her stop— or slit your own throat to end your misery." He shook his head. "*And* she doesn't listen. Ever. I wouldn't wish her on my worst enemy."

Grainger leaned forward and waggled his index finger at Harry. "Marry her and I'll never invite you here again. I value my sanity too much. Good God, man, I swear I lose a little more intelligence with every word she utters."

Grainger was making rather too much of the matter.

"So then why did you invite her to this house party?" Granted, this had not been the usual *ton* country gathering. The guests were older—none of the just-out-of-the-schoolroom girls here. A few were widows with young children in tow, which would make sense if Grainger was considering remarriage. Grainger's wife had died several years ago, just days after their son was born.

"I was afraid I could see the way the wind was blowing with you. I don't *want* to have to cut your acquaintance. I was hoping extended exposure to her would bring you to your senses." He grinned and said hopefully, "And has it?"

Harry's senses had never been at issue. "You seem to be missing the point here, Grainger. I need an heir. Ergo, I need a wife."

"But perhaps not this particular wife." Grainger poured them both more brandy. "What's the rush? You're not even thirty yet."

"True, but my brother's sudden death—Walter was only thirty-five, you know—has made me—" Might as well lay it all out on the table. "Well, mostly my mother and sister-in-law acutely aware of the uncertainty of life. I could overturn my carriage leaving here and break my neck."

"Which might be preferable to marrying Lady Susan."

Harry almost snorted brandy out his nose. "I wouldn't say that." Though if he were being brutally honest, he didn't completely disagree with Grainger.

I can't really prefer death to marrying Lady Susan, can I? No, of course not.

Grainger cocked a skeptical brow, but didn't argue the point. "Don't you have a cousin or some relative who will inherit if you should meet an untimely end?" he asked instead.

Harry nodded. "Yes. A very distant cousin in my great-grandfather's brother's line."

"Ah. Now that would be quite the calamity, wouldn't it?" Grainger said with a perfectly straight face.

Of course, Grainger wouldn't see the problem in letting . . . Harry wasn't even sure of the fellow's name who was next in line to be earl. Searching among the distant leaves of the family tree was precisely how Grainger had succeeded to his title. Until early this spring, he'd been merely Edward

Russell, London solicitor—and then the fourth Duke of
Grainger, along with his wife and children, had died suddenly and unexpectedly of influenza.

Harry shrugged, acknowledging Grainger's point. "Perhaps it wouldn't, but Mama and Letitia aren't eager to have
their comfortable lives upended."

Grainger's other brow rose as well, and then both settled
into a frown. Clearly, he was biting his tongue.

Well, Grainger wasn't saddled—er, *blessed*—with female
relatives.

"Don't make it bleed," Harry said. Grainger grinned.

"And it's not just them, of course," Harry continued. "I
have a responsibility to all the people on the estate." He
might not have given a thought to being earl, but his years
in the army and working for the Crown had impressed
upon him the need to look out for the people who depended
on him.

Grainger still looked unconvinced. "I see. Well, then, I
am very sorry to have put a spoke in your wheel. I hope—
well, I don't actually hope because I think it's a dashed bad
idea, but if you're really set on it, then I imagine you can
propose to Lady Susan in the morning."

Harry grunted and took another swallow of brandy. He'd
never been enthusiastic about offering for Lady Susan, but
now suddenly he felt trapped.

Blast Grainger for cracking open the door to his prison.
He was very tempted to bolt. It must be the brandy's fault.

He took another swallow. "So, *do* you have an urgent
matter of some sort, Grainger, or was that just a ploy to get
me away from Lady Susan?"

Grainger poured them more brandy. If Harry were the
suspicious sort, he'd suspect the duke was trying to get him
drunk enough to disregard the urgings of his better, more
responsible self.

"I do, actually," Grainger said, "though it's not really urgent."

Harry might have growled, because Grainger smiled.

"It requires some discretion," Grainger said, "and I know you've done some discreet inquiries for the Crown."

I shouldn't *rise to the bait. . . .*

He couldn't help himself. "Tell me."

Grainger reeled him right in, though at least the duke permitted himself only the smallest smile as he did so.

"I've been going over the estate books," Grainger said. "They are a bit of a mess."

Harry nodded. Darrow's books hadn't been that bad, but it was always a challenge to jump into the middle of matters with which one had no previous experience.

"As far as I can make out, for over a decade the estate has been supporting someone or something in a village called Little Puddledon."

Harry frowned. "Never heard of the place. And what do you mean, someone or *something?*"

Grainger shrugged. "The entry just lists the recipient as *JSW*. It could stand for Joseph Samuel Withers or the Just Society of Weasels."

Harry snorted. "I'd say that unless the previous duke had an affinity for weasels, JSW must be his bastard."

The duke grimaced. "Yes, that thought had occurred to me."

"What did the old duke's man of business say it was for?"

Grainger ran his hand through his hair. "That's the devil of it. The fellow was at the estate when the influenza hit, and he, too, died of the disease. No one else seems to know anything about the matter."

Harry frowned. "That's odd."

Grainger nodded. "Very. However, it is only a small sum, paid out once a year, so perhaps it's understandable that it was overlooked. I certainly haven't felt it a priority to sort out before now." He shrugged. "This year's payment was to go out two weeks ago, but I stopped it until I could discover the particulars. I was planning to go down to Little Puddledon as soon as this gathering was over to see what I could find out."

It was Harry's turn to cock an eyebrow. "The Duke of Grainger is going to visit an obscure village? That will get tongues wagging at record pace."

Grainger laughed. "I doubt anyone will recognize me, but I hadn't intended to announce myself. I was going to ride down on horseback and use my family name instead of my title. However"—he gave Harry a hopeful look—"I freely admit I have no experience in skulking about."

"And I do." Harry could see where this was going.

"Precisely. It could get rather awkward, depending on what I find, if my identity *was* discovered. So, I thought, given the fact that you *do* have experience with, er, sneaking about, you might be a better person to investigate." He grinned. "And it would give you a break from Lady Susan and the entreaties of your female relatives."

True.

"Though I've often wondered how you managed not to call attention to yourself on the Continent." Grainger gestured at Harry's temple. "With your silver blaze, you might as well have a placard with your name pasted to your forehead."

His silver strands, contrasting starkly with his dark hair, did make him stand out in a crowd, though he would be surprised if anyone in Little Puddledon knew of the Graham streak. "It's not a problem that a little blacking won't fix."

The thought of getting away from Mama and Letitia—and Lady Susan—and getting back to a semblance of his old life, even for a short time, was extremely appealing.

It will only be for a few days. Lady Susan won't marry someone else that quickly.

It was rather telling that the thought she might came with a jolt of relief.

I'll take this one last frolic and then I'll settle down to be a model earl.

Harry hesitated only a moment longer. "Very well. I'd be happy to see what I can discover." *Elated* might be a more accurate adjective. "I'll leave in the morning."

Grainger raised his glass. "Splendid. May I suggest departing early, before the women are up? I'll tell them you went off on an urgent matter for me"—he grinned—"and I promise not to reveal your destination."

Chapter Two

Sunday, Little Puddledon

Penelope Barnes sat next to her daughter, Harriet, and studied the vicar as he climbed the steps to the pulpit.

Sadly, the Reverend Godfrey Wright had not miraculously transformed into a prince while she'd slept. His slightly bulging, watery blue eyes still reminded her forcibly of an amphibian. Add to that his thinning brown hair, beakish nose, receding chin, and the pronounced paunch currently concealed by his vestments—

Ugh.

Single men aren't thick upon the ground in Little Puddledon, you know, she reminded herself sternly. *Godfrey is your best—your only—chance of getting Harriet out of the Home.*

She would do anything for Harriet, even marry Godfrey.

And, really, what did it matter? Harry Graham was the only man who had ever made her heart beat faster. She must be sensible, and Godfrey was a sensible choice. At thirty, he was old enough to have put aside youthful foolishness but not so old that he was teetering on the edge of his dotage.

A hideous image of Godfrey naked and approaching their

marital bed sprang unbidden and far too fully formed into her mind. Bile rose in her throat.

Old and feeble might be better.

Nonsense. She frowned and sat a little taller to banish the sinking feeling in her stomach. She'd like to give Harriet a sister. She'd been an only child herself and had always wanted a sibling. Godfrey was a man of the cloth, focused on the spiritual rather than the physical realm. He must have mild appetites. In all likelihood, she'd have to do her conjugal duties only infrequently—just often enough to conceive. If she was lucky, they'd accomplish that goal on their wedding night.

She was more than willing to undertake any other wifely duties in exchange for a roof over her head and Harriet's. A roof that did not also shelter Verity Lewis.

"Stop it!"

Pen jumped and looked at her daughter, though not before she saw Godfrey freeze midword and swivel his head toward them.

Blast! She couldn't have the man taking a disgust of Harriet now.

Her strong-willed daughter gave no sign she noticed the attention. Her entire focus was on Verity, the eleven-year-old girl sitting in the pew behind them. Verity's eyes were demurely studying her hands clasped loosely in her lap. She was the picture of innocence—if one ignored the faint smirk on her lips and the fact that Martha Hall, Verity's main partner in crime, was giggling next to her.

Dear Lord, what has that girl done to Harriet this time?

Pen felt a now-all-too-familiar lurch of anger, pain, and despair as she leaned over to whisper to her daughter, "Shh. You are disturbing Mr. Wright and the rest of the congregation, Harriet."

Verity was the reason Pen needed to get Harriet out of

the Benevolent Home for the Maintenance and Support of Spinsters, Widows, and Abandoned Women and their Unfortunate Children as soon as possible.

Pen had been toying with the idea of marrying Godfrey since shortly after he'd arrived in the village that spring—she'd been getting very tired of sharing a house with so many women and had wanted Harriet to grow up in a real family. But in the days since Verity and her mother, Rosamund, had stepped through the Home's door, her resolve to bring Godfrey up to scratch had hardened.

She'd tried to give Verity the benefit of the doubt. New girls often had a difficult time adjusting to the Home. Verity and Rosamund had only been there ten days—yes, Pen had been counting—but each day had been worse than the one before. Verity was turning all the other girls against Harriet.

Each snigger, every rude whisper, infuriated Pen, and the hurt and confused looks on Harriet's face lanced her heart.

She'd managed to hold on to her temper until yesterday morning when she'd overheard Juliet Walker, Harriet's best friend—her *only* friend at this point—tell Harriet that Verity said she couldn't play with her anymore.

The memory *still* made Pen's blood boil, even here in the Lord's house.

And she'd swear something else had happened this morning. Harriet had been unusually subdued when she'd come out of the dormitory to go to services.

Harriet's blue eyes—so much like her own—flashed. "Verity pulled my hair, Mama," she said in a furious whisper.

Pen couldn't help it—she glanced back at Verity.

Verity's smirk grew.

The nasty little cat. I'd like to—

No.

She forced herself to take a calming breath. Much as she'd like to box Verity's ears, Verity *was* only a child—an obnoxious, scheming one, perhaps, but a child nonetheless.

"Perhaps it was an accident," she said.

Right. Neither she nor Harriet believed that.

Harriet's expression turned mulish. "No, it wasn't. She—"

Pen put her hand on Harriet's arm, certain she could feel Godfrey's frown piercing through the back of her head. Whenever he disapproved of something—which unfortunately was rather often—his nostrils flared and then his nose wrinkled up as if he'd caught a whiff of Farmer Smith's pigs.

"We'll talk about it later. Now do pay attention to Mr. Wright."

Harriet's brows angled down so steeply they almost met, and her lower lip pushed out in a furious pout, but she held her tongue, thank God.

Pen relaxed slightly and turned back to face Godfrey. He sniffed and then began his sermon, droning on—

No, he was delivering an insightful . . . er, an interesting . . . well, an earnest . . .

Oh, why dissemble? Godfrey's sermons were an invitation to untether one's mind and let it wander where it willed.

She pasted a rapt expression on her face at twenty seven, she'd perfected the skill of masking boredom with a false façade—and mulled over her problem. Even if she could get Godfrey to propose today, they would have to wait three weeks for the banns to be read. She couldn't let Harriet suffer that long. Something had to be done about Verity today.

She'd mentioned the matter to Jo after the incident with Juliet—the Home was Jo's creation and she oversaw all its operations—but Jo was a bloody saint. She'd counseled patience and understanding. Turning the other cheek.

Bugger that. This was *Harriet* she was talking about. Jo didn't have children so she couldn't understand how fiercely the need to defend Harriet burned in Pen. She'd stand up to the Prince Regent himself to protect her daughter.

I'll even threaten to leave the business if I have to.

She stiffened. That thought hadn't occurred to her before. *Would I really quit?*

A yawning hole opened in her stomach. The Benevolent Home had been the branch she'd grabbed just as life had been threatening to sweep her and Harriet over a cliff. If Mrs. Simpson, Aunt Margaret's friend, hadn't told her about the place the day after Aunt Margaret died, Pen would have been sleeping under a hedgerow with her eight-month-old baby.

Her arrival had been good for the Home, too. She'd known enough about farming—her father had often been too drunk to tend their own fields so those duties had fallen to her—to manage the orchards and other crops and nurse the all-but-abandoned hopyard back to life. She and Caro Anderson, another Home resident, had come up with the idea of adding brewing to the many money-making efforts Jo had tried in the constant battle to keep the Home afloat on a sea of expenses, and they'd succeeded beyond their wildest dreams.

They weren't out of the woods yet—far from it. The weather the last two summers had been terrible, cutting their harvest to almost nothing, but they'd made it through and this year looked to be much, much better. The hop plants were groaning with cones almost ready for harvesting.

Could she really give all that up?

Yes. Yes, she could. Harriet's happiness was more important than *anything* else. And it wasn't as if she'd be twiddling her thumbs all day. She'd have a new position to fill—vicar's wife. She'd be busy seeing to Godfrey's comfort as well as the needs of his parishioners.

Her stomach twisted. The less she thought about Godfrey's comfort, the better.

"*Ow!*" That was Verity.

Pen's attention snapped back to the girls. The brim of

Verity's bonnet was askew, and Verity's hands cradled her head.

Harriet's hands hefted a hymnal.

"Touch me again and I'll hit you harder," Harriet hissed into the sudden quiet.

The congregation sucked in its collective breath in horror—or in anticipation of a shocking, scandalous row. Godfrey cleared his throat.

Flight was the only option. Pen grabbed Harriet's arm and bolted out of the pew, dragging her daughter behind her, down the aisle to freedom. "Excuse us. Pardon me. Harriet needs some air."

"Mama," Harriet said as the heavy wooden church door closed behind them.

"Not yet." The odds were good that at least one of Godfrey's flock would be struck by a sudden attack of curiosity and follow them.

Harriet let Pen hustle her down the church steps, along the village green, over the bridge, and halfway up the hill to the manor before she protested. Then she dug in her heels and jerked her arm free.

Pen stopped too, turned to face her daughter—and felt her heart seize. Harriet looked so much like Harry at that moment with her unflinching gaze, hard jaw, and fierce intensity. Pride, love, and worry started to churn in Pen's belly. Such self-assurance and independence were admirable in a man, especially a man who was now an earl. They were far less of an asset in a young fatherless girl.

"I'm not sorry I hit Verity, Mama. She's mean."

"Harriet . . ." She should not encourage violence, much as she might agree with her daughter. "Verity is new to the Home. You know it's always difficult for girls when they first arrive."

Harriet's eyes narrowed and her jaw hardened to granite.

"I *know* that. I *tried* to be nice to her, but she won't stop picking on me."

Anger flared in Pen's breast again. She struggled to keep her tone even. "I'll have a word with Miss Jo—"

"Verity called me a *bastard*, Mama!"

Pen froze, mouth agape. Then her heart started to thump so hard she was afraid it would break free of her chest.

Calm down. Verity can't know. Little Puddledon is a small, obscure village in Kent. No one ever goes to London, and no one from London—or Darrow—comes here. We're safe.

Verity and her mother were from London.

Her heart thumped harder. She had trouble breathing.

"I told her you were a widow, Mama. That Papa had died fighting N-Napoleon." Harriet swallowed. "She *laughed* at me. And then she pointed at my hair and said it *proved* I was a bastard."

Oh, God. Oh, God.

Breathe. You can still bring this about.

"If you mean your streak, I told you it was caused by that fever you had."

The moment Pen had realized she was increasing, she'd known she had to leave Darrow and never come back. Even if she'd been willing to marry the man her father and the earl had chosen for her, there could be no hiding who her baby's real father was once that silver blaze appeared.

Well, or worse, everyone would assume she'd consorted with Walter, and Harriet was just another of Walter's whelps. The estate was littered with them.

But then the streak *hadn't* appeared. Year after year Harriet's hair had remained as dark as night. Pen had begun to hope it would stay that way forever.

She'd been relieved and, well, yes, also a little sad. To be honest, in her heart of hearts, she'd wanted some visual reminder of Harry.

I used to tease him that he'd trapped a moonbeam in his hair.

He'd been completely revolted by the notion.

And then this year, shortly after Godfrey arrived in Little Puddledon, Harriet had taken ill. When she'd recovered, a thin ribbon of silver shimmered from her temple. It wasn't terribly noticeable. When she wore a bonnet, or combed her hair in her usual fashion, no one could see it. Up until now, she and everyone else had accepted Pen's fever explanation.

"That's not what Verity says. She—and her mother— called it the 'Graham streak' and said only the Earl of Darrow's family has it."

Pen's heart sank. Surely there must be others with the distinctive mark. Could she claim Harriet's father was descended from the distaff side of the family? Had Harry's father had a sister? She couldn't remember.

And that would just be adding one more untruth to the many she'd told already. Better to stick to her original story.

She'd taken too long. Harriet had her father's sharp intellect and unflinching courage.

"It's true, isn't it?"

"Ahh." Suddenly, she couldn't lie any longer. The moment she'd been dreading for years had finally arrived. "Er . . ."

It was so very hard to find the words.

Harriet's face began to crumple, but she caught herself. She straightened as if a poker had been shoved down her back. "You *were* the earl's wh-lightskirt, just like Verity and her mother said, weren't you?"

"No, I wasn't."

"And all those stories you told me about my father were lies."

Pen felt as if she'd been kicked in the gut. "No!"

Oh, blast. So many lies to unravel, though the one about having a husband lost to war had been Aunt Margaret's idea. Pen had been too confused and frightened and sad when she'd landed on her aunt's doorstep to object. And the story hadn't been that far from the truth—Pen's heart's truth, at least. She'd *felt* married.

She'd known from the beginning Harry wouldn't actually marry her, of course—earls' sons didn't marry farmers' daughters—but it hadn't mattered. She'd loved him as only a naïve seventeen-year-old girl could—blindly, passionately, completely. *Defiantly.* And she truly believed he'd loved her—as much as a randy eighteen-year-old boy getting ready to go off to war could love anyone.

No wife could have worried more for a husband than she had for Harry while he was on the Continent. She'd scoured every news report, terrified she'd see his name among the casualties.

"Harriet . . ." Pen stepped closer. If she touched her daughter, if she put her arm around her, she could make her understand.

But Harriet dodged her, backing toward the stile that would take her over the fence and off across the fields.

Pen's hands fell awkwardly to her sides. "I . . . It was easier . . . It never seemed important." She twisted her fingers in her skirt. "I would have told you when you were older."

Or would she have? Perhaps she'd hoped they could live forever in this happy fiction. And really, what *did* it matter? It wasn't as if Harriet had wealth and security depending on her legitimacy. Girls couldn't inherit their father's titles or lands.

Harriet's face was flushed and her words came in quick little gasps. "Verity's mother said . . . my real father . . . d-died last year."

What?! That was ridiculous. Pen had read newspaper accounts of Harry's social exploits throughout the Season. Betting seemed to have him offering for the Earl of Langley's daughter at any momen—

Oh. Of course. Rosamund and Verity thought *Walter* was Harriet's father. It was what everyone would think.

Ugh. Her stomach twisted.

Harriet sniffed, fighting to hold back her tears. "I *could* have met him, and now I can't."

"Harriet—" *It might be simpler if I let her believe—*

No, she was done with lies. And she didn't want Harriet thinking the profligate, *cheating* Walter was her father. Pen's stomach turned again. Or that Pen had slept with a married man. Worse. When she'd conceived Harriet, Walter had not only been married, he'd had one daughter and another on the way.

"Harriet, stop. Your father is the current earl."

An odd look—some mix of confusion and shock—flitted over Harriet's features.

Pen reached for her again—and again Harriet backed away. She now had one foot on the stile.

"So, so he doesn't c-care about me?" Harriet's voice wavered with pain and uncertainty.

Dear God, Pen hated to see her strong, fearless daughter look so fragile.

She would fix things. She'd marry Godfrey. Then Harriet would have a father and a room of her own. She wouldn't have to be around that nasty Verity all the time. Wedding Godfrey would solve all their problems.

"He doesn't know about you."

Harriet's eyes widened as her jaw dropped—and then anger twisted her features into a dark scowl. "You didn't tell him?" The words were sharp and heavy with accusation.

Pen shook her head, a wave of sick helplessness washing over her at Harriet's fury, bringing with it the memory of how helpless she'd felt when she'd discovered her pregnancy. "I couldn't. He'd left for the Continent before I knew I was increasing. He was in the army. I didn't know how to reach him."

Harriet wasn't satisfied with that answer. "But he came home months ago, didn't he? You could have told him about me then."

Yes, she supposed she could have. "There was no point in that."

"What do you mean? He might have married you. We could be a family!"

Harriet had grown up in Little Puddledon. She was too far removed from the peerage and polite society to understand how these things worked.

"No, we couldn't. He wouldn't have married me, Harriet. I'm only a farmer's daughter. Earls don't marry so far beneath them."

"But I'm his daughter."

Pen's heart broke at the pain in Harriet's voice. Perhaps that had been her real reason for not writing Harry—by not putting the matter to the test, she'd been able to keep alive a faint hope he would indeed care about their child.

Silly. It was more likely Harry had followed in Walter's footsteps—well, *footsteps* weren't precisely what he'd have been following in—and had a raft of illegitimate offspring.

"It doesn't matter, Harriet. You're *my* daughter. I've taken care of you all these years. I'll always take care of you." Perhaps Harriet would feel better if she knew Pen's plans. "When I marry Mr. Wright—"

"Marry Mr. Wright?!" Harriet sounded—and looked—horrified. "The vicar?"

"Well, yes, of course the vicar." Pen tried to keep the annoyance out of her voice, but without much success. "That's the only Mr. Wright in the village."

"He's asked you to marry him?" From Harriet's tone, the man might just as well have asked Pen to dance naked down the church aisle.

"Not yet, but I'm quite certain he will." Pen smiled in what she hoped was a comforting fashion. "And then we'll have a real home. You won't have to deal with Verity and the rest of those girls all the time."

Harriet was shaking her head, looking distinctly ill. "Marry Mr. Wright?" she repeated in a hollow voice.

"Y-yes." This certainly wasn't the reaction Pen had expected.

"He's . . . he's *horrible*."

"No, he's not." Godfrey might be a bit pompous and sanctimonious and, well, boring, but he wasn't horrible.

"Yes, he is. He looks just like an ugly, sneaky *toad*—"

"No, he doesn't."

"—and wrinkles his big nose when he sees me, as though I stink." Harriet's eyes narrowed just like Harry's used to when he was angry. "I *hate* him."

"Harriet!" Where had her calm, controlled daughter gone?

"And he won't marry you when he finds out you're a wh-*whore*."

"*Harriet!*"

"That's what Verity called you." Harriet was shouting now, but Pen heard the quaver in her voice as well. "You had a baby and you weren't married." She sniffed furiously and swiped a few traitorous tears from her eyes. "And he'll look down his long, ugly nose even more at me because I'm a *bastard*, conceived in *sin*."

"You're not." Now she was the one feeling ill. "And he won't." Godfrey was a vicar. Surely, he'd embrace charity.

But Harriet was gone. She'd scrambled over the stile and was now running across the field, taking Pen's heart with her.

Should I follow her?

No. Harriet was like Harry in this, too. She needed time alone to come to terms with her feelings—she *had* had a lot of unpleasant things to deal with all at once. She'd come home when she was ready.

Pen started back up the road to the manor, though now she felt as if she were dragging herself through treacle.

Godfrey won't really hold Harriet's birth against her, will he?

She scowled down at the dirt. *I won't let him.* The moment she saw—or suspected—anything of that nature, she'd let the man know in no uncertain terms that she would not tolerate it. She would do anything for Harriet. Even lie.

If he hears the gossip, I'll deny it.

She'd been taken unawares this time, but now that she knew what Rosamund and Verity were saying, she could come up with a convincing story, one that hewed as much to the truth as possible. She wasn't an accomplished liar. She would have to keep the tale simple. . . .

Ah, now she had it. She'd say her dear departed Mr. Barnes was descended from a Graham by-blow, a female born on the wrong side of the blanket. Surely that would work. Godfrey had a powerful reason to believe whatever she said. He wanted her in his bed.

She repressed a shudder and quickened her pace, forcing her thoughts to the safer topic of her hop garden. She'd check the plants when she got home and pluck off any nasty bugs she found lurking there. It wouldn't be much longer before the cones were ready to harvest and she could stop worrying—about the hops, at least.

If only she could pluck the nasty words and hurtful looks from Harriet's heart as easily.

Chapter Three

Pen brushed off her skirts as she left the hopyard and headed up the path to the house. She'd spent the last—she glanced at her watch—almost three hours carefully tending her hop plants, keeping a sharp eye out for any sign of mildew or greenflies. So far, so good.

If only raising a child was as straightforward.

She bit her lip, trying to will away the worries infesting her thoughts as destructively as any garden pest, but no matter what she did, they kept coming back to devour her peace.

Maybe she should have told Harriet the truth about her birth years ago, but she'd thought her too young to understand. Why did she need her life complicated with things that had happened so far in the past and which neither of them could change?

No, the fault went further back than that. She should never have gone along with Aunt Margaret's widow story—and yet it had saved her and Harriet years of being judged and excluded.

What you really *should never have done was let Harry under your skirts.*

Ha! Most of the time her skirts had been discarded long before Harry touched her.

She smiled, remembering. That summer with Harry had been wonderful, the best thing—besides Harriet—that had ever happened to her. She'd never before—or since—felt so alive and, well, *real*. Everything—every feeling, every smell, every touch—had been so intense: brighter and sweeter than at any other time in her life. Instead of going through her days enduring or hoping for something in the future, she'd lived in the present, savoring each moment, storing it away to cherish later, after Harry was gone.

She'd always known he was going.

And then she'd got Harriet, and as hard as it was to be an unmarried mother, she'd never once regretted it or wanted to be free of her daughter. Harriet was a living piece of Harry, but she was also precious in her own right.

Precious, but maddening, too.

Pen desperately wanted to go in search of her, but she knew talking to her now would do no good. In fact, it would likely make things worse. She had to let Harriet work things out on her own. She'd come to Pen when she was ready.

She flicked a bead of sweat off the tip of her nose as another worry intruded.

Is Harriet right? Will Godfrey think me a whore when he hears the rumors and wash his hands of me?

Something that felt suspiciously like panic formed a tight knot in her chest.

No, surely not, but she'd best not give the story time to reach him—if it hadn't already. She glanced at her watch again as she entered the yard with the service buildings. She'd go down to the Dancing Duck in a little while and catch Godfrey as he was leaving after his big Sunday meal. Perhaps she could get him to propose today.

"Pen!"

She looked over to see Caro striding toward her from the brewhouse.

"Jo wants to see us."

"All right." Good. She had some time before she had to leave to ambush—er, talk to Godfrey. Meeting with Jo would give her the chance to mention again the problems Verity was causing Harriet—not that anyone could have missed the drama in church earlier.

"All still good with the hops?" Caro asked rather anxiously as they walked across the yard.

"Yes, but you know that already. I've seen you sneaking out of the hop garden. You've counted each cone, haven't you?"

Caro laughed. "I've tried, but I'm happy to say there are too many for me to keep track of. Still, I've heard you mutter about bugs and blight, so I'm not breathing easy yet. Could we still lose the crop?"

"Yes." No point in beating around the bush. Caro knew very well that there were no guarantees in farming. The last two freakishly cold summers had taught her that, but even something as simple as a sudden storm at the wrong time could put paid to their entire crop. "That's why I check the plants so often. But I'm optimistic—*cautiously* optimistic."

"Thank God for that," Caro said as she opened the door to Jo's office.

"Thank God for what?" Jo asked. She was sitting behind her desk, her big ledger open before her. Freddie, her brown and white spaniel, came over to be petted before returning to sprawl at her feet.

"So far, the hops are doing well," Pen said, taking the worn, red-upholstered chair she always did.

"And—fingers crossed—if we get the harvest it looks like we will, I can increase production, which means I can expand our distribution." Caro sat on the edge of the other chair that faced Jo's desk and leaned forward, almost vibrating with excitement. "I'm sure I've told you both that the Rooster's Tail in Tuddlegate and the Drunken Sheep in Westling have asked about getting more Widow's Brew. I've had to put them off because I was hard-pressed to produce enough for the Dancing Duck, but now—"

"Don't count the hops before they're off the bine," Pen warned. She wasn't particularly superstitious, but she hated to tempt fate—even with crossed fingers.

"Yes, yes. Of course. But as soon as we know for certain how big the harvest is, I'll contact those public houses again." Caro bounced slightly on her chair. "And Mr. Harris, the owner of the Drunken Sheep, has a brother with a tavern in London. If our ale keeps doing well at the Sheep, I'm certain he'll recommend it."

Caro's brow furrowed and she tapped her pursed lips with her index finger. "I'll probably have to see about hiring another man to help in the brewhouse. Albert's getting too old for all the lifting, though don't tell him I said that."

Jo's brow was now furrowed, too. "What about Bathsheba and Esther? I thought you said they were managing quite well." She gestured at the ledger. "We don't have money for extra wages, so I'd much rather you utilize the women who live here."

Caro smiled the way she did when she wanted to cajole someone into doing something they didn't want to do. "They *are* managing well, but you know there's a lot of heavy lifting and carrying involved in brewing. Bathsheba and Esther are both strong—quite likely as strong as Albert—but they are not as strong as a young man would be. I'm sure the increased production would pay for one man's wages with plenty left over to go toward the Home's support."

Caro was so ambitious, she sometimes lost sight of reality.

"Even if we have a stellar harvest, we can't compete with the London breweries," Pen said. "Their facilities are much, much larger than ours. I've heard they can host dinner parties for hundreds of people in just one of their vats."

Caro scowled at her. "I *know* that, but I still say it would be a very good thing if we got our beer into the London market." She grinned, her imagination clearly galloping away with her again. "We can ask a better price because the supply will be limited."

"Anything we can do to bring in more money would be a good thing," Jo said, her voice tight with worry.

Oh, Lud. "Still no word from the new duke?" Pen asked. Jo had been fretting their support would evaporate ever since she'd read that the old Duke of Grainger and his family had succumbed to influenza.

"No." Jo rubbed the spot between her brows where a deep line had begun to form. "This year's funds have yet to arrive."

Pen felt her stomach drop. If the new duke cut off his support—

No need to panic yet. "They're only two weeks late, aren't they?" she asked.

"Yes." Jo sighed, her shoulders drooping. "But they're never late."

Caro made a sound that closely resembled a growl. She looked as if she'd like to push the man into her large copper when it was full of boiling wort. "The duke can't cut us off."

"Yes, he can," Jo said. "You know we're only squatters here."

Unfortunately, that was true. Puddledon Manor had once belonged to Jo's husband, Freddie, Lord Havenridge. He'd wagered it and all his other unentailed property on the turn of a card—and lost. And then like the coward he was, he'd promptly put a bullet through his brain. When the winner— the previous duke—had come round the next morning to forgive Freddie's debt, he was appalled to find Jo a new widow with no one to turn to.

He'd let her stay at Puddledon Manor and had contributed to her support for over a decade.

"The old duke must have made some provision in his will for you—for us," Pen said.

"I don't know." Jo sighed again, making Freddie whine and bump his head against her leg. She stroked his ears. "He had no duty toward me. I think he just felt guilty about Freddie—"

The dog, recognizing his name, beat a tattoo on the floor with his tail.

Jo looked down at him. "My husband, not you, you silly creature."

Freddie's tail wagged faster and his brows rose. He put his paws on Jo's knee and licked her face.

"Now don't slobber all over me, sir," she said, laughing. Then she looked back at Pen and Caro.

"I think the money was the old duke's way of assuaging his conscience as much as helping me. He might not have made any formal arrangements." She worried aloud as she'd been doing rather frequently of late. "The new duke is well regarded as far as I can tell from the newspapers. He's a former solicitor, a widower with a young son. I'd hoped he'd be compassionate. The amount we get isn't large. It's only a few pence compared to the vast wealth he now commands. It can't make much of a difference to him, but it's vital to us."

"Perhaps that's the problem," Pen said. "Sometimes people new to riches are the stingiest."

"Yes." Jo swallowed and then bit her lip. "He could even decide to make us vacate the house, and then what would we do?"

"Write to him." Caro was always one to take the direct approach. "I told you to do that the moment we learned he would succeed to the title, if you'll remember."

Unfortunately, Caro could also be a bit of an I-told-you-so.

"Perhaps it's just an oversight or a miscommunication that he'll fix as soon as he's aware of it," Pen said.

"And if he did mean to stop his support," Caro added, "writing him will give us a chance to argue our case. As you say, he was a solicitor. He should appreciate well-organized facts and figures. In any event, it's better to find out where things stand now than to waste time guessing and worrying. The sooner we know, the sooner we can make plans."

Jo nodded. "You're right, of course. It would be good, though, if I could show him we aren't just hanging on his sleeve. I can't afford to buy Puddledon Manor from him, but if I can convince him that we have a plan to become financially independent—reduce and finally eliminate his charity, perhaps even pay him rent—he might let us continue here."

Caro nodded, sitting up straighter and shaking her index finger at Jo to emphasize her point. "And that's another reason I want to get Widow's Brew into the London market. It will prove to the duke and everyone else that we have a successful business." She grinned. "And, who knows? Some of his friends might take a liking to our beer and argue in our defense. The duke might even decide to *increase* his support."

There Caro went spinning ambitious dreams again—

No, it was a good thing Caro had such big dreams. They might not always reach them—they definitely hadn't the last two years with the poor harvests—but her dreams gave them all a goal.

"And it's not as if he needs this little house," Pen said. "He must have a number of large estates now."

"Yes." Jo sounded more determined. "I'll write him"— she faltered—"soon." She looked down at the ledger. "If only the last two years hadn't been so dismal. I've been going over our books and have found a few places where we can economize, but . . ." She shook her head. "If we can increase brewery production, that would be wonderful."

Then she looked up and grinned—well, her expression was more a grimace. "It's not as if any of our other money-making attempts have been successful."

True. They'd tried taking in mending, knitting shawls, baking cakes, and any number of other domestic activities all with equally disappointing results. Either the women who lived at the Home weren't enthusiastic and produced inferior goods, or the villagers preferred to do such things for themselves. It wasn't until they turned to the old brewhouse on the manor grounds that they hit upon an income-producing scheme that met with enthusiasm on all sides.

"There's not much we can do until the harvest is in," Pen cautioned once more. "It looks good now, yes, but that could change."

"But don't wait to write him," Caro said. "Better to tell him now how good the harvest looks to be. If something dire does happen after his money is in our coffers . . ." She shrugged. "It's not *that* much money. He's not going to come down to Little Puddledon to snatch it back."

Caro was by far the . . . bravest businesswoman of the three of them.

"Er, r-right." Jo closed the ledger and stood, causing Freddie—and Pen and Caro—to get to their feet as well. "I can't say I agree with that approach completely, but I do see that we can't afford to wait until the hops are safely drying in the oast house to contact him. I'll write him tonight." She blew out a long breath. "I only hope the man will be persuaded."

"I'm sure he will be," Pen said. "What sort of gentleman would throw a houseful of women and children out into the street?"

"Yes." Jo brushed an invisible speck off her desk. "I've followed reports of him in the newspapers, and I got the impression he was a kind man, intelligent and principled."

Caro's expression turned cynical. "Let's hope you are

correct. The fact that he's new to the peerage does give me some hope, however . . ." She pulled a face. "It's usually not a good policy to trust the nobility to do the right thing."

And then she looked at Pen with what Pen would swear was sympathy. "As Pen must know all too well."

Pen's heart leaped into her throat, and then somehow managed to pound loudly in her ears. "Wh-what do you mean?"

Jo frowned and touched Pen lightly on her arm. "On the walk back from church, Rosamund told everyone that Harriet's real father was the previous Earl of Darrow."

Pen opened her mouth to protest—and stopped. Did she truly want to get into the whole tale now? She glanced at the clock on the mantel. She needed to leave soon if she was going to waylay Godfrey. And she *had* to waylay him today. Clearly, time was running out.

Caro was shaking her head. "I don't know why it didn't occur to me the moment I saw that silver streak in Harriet's hair. It's quite distinctive." She frowned. "Well, yes, I do know why. It showed up so suddenly. And I believed your fever story—it seemed odd, but I suppose fevers can do odd things. Not to mention the fact you'd told us you were married to a farmer." Caro waggled her brows at Pen. "I'd always thought you quite the prude. I still find it hard to believe you were an earl's mistress."

Pen sucked in her breath. Hearing Caro say it out loud like that . . . What she'd done with Harry sounded so sordid, but it hadn't been.

"Not that we mean to be critical, of course," Jo said quickly. "That's what the Home is for, isn't it? To serve as a refuge for women without any other support, especially women with children." She frowned at Caro. "We don't judge. Women all too often are at the mercy of predatory men. There's nothing to be ashamed of."

Pen wasn't ashamed, and Harry hadn't forced or tricked her. She'd chosen freely. She'd loved him—and she'd got her

daughter, who was her life, from what they'd done together.
She didn't regret a single thing.

"Your past—anyone's past—is none of our affair," Jo said
in a calm, soothing tone as she sent Caro another speaking
look.

Caro ignored her. "I say, Pen, you don't suppose you could
get some money from the earl, do you? I would think he
owes you something as you're his niece's mother. That could
help us with expenses in case the duke proves difficult."

*If Caro knew the truth, she'd not let me leave this room
until I wrote a begging letter to Harry.*

"I am *not* going to pick the Earl of Darrow's pockets."
She stood and glared at Jo. "And you need to speak to
Rosamund, Jo. I won't have her spreading stories about my
daughter."

"Yes, I'll—"

Pen didn't let her finish. "And she needs to control Verity.
The girl has turned everyone against Harriet. She—"

She caught sight of the clock on the mantel. Good Lord!
She was going to miss Godfrey. "I have to go. I have an, er,
appointment in the village."

She had to get to Godfrey before the story did—though
it might already be too late for that. She started for the
door. "Talk to Rosamund, Jo. I won't let her or Verity torture
Harriet any longer."

Pen jerked the door open and half ran out of Jo's office.
She didn't slow down until she reached the big oak just
before the bridge. Then she stopped and took several
deep breaths. She needed to appear calm. Godfrey would
notice if—

No, Godfrey probably wouldn't notice if she was angry
or upset. He was not the most observant individual. But
someone else might. No need to give the gossips another
bone to chew on.

She smoothed her skirt. Godfrey took his midday meal

at noon each day and left the Dancing Duck at two after consuming a hearty plate of mutton and several glasses of Widow's Brew.

It was now one fifty-eight.

She took another deep breath, adjusted her bonnet to what she hoped was a complementary angle, and, at precisely one fifty-nine, strode purposefully across the bridge toward the tavern.

She'd timed things perfectly. The door opened just as she was passing, and Godfrey emerged.

"Mrs. Barnes!"

"Mr. Wright." He couldn't hear the hollowness in her voice, could he?

Show some enthusiasm! Godfrey is the answer to your prayers.

She forced a bright smile. "How lovely to see you."

Why is he inspecting my bodice so thoroughly?

She was used to him darting glances at it, but today he wasn't even trying to mask his interest.

Perhaps that was good. It might mean he was having trouble controlling his male urges—weak as they may be— urges that would provoke him to offer for her if she played her cards right.

I never thought of Harry's urges.

With Harry, she'd thought only of love—and, well, her *own* urges. However, since she had no love nor, to be brutally honest, even the faintest urge where Godfrey was concerned, she would have to hope his animal instincts carried the day.

My urges are all maternal now. The only thing—the only person I care about is Harriet.

He bowed. "I was planning to walk along the stream, *Mrs.* Barnes. Aids the digestion, don't you know. Would you care to accompany me?"

Unease slithered down her back and she hesitated. Had he stressed the word *Mrs?* Why?

It must be my imagination.

Of course, it was her imagination. She was just a little off balance after her meeting with Jo and Caro. "Yes, thank you. That would be very pleasant."

She rested her fingers on Godfrey's sleeve, and his hand came up to cover them.

Well, more like trap them, pinning them to—

Stop. This is Godfrey, remember. Stuffy, boring, mild-mannered, God-fearing Reverend Wright.

She let him lead her down to the well-trodden path and along the stream toward the rectory. She had about ten minutes to charm him. That might not be enough time.

She slowed her steps.

Godfrey didn't, and since he still held her hand against his arm, she could either pick up her pace or get dragged through the dirt.

She picked up her pace. "Do you have someone waiting for you at the rectory?" That would be unfortunate, but there was nothing to be done about it. She would have to make the most of what time she had.

"Oh, no."

"So, then, er, what's the hurry? I mean, can't we enjoy the, ah, view?"

He smiled down at her. In another man, his expression might be considered wolfish, but this was Godfrey. Perhaps his mutton hadn't quite agreed with him.

He waggled his brows. "I have a *much* more interesting view I wish to contemplate."

"Oh?" How odd. She knew this path very well. It was pleasant enough, but the view was basically the same all along the way. One might encounter some wildlife—ducks or other waterfowl, a turtle perhaps, occasionally a snake—but otherwise one saw just water and fields and trees. "What do you mean?"

"I hope to see lovely, rose-tipped"—his brows waggled

again!—"h-hills, a beautiful, er, field." His tongue darted out to wet his plump lips. He was almost panting. "And then a tangled thicket and a dark, *hot* tunnel."

He was definitely panting now, and his hand squeezed hers almost to the point of pain.

"I don't know what you're talking about." She sniffed as discreetly as she could. Had Godfrey imbibed too many Widow's Brews with his meal? She couldn't smell any alcohol, but he certainly seemed drunk. Perhaps it would be wiser to remember some pressing engagement—

No, *engagement* was precisely what she was looking for and she wasn't going to find it by turning tail and running.

"You will. You will." His voice was oddly husky.

The unease that had slithered down her back earlier fluttered into her chest.

I shouldn't go with—

Don't be silly. This is Godfrey, *the vicar. He's harmless.*

She let him pull her along, past the turnoff for the rectory, past the old rickety footbridge that Farmer Smith had built to get to church, past the bench someone else had put on the bank—

Her heart sank as they passed the bench and she realized she'd been hoping that *that* had been Godfrey's destination.

Then they reached a point where the main path moved away from the stream. Godfrey veered off on a narrow, overgrown trail Pen had never noticed before, not that she'd spent any time exploring this area. There was no room to walk two abreast, so Godfrey towed her along behind him.

"Where are we going?" Pen put up her free hand to keep from being smacked in the face by a branch Godfrey had just pushed by and hadn't had the courtesy to hold for her. "Besides toward the stream." At least there were no hills, rose-tipped or otherwise, between them and the water.

"You'll see." He leered—well, that was the best she could

describe his expression—back at her. "It's a place where no one will disturb us."

She laughed nervously. "I hope it doesn't involve a thicket or a tunnel."

Godfrey sniggered. "Don't play coy, Penelope. You want this as much as I do."

"W-want wh-what?" She considered taking issue with his use of her Christian name, but decided to let it go this time. The fluttering had moved from her chest to her throat, making it difficult to keep her voice steady.

He *must* have overimbibed at the Duck.

The narrow path opened up into a small clearing with a large willow tree. Godfrey pulled her under the willow branches and then backed her up against the trunk.

"Want *this,*" he said, and his lips—his wet, slobbery, flaccid lips—came down on hers.

Thank God she'd had the presence of mind to close her gaping mouth before they landed. Her hands shot up to brace themselves against his chest, ready to shove—

Remember Harriet!

Right, Harriet. She would endure anything for Harriet, even this.

Though thinking of Harriet in this particular situation made her think of Harry and how different she'd felt whenever he'd kissed her.

Could she pretend Godfrey was Harry?

No. Harry had never smelled of onions and garlic, and, more to the point, he'd never attacked her this way. He'd have noticed if she'd been at all reluctant and would have stopped at once.

Not that she'd ever been reluctant. More times than not, she'd kissed him first.

At least Godfrey's paunch seemed to be shielding her from his—

Ugh! He's trying to force his tongue into my mouth!

She locked her teeth together. Time for some shocked protest. She couldn't risk saying anything—if she opened her mouth, his tongue would strangle her—so she shoved on his chest.

Nothing happened. He might not even have felt the push.

She shoved harder. Still nothing.

She kicked his shin.

At last! He lifted his head—and *chuckled*.

"No need to pretend, my dear."

The fluttering in her throat froze and dropped like a shot bird to land with a heavy thud in her stomach. "Pretend?"

He tugged her bonnet's ribbons free, and then sent her hat sailing away.

"Hey!" She turned her face to follow its trajectory. It landed, at a rakish angle, on a bush.

His clammy hand turned her face back to his. "You're as eager for it as I am."

It? This sounds like a proposal, but not one of marriage.

"Eager?" She *might* be misunderstanding. Godfrey was a man of the cloth, after all. One would think he'd wait to engage in anything of a carnal nature until he had God's blessing.

Apparently, one would be wrong.

"You're like a bitch in heat."

"Mr. Wright!"

His other hand planted itself on her hindquarters. "And I'm here to satisfy your needs—and mine." He pulled her hard against him in such a way that his paunch no longer hid his, er, firm resolve.

His doesn't feel as big as Harry's—

She forced that thought from her head. She had to focus. Why would Godfrey think she'd welcome illicit relations? He *must* mean marriage. . . .

He certainly had an odd way of courting her. But he was a vicar. What else *could* he mean?

She would find out. She certainly wasn't going to let him maul her unless he intended to make her his wife.

"Godfrey, you're frightening me. I don't—"

He laughed again. "Lord, you play a demure widow so well. You had me completely gulled."

Everything inside her stilled. *Dear God. He knows.*

"I heard the story as I ate my lunch at the Duck. You can imagine my shock to discover you were the old Earl of Darrow's whore."

"I wasn't." Her mouth was dry, but she managed to say the words clearly. Firmly.

Godfrey shrugged. "Ah, well, perhaps you prefer the term *mistress.* I suppose it sounds better. Same thing, though. You spread your legs for the man."

He smiled in a very unpleasant fashion. "And you'll spread your legs for me, too, won't you? I'll admit I've been lusting for you. Was almost on the verge of offering to marry you. Lucky for me I discovered in time that you'll sell your favors at a much lower price." He frowned for a moment. "What *is* your price?"

Horror had been growing in her, icy bit by icy bit, with each word the man uttered. His final question magically transformed the ice to fire. Red-hot fury exploded through her.

"Your ballocks!" she yelled, and drove her knee up between his legs.

Chapter Four

Harry stood in the shade and looked upstream as his horse drank. He hoped to God he was almost at Little Puddledon. He'd left Grainger's yesterday morning thinking he'd only an hour or two's ride before him, and here it was almost two o'clock in the afternoon the next day and he *still* hadn't reached his destination. He'd had to deal with washed-out bridges; rutted, meandering roads; and confusing—or nonexistent—road signs. Stopping to ask directions hadn't helped, either. He'd swear the majority of people he'd encountered, even those employed by inns, had never strayed more than a mile from their homes.

It was no wonder Grainger knew nothing about whatever was going on in Little Puddledon. Frankly, Harry had begun to think it was a fairy village, appearing and vanishing with the mist.

He took out his handkerchief and wiped his face. It was beastly hot.

When he'd stopped for a meat pie and a glass of beer at that tavern in Westling—the Drunken Sheep—the barmaid had assured him Little Puddledon was only a few more miles down the road. Perhaps it was—as the crow flew. It hadn't helped matters that not one but *two* bridges were out, forcing him to make several more befuddling detours—and he prided himself on having a good sense of direction.

He eyed the stream. No, he wasn't yet thirsty enough to join Ajax. He was holding out for a nice, tall mug of Widow's Brew, the beer he'd had at the Drunken Sheep and which the barmaid told him was produced in Little Puddledon by a group known as the Benevolent Home for the Maintenance and Support of Spinsters, Widows, and Abandoned Women and their Unfortunate Children.

Quite a mouthful—and perhaps the answer to Grainger's mystery. It sounded like the perfect place to park an illegitimate child or two.

He put his handkerchief back in his pocket. He'd know soon enough—if only he could find his way to the blasted village.

Ajax raised his head, finally finished—

No. Now he heard it, too. The snap of a twig, the crunch of leaves . . .

The back of his neck prickled. Someone was here, watching him. Where?

If I'd been this inattentive on the Continent, I'd be dead.

He turned his head casually, following Ajax's gaze to . . . Oh.

His horse was the one under surveillance.

"Would you like to meet Ajax?" he asked the young girl lurking in the shadows by an overgrown bush. Her green dress and old straw bonnet had helped her blend into her surroundings.

She gave him a considering look, and he waited while she took his measure. Then she looked back at Ajax. "Does he bite?"

He must be honest. "No, not if you approach him correctly. Any animal might bite if frightened."

She nodded, and came closer. "He's very large, isn't he?" She gave Harry a wide berth, keeping the horse between them. Wise girl to be as cautious of a strange man as a strange horse.

"He's a little taller than average." Though Harry could see how the girl would think Ajax enormous, especially if she hadn't grown up around Arabians. She was likely only about four feet tall, a foot below Ajax's withers, and thin. He didn't know much about children, but if he had to guess, he'd say she was somewhere around his middle niece's age, so nine, give or take a year. "He likes to be petted on his shoulder or neck."

She reached up to put her hand cautiously on Ajax. Her long fingers were pale and delicate against the horse's chestnut hair, but the cuff of her dress was frayed. The fabric was serviceable, not fashionable like the dresses his nieces wore.

Clearly, she was not the squire's or the vicar's daughter. Not only would she be better dressed if she were, she'd likely not be allowed to roam the countryside unattended, and she'd be busy with lessons in needlework and numbers and such. Yet her diction and general behavior made him think she *was* from the gentry.

She laughed as Ajax's neck twitched beneath her hand. The horse turned his head to look at her. "He has such pretty eyes."

And then Ajax nudged her with his nose and she laughed again, looking up at Harry to share the joke.

Something about her expression seemed oddly familiar. Or perhaps it was her eyes. They were a striking blue, light and clear with a dark rim around the iris.

And then Ajax, the bold fellow, used his nose to knock her hat off, sending the dark hair she'd stuffed up into it tumbling down over her shoulders.

The dark hair with its silver streak.

Good God! The girl's Walter's by-blow. That's why she looks so familiar.

Years of experience operating behind enemy lines and in

the halls of diplomacy threatened to fail him. Fortunately, the girl dove for her hat, and that gave him a chance to recover. By the time she'd scooped it up and jammed it back on her head, he'd schooled his features to bland friendliness.

She gave him a look, part defiance, part unease. Clearly, she knew the silver mark meant something.

Of course, she knew. She might live in a rural backwater, but this was still England. His family's distinctive blaze was no secret. Thank God he'd darkened his own hair.

He bowed slightly. "I apologize for Ajax's impertinence. I believe he hoped you had a carrot or an apple hidden away."

Her wary look faded and she giggled. "I'm sorry, Ajax," she said, petting the horse's neck again. "I wish I had a treat for you."

Had her mother written Walter for money? He didn't remember coming across any unusual expenditures when he'd gone over the estate records, but he would quiz his manager and examine the books again when he got home. Walter might have concealed it, not wanting his wife to find out.

Ha! How ironic that he'd come here on Grainger's behalf only to discover that *he* had an illegitimate relative in the village. Was the area teeming with the nobility's bastards?

He'd best get on with it and find out. "I wonder if you could help me."

Her hand froze on Ajax's neck, and she looked up at him guardedly.

Oh, Lord. Now he'd alarmed her. He spoke quickly before she could flee. "I'm trying to find a village called Little Puddledon. I've asked any number of people along the way, and everyone assures me that it's just up the road—but it never is."

Ah, she was giggling again.

"I'm beginning to think the place doesn't exist."

"Oh, it exists." Her eyes danced with mischief. "It's just up the road."

That surprised a laugh out of him.

It was too bad Walter had never met the girl—well, he didn't know for a fact whether Walter had met her or not. But she clearly had a lively wit.

I'll have to make certain she's taken care of properly. I'm head of the family now.

For once, that responsibility didn't feel like a burden.

"No, truly, it is." Her brow wrinkled with earnestness. "If you just keep to the road, you'll be there in no time."

"Promise?"

She nodded vigorously.

"And is there an inn in this elusive village?"

"Yes. The Dancing Duck. You can't miss it. Little Puddle-don is rather . . ." She grinned again, the impish look back in her eyes. "Little."

"Ah." He laughed, but he struggled with an odd breathlessness, too. "Thank you. I'll be on my way, then."

She smiled shyly. "Good-bye, sir." She gave Ajax one last stroke. "Good-bye, Ajax."

Harry couldn't manage more than a nod and a wave as he swung into his saddle and urged Ajax into motion.

What *was* it about the girl's expression that gave him such a feeling of . . . ? He searched for the right word. *Recognition.*

This time he knew it wasn't Walter she reminded him of. Walter had never looked impish.

Of course, Walter had been seven years older than he. Harry's earliest memories of him were of a churlish, pimple-faced fellow who had zero interest in his younger brother.

Ajax suddenly quickened his pace, and Harry pushed the girl from his thoughts. "Are we *finally* there?"

They were. As soon as they came round the next curve, he saw stone houses lining the lane, and then just a few moments later, the village green with its church and—yes, the Dancing Duck—came into view. Splendid.

He rode into the innyard—and the ostler's eyes almost popped out of his head. Unlike the girl by the stream, this man knew an Arabian when he saw one.

"Ohh, milord," the man said reverently. "The horse, milord. I've not seen such a fine one in Little Puddledon afore."

Perhaps he should not have ridden Ajax if he wished to avoid attracting attention.

"Yes, Ajax is a fine fellow, aren't you, Ajax?" Harry said, patting his horse on the neck. Then he swung down, took his saddlebag, and smiled at the man.

The ostler spared him only the briefest glance. He'd taken Ajax's bridle and was murmuring horsey praise. Ajax's ears twitched and he nickered his approval.

Harry had been quite forgotten.

"I'll leave him in your capable hands then, shall I, Mr. . . . ?"

"Thomas, milord. Just Thomas." The man tore his eyes away from Ajax briefly. "Ye can be sure I'll take good care of this handsome fellow." He tilted his head toward the front of the inn. "Ye can ask Bess about a room." Then he led Ajax off.

The Dancing Duck was like every other small hostelry Harry had ever stayed in. He entered through the tavern, ducking his head to avoid banging it on the low lintel, and glanced around. Fortunately, it was a few minutes after two o'clock, so most people had finished their midday meal and left, but there were enough men lingering over their mugs that he knew he'd end up being the main topic of the day's gossip.

Well, that was to be expected. Any new face in a small village provoked intense interest.

He removed his hat—thanking God once more that he'd blackened his streak—smiled, nodded, and walked over to a short, plump woman who seemed to be in charge. "Good day, madam. I wonder if you could tell me where I might find Bess? I was told she was the one to see about a room."

The drone of conversation behind him had all but stopped. He imagined the men's ears twitching like Ajax's, trying to catch every word he uttered.

"I'm Bess," she said, looking him over carefully.

At least his clothes wouldn't betray him the way Ajax's all-too-obvious bloodlines had threatened to do with the ostler. His breeches, waistcoat, and coat were plain, worn, service-able items he'd bought from one of Grainger's tenants.

Hmm. Now that he thought about it, he'd better come up with a plausible story to explain Ajax before he saw Thomas again—or to have ready when the news of an Arabian in the stables went through the village men.

Oh, blast. Bess had finished her inspection and was now tugging her bodice lower, giving him a sultry look from under lowered lashes. She was a pleasant-enough looking woman, but he was not interested in bed play at the moment.

"Come this way, Mr. . . ." Bess let her voice trail off as she raised her brows inquiringly.

At least they'd stepped beyond the men's hearing. "Graham."

Her brows rose higher. "Oh? Are you part of the Earl of Darrow's family, then?" She glanced up at his temples. "Though I see you've missed the silver streak."

So, the girl by the stream knows she's Walter's by-blow.

"Right." He gave Bess his best smile, hoping to distract her from pursuing that line of inquiry. He could deny the connection, but he'd found it best not to lie outright unless forced to.

His smile worked rather better than he'd intended. Bess blinked and then gave him a slow, suggestive smile of her own before turning to lead him up the stairs, her hips sway-ing provocatively in front of his nose.

"You're in luck, Mr. Graham," she said as they reached the landing. "Our nicest room happens to be available."

She opened a door at the end of a short corridor and stepped aside—barely—so he could brush past her. Then she followed him into the room.

The *small* room. If this was the best the inn offered, he'd hate to see the worst.

He put his bag on the floor and then stepped round it to look out the window. Ah, he could see the stream below and what looked like a path along it.

"What brings you to Little Puddledon, if I may ask, Mr. Graham?"

He looked back at Bess. Good. His bag was acting as the wall he'd intended, keeping her at a distance. He'd been afraid she was going to try to plaster herself up against him.

She smirked. "Though I suppose I can guess. It must be Harriet, right? I mean, we've all noticed her hair, but I never imagined until just today—no one did—that she could be the last earl's daughter. And now you show up. It can't be an accident, can it? That's what I say."

Harriet. So, that's the girl's name. And what happened today?

Best play dumb. "I'm sorry. Who's Harriet?"

His carefully bewildered tone must have been convincing because Bess frowned. "You didn't know about Harriet?"

"No." He could answer that truthfully. Until he'd stumbled upon her at the stream, he'd had no inkling she existed. "I came to sample the beer I understand you make here." At least something useful had come from his many stops to ask directions.

"Oh." Bess frowned, clearly having some difficulty adjusting her thinking. "You mean Widow's Brew?"

"Yes."

"I see." She obviously didn't see, but at least she was willing to move on from Walter's daughter. "Well, then, you've come to exactly the right place. I'll pour you a large tankard down in the tavern, shall I? And if you like it, perhaps you'll put in a good word with your friends in London. I mean, being related to an earl, you must have friends there, right?"

She paused, clearly expecting a reply, so he nodded. It was true. He'd reconnected with some of his military and school friends and had finally begun to find his place among the *ton*.

"That's very good. Caro—she's our brewer—has been dying to get our beer into a London tavern or two. She'll be delighted to meet you."

She stepped back to the door—and Harry tried not to sigh with relief.

"Now, shall I pour you that tankard? Most of the men downstairs are finishing up and will be leaving soon, so I'll be able to spend some time answering any questions you might have"—she gave him a coy look—"about anything."

She was giving him an opportunity he could not refuse—but he was going to refuse it, at least for now. The trick would be to decline gracefully enough that he didn't offend her and lose a source of information.

"Thank you, but after hours in the saddle I feel the need to stretch my legs." He smiled to take the sting out of his refusal. "Perhaps I could take you up on your kind offer later?" *At least the part about the beer.*

She pouted briefly and then shrugged. "Suit yourself. You know where to find me."

"Thank you. Oh, and before you go"—he gestured at the window—"I see what looks like a path down by the stream. Is that a pleasant walk?"

"If you like looking at water. Take it upstream and then come back through the village." She grinned. "When you return, I wager you'll be ready for that nice tall tankard of Widow's Brew."

"I'm sure I shall be."

He waited until Bess had left and then hurried down the stairs. He took a quick look in to be certain Ajax was well settled and then headed for the water, turning upstream as Bess had suggested. He did need to stretch his legs, but he also needed time to think.

He should have adopted an alias rather than use his family name. Graham was rather common, but once he'd seen the girl—Harriet—he shouldn't have risked people making the obvious connection. Stupid of him not to think of that. He really *was* losing his touch. Now he would have to—

A flock of crows erupted from a stand of trees up ahead, cawing and wheeling through the sky over the stream. Something must have startled them. A stag? A wild boar? He'd keep an eye out—

And then he heard what sounded like a woman's scream followed by a male roar of pain or anger.

He broke into a run.

Godfrey knew an impressive number of swear words for a vicar.

Pen scrambled away from him, backing toward the stream, while his hands were busy gripping his . . . legs. It must hurt too much to touch the part she'd injured.

I wish I'd hit him harder.

He'd been holding her too tightly for her to get a really good angle on her target or as much force behind her thrust as she'd wanted.

"You bloody bitch."

"Tsk, tsk, Godfrey. What would your congregation say to such language?" She should be frightened, but the churning emotion in her gut didn't feel like fear. It felt like anger.

She also should run while Godfrey was incapacitated. He

was much larger than she—not that much taller, but far heavier—and he had a man's strength.

But he was between her and the path. Even if she made it past him, she'd still have a distance to run to the village and safety. Not far, but far enough that he could catch her before she got there.

She'd rather deal with him now, face to face, than have him run her down like a hunted animal, grabbing her from behind.

She took several deep breaths. And she should try to be calm. She still had to live in Little Puddledon and attend Sunday services in Godfrey's church. Having a rational conversation about the matter would be better than shrieking at him.

She should treat this as a simple misunderstanding and be thankful she'd discovered his true nature before she married him. Harriet was right. He *was* horrible.

"You'll pay for this, you slut," he said through clenched teeth.

Slut?! A dam broke inside her, and years of anger, fear, and powerlessness flooded out.

Bugger calm and reason.

She grabbed a sturdy stick off the ground. "You're the one who's going to pay."

"I don't think so." He laughed—well, that's what the noise sounded like, but there was no humor in it. Rather, she heard anger and disgust, though the fact that he was looking at her as if she were a piece of dung he'd just discovered on his shoe might be influencing her opinion. And yes, his beak of a nose had wrinkled just as Harriet said it would.

"Here I thought you were a respectable widow. Zeus, how you played me for a fool." He stepped toward her.

She was happy to note that he winced a little when he moved.

"Don't come any closer." She brandished her stick. "I

won't hesitate to use this"—she let her eyes drop briefly to his fall—"where it will do the most damage."

Did Godfrey suddenly look a bit green about the gills? At least he stopped his forward motion.

"You're a woman." His lip curled. "I can overpower you easily."

She gripped her stick more tightly. "I'm a woman who works with her hands every day. I'm strong"—she pointed her stick at her target—"and I have very good aim."

And she was bluffing. Yes, she was strong—for a woman. It was hugely unfair that the female of the species was at such a disadvantage when it came to physical strength. She would just have to make up for the difference with a cool head—and unerring aim.

Fortunately, Godfrey decided not to put it to the test, at least not yet. "I almost offered for you, you know," he said, tugging on his waistcoat and then, with false nonchalance, clasping his hands together in front of him so they offered his male bit some protection. "I almost opened my house to you and your"—his nose wrinkled again—"bastard."

Her grip on her stick tightened so much her knuckles turned white. Perhaps anger would make her strong enough to beat Godfrey's supercilious expression off his ugly face. "Don't you *dare* call Harriet that."

"Why not? It's what she is."

"It is not."

"Do you prefer the term by-blow, then? Love child?"

Harriet is *a love—a* loved—*child.*

She suddenly remembered how powerful she'd felt with Harry. Her love had burned so brightly that nothing—not her father, not her reputation, not all the rules of behavior she'd grown up with—had mattered. All those things had been as insignificant as a candle in the noon sun.

She'd been young and naïve then, but so very brave.

As only the young can be. Being on one's own with a child to support had taught her that the young were often fools.

Godfrey shook his head. "Thank God I discovered the truth in time."

She slashed her stick through the air, almost blind with anger. "No, thank God *I* discovered the truth in time. You are no more than a whited sepulcher."

Godfrey flinched, but recovered quickly. "Isn't that a bit like the pot calling the kettle black?" He took a step forward.

Pen thrust her stick toward his groin as she took a step back. "*I'm* not a vicar. I work with hops, not holiness."

She was not going to explain herself to him or to anyone, and she certainly wasn't going to ask for forgiveness. She hadn't done anything that she felt in her heart of hearts was wrong.

Though of course everyone else would think it wrong. They would look at her the way Godfrey was looking at her now. They'd see a woman damaged. Dirty. Worthless.

A whore.

And, more importantly, they'd see Harriet as a mistake, a child who would be better off if she'd never been born.

Which was why Pen had pretended to be a widow all these years.

"So, you want to talk about agriculture? About plowing and sowing?"

Her eyes narrowed—and she noticed he was coming closer again. She poked her stick in his direction and he stopped.

Unfortunately, his mouth didn't. "Have you been letting all the other village men plow your field?"

"W-what do you mean?" The words slipped out before she could stop them. She could tell what he meant from his insulting tone.

"Come on. It's only fair you give me what you've given them." His lips turned up in a grotesque smile. "Think of it as tithing."

Good God, how could she ever have considered marrying this jumped-up, sanctimonious scoundrel? "You're despicable."

"I promise you you'll like it." Godfrey cupped his fall. "My friend here always leaves the ladies begging for more."

Her stomach heaved at the thought, but she forced herself to ignore it. "Ha! If you hear begging, it's for you to hurry up and be done."

Lord, I shouldn't have said that.

His face darkened like a thundercloud, and then in a flash he was on her, ripping the stick from her hands and jerking her up against his chest. His arms across her back felt like iron bands.

She tried to knee him again, but he was holding her too tightly. She couldn't move. And then he smashed his mouth down on hers and tried to push his tongue between her lips.

She kept her jaws locked.

Stay angry. Fight. Don't let him do this.

He pulled his head back to glare at her. "Stop resisting."

"And let you rape me?"

"It's not rape. You want it."

She shoved against his chest, but couldn't move him even an inch. "Ask your aching cock if I want it." *Maybe I can strangle him with his cravat.*

She reached for his neckcloth, but he trapped her hands with one of his before she could grab it. The arm around her back tightened.

Oh, dear God. Now she was in a worse position. Without her hands to exert any force against him, he'd closed the last space between them. She could feel his hard cock pressing against her.

"You're a whore. You can't be raped."

"I am *not* a whore." *I have to break free. I won't—I can't— let Godfrey do this. What if he gets me with child? I—*

I have to remain calm and watch for the slightest opportunity. "But even if I were, my body is *mine*. No one gets to decide who . . . touches it but me."

He was panting now. He dragged her back to the willow, pinning her against the trunk. She felt his hand fumble with his fall. "Spare me your maidenly airs. We both know they're an act."

"They're not." Did she hear branches snapping, feet pounding down the narrow path?

It was likely just the blood rushing in her ears.

"Is it money you want? I'll pay you." He grinned. It was the most horrifying expression she'd ever seen. "I'll pay more if I'm pleased. Try to please me, Penelope."

He must have got his fall's buttons undone because now he was fumbling with her skirt, pulling it up, higher and higher, past her calves, her thighs—

"No!" She screamed and tried to slam her head into his face. She didn't get a flush hit, but managed a glancing blow to his chin. She felt him flinch.

"You bloody bit—*aurgh!*"

Suddenly she was free.

She blinked. How—

Oh. Godfrey's hands had more important things to do than molest her. They were busily clawing at an arm clad in blue broadcloth that had appeared across his throat.

"Aurgh!" Godfrey said again. "Gaa gaa gaa!"

Who was her savior? She looked up—but the man had twisted around, putting his body between her and Godfrey. All she could see was his back.

His back was very nice—broad with wide shoulders. He was a good six inches taller than Godfrey and clearly in far better condition.

Good God, if this man decides to rape me, I'll have no hope of freeing myself. I should run.

But the men were between her and the path. Perhaps she could go over or through the stream. She moved toward the water, trying not to bring any attention to herself.

The stranger removed his arm from Godfrey's neck.

"Bloody hell, sir, what do you mean by this?" Godfrey massaged his throat. "I'll thank you to take yourself off. You are interrupting my sport."

"Not sport. Rape."

She paused in her retreat. The voice was educated and vaguely familiar. Who could it be? Not a villager—Godfrey would have called him by name if he were.

She looked at Godfrey to see if he showed any signs of recognizing the fellow.

He didn't.

And then without conscious thought, her eyes dropped to Godfrey's fall. His pale pink rod peeked out at her.

Blech.

Godfrey made a dismissive sound, a cross between a laugh and a snort. "Oh, no, my good fellow. You've misconstrued the situation entirely. The woman's a common slattern, a—"

The man's fist connected with Godfrey's jaw in a dull thud. Godfrey's head snapped back, and the rest of his body followed to measure its length on the dirt and dead leaves, sending a red squirrel scampering away in alarm.

Pen pressed her lips together to keep from cheering.

She shouldn't cheer—she still had no notion who the stranger was. He might turn against her next. She saw the stick she'd dropped when Godfrey had accosted her and picked it up.

Godfrey scrambled to his feet. "You blackguard! Cur! I'll teach you some manners." He threw a punch.

In one fluid motion, the other man blocked it and sent

Godfrey crashing back to earth, nose spurting blood all over his cravat.

"Bloody hell"—except it came out more like *buddy hell*—"you broke my nose," Godfrey said, sitting up and using his handkerchief to try to stem the red flood.

"Unlikely. But if you try to hit me again, I *will* break it." The man straightened his cuffs. His back was still to Pen. "Now apologize to the lady."

Godfrey snorted—and then winced in pain. His eyes over the rapidly reddening handkerchief glared at the man and then glared at Pen. He got laboriously back to his feet.

"My apologies if I gave offense," he said to a point somewhere over her head.

If he gave offense! She'd like to—

"Let it go, Pen. Accept the man's weak apology before I'm forced to kill him."

Good God! It couldn't be—

"Harry?"

Chapter Five

"So, you know each other, do you?"

Godfrey's words were muffled by the roaring in her ears.

It's Harry. Oh, God. It's Harry!

She felt lightheaded, her heart pounding so hard she thought it might tear a hole in her chest, her lungs struggling to draw air. She planted one end of her stick on the ground, using it like a cane to steady herself, and studied him.

He was older, of course. There were lines at the corners of his mouth and eyes that hadn't been there before. And he seemed more . . . he looked more . . .

The only way she could describe it was *solid*.

The slim boy she'd loved had turned into a man.

Does he know about Harriet?

A hard ball of ice formed in her stomach. She was afraid she might be sick.

Godfrey sniffed. "Is he one of your custom—"

Harry's fist sent Godfrey back into the dirt. Fortunately, Harry's hat remained firmly on his head.

If Godfrey sees the silver streak, he'll know at once what Harry is to me.

Was. What Harry *was* to her. Had been. Their relationship was very much in the past.

Something that felt like longing stabbed through her.

Ridiculous. Yes, she'd loved Harry once, but that was a decade ago. He'd changed. *She'd* changed. They most likely had nothing in common.

Except Harriet.

Has he come for Harriet?

Panic joined the stew of emotions roiling her gut.

"You bloody *bastard*." Godfrey had managed to get to his feet again. "I'll have you know I'm the vicar here."

"Good for you. Now go away," Harry said dismissively, focusing instead on Pen.

She searched his face, but she might as well have been looking at a shuttered house for all she could glean from his expression. He hadn't used to be so inscrutable.

What can he see in my *eyes?*

Likely far too much. She looked at Godfrey instead.

His face was the same shade as the blood spattered on his cravat. "You can be certain I shall write at once to my patron, the Duke of Grainger, sirrah. He will not like to hear that you have abused one of his vicars."

That got Harry to look back at him. "He'll like it even less when I tell him one of his vicars is a rapist."

Godfrey's jaw dropped and his face went from red to white and then back to red. "I am no such thing!"

"Only because I arrived in time to stop you."

"I . . . The woman is a—"

"Say what I think you mean to say and I'll break your jaw as well as your nose."

Godfrey snapped his mouth shut, but only for a moment. "I promise you I intend to write the duke at once."

Harry shrugged. "You may do as you please."

"Indeed." Godfrey cleared his throat and shifted from foot to foot. "I must ask you your name, sir."

Was Harry going to tell Godfrey that he was the Earl of Darrow?

Apparently not.

"Harry Graham."

"I see. And—" Godfrey's mouth hung open, frozen for several beats. He frowned. "Graham as in the Earl of Darrow's family?"

Or as in the Earl of Darrow.

"Yes. But you can just tell Grainger it's his friend Harry. I'm here on his business, so he'll know whom you mean."

"Ah."

Pen thought she could see Godfrey's Adam's apple bobbing nervously even from her vantage point several yards away.

Harry's smile had an edge. "I do think he'll be more inclined to believe a friend than an, er, employee he's never met, don't you?"

"Um."

"In fact, now that I consider the matter, I think you might be wise to explore other employment opportunities. I very much doubt Grainger will wish to keep on a vicar who's a rapist."

"I didn't . . . That is, she—"

"Do you *really* wish to feel my fist again?"

Godfrey looked at her. "Mrs. Barnes, I do apologize but you must see I made an honest mistake."

An *honest* mistake? *She* would like to punch him in the nose—or in an organ much lower on his person. "You forced your attentions on me when I clearly didn't want them." Didn't want them? That was a colossal understatement. "I was trying to fight you off. That is not a mistake, honest or otherwise. It is an attack. If Mr. Graham had not arrived when he did, you would have r-raped me."

She started to shake as the realization hit her just how close she'd come to being violated.

I can't lose control now.

She tightened her grip on the stick and took several deep breaths.

Godfrey's mouth had flattened into a thin, tense line. He turned back to Harry. "Mr. Graham, I must tell you that this woman is living under false pretenses. She holds herself out as a widow, but she has an illegitimate daughter—" He shot her a glance before looking back at Harry.

"Since you say you are here on the duke's business and not your family's, perhaps you are unaware that this woman is the former earl's whore."

Harry's fist connected with Godfrey's stomach this time.

Godfrey bent over, gasping.

"You are quite a slow learner, aren't you?" Harry's voice was hard and cold—she'd never heard that tone from him before. "I advise you to leave without saying another word—here or anywhere. I really do not wish to kill you, but you are sorely trying my self-control. Do I make myself clear?"

Godfrey nodded.

"Good. And button your bloody fall."

Godfrey fumbled with his buttons as he scuttled off. He looked cowed, but Pen was certain Harry's threat wouldn't keep him from telling the first person he encountered the entire story.

Oh, who cared? It didn't matter any longer. The reputation she'd worked so hard to build was gone no matter what Godfrey did.

"Pen." Harry had come over and put his hands on her shoulders. "Don't cry."

"I-I"—she sniffed—"I'm not c-crying."

"Of course, you're not."

His hands exerted the slightest pressure and she gave in,

dropping her stick and collapsing against him, burying her face in his coat and sobbing. It felt so good to have his hard chest under her cheek again and his strong arms round her back.

But it was so foolish, too. She knew even as she sobbed and snuffled that Harry would go back to his estate tomorrow or the next day and she'd be here with Harriet—

She *would* be here with Harriet, wouldn't she? He'd not try to take her daughter?

Their daughter.

But he wouldn't do that to her. She knew he wouldn't. What did he want with Harriet? No, he would leave and she would stay. There would be no escaping or even sharing her responsibilities.

Not that she wanted to escape them. Of course not. She was quite able to handle matters on her own. It was weak of her to buckle under a little difficulty like this.

She forced herself to raise her head. To step back out of the warmth and support of Harry's arms.

Little Puddledon is where I belong now. I have a job to do—Jo and Caro and the rest of the Home depend on me. And I have Harriet to raise. I'm strong. I'll manage.

"Harriet's mine, isn't she, Pen?"

Oh, Lord. She'd used to imagine what it would be like if Harry suddenly appeared and asked her that question, but she'd stopped thinking about it years ago. What should she say?

Should I lie?

No. If he'd seen Harriet, he already knew the answer. *He* would never think she'd warmed Walter's bed.

"Yes."

His face stilled, shuttered again. What was he thinking?

"You didn't used to hide your feelings." Oh blast, she shouldn't have said that. She would call the words back if she could. The time when they'd been close and had shared everything—or at least she'd thought they had—was long gone. They were both different people now. She must remember that.

His lips curved into a small, guarded smile. "I've learned to be more cautious."

Cautious. That was what she should be. What she usually was. But he looked so familiar, so much like the Harry she'd known, that she had to fight to keep from falling into her old ways.

To do that would lead to disaster. Exactly what sort of disaster she couldn't say, but she felt as if she was teetering on the edge of a precipice. She should step back before she plummeted into the abyss.

"You've met her?" she asked, her mouth so dry her voice came out scratchy.

He nodded. "On my way into the village. I stopped by the stream to let my horse drink. She saw Ajax and came over to pet him."

"She likes animals." Pen felt a sharp pang of regret. If Harriet were Harry's legitimate daughter, she'd have grown up with horses. She'd likely have her own pony.

I'll go mad if I let myself think that way. "Did you tell her you were her father?"

"No." His brows snapped down into a scowl. "I didn't know I was—the thought never occurred to me. You hadn't told me about her, and I didn't know you were here. I thought she *was* Walter's. He certainly had plenty of by-blows."

She flinched. *By-blow.* It sounded so . . . disposable. Unimportant. Common.

How many by-blows does Harry have?

It was none of her concern.

Back when she'd imagined telling Harry he had a daughter, she'd never pictured it would be like this—that he'd be so . . . annoyed.

"And everyone—that arse of a vicar, Bess at the inn—

seems to think she's Walter's. Is that what you told them—told her?" His jaw hardened. "Is that what you told Walter? Did you try to get money out of him?"

How dare he! Her hand flew up to slap him, but he grabbed it before she could make contact.

"Careful. You saw what I did to the vicar."

"I'm not afraid of you."

Something flickered in his eyes, but it was so fleeting, she couldn't tell if it was anger or regret or something else.

"You should be," he said. "We are very much alone here." A rather chilling smile curved his lips. "You are at my mercy."

Fear shivered in her belly—

For God's sake, this is Harry.

She tugged her hand back. "Stop it. You're not funny."

"I didn't mean to be."

His voice still sounded slightly threatening, but this time she saw a glint of the old Harry in his eyes.

"I've known you since you were a boy, Harry Graham. I know you would never hurt me—or any woman."

He frowned, his eyes serious now. "It's been—what? Almost ten years. I've changed, Pen."

The fear stirred again, but she quashed it. "Not that much. And I also know you don't really think I'd try to get money from Walter. I'd rather starve to death."

"But would you let Harriet starve?"

Lud! He knew her too well. "Perhaps not. Fortunately, I never had to face that question." She considered it now. It took only a moment to decide what she would have done—or hoped she would have done.

"Yes, if I'd exhausted every other option, I'd have swallowed my pride and come begging to Walter. Not that it would have helped. I'm quite sure your brother would have slammed the door in my face—or would have had his butler do it."

She thought a moment more. "And then I would have pounded on it all the harder." She would do anything for Harriet, even take on the Earl of Darrow.

She frowned at the current Earl of Darrow.

Harry stared at her an extra beat or two, and then grinned, looking more like the boy she'd known. "Fearless as ever. Lord, I've missed you, Pen."

If only she *were* fearless. And she'd missed him, too, but stopped herself from saying so. She could not begin to lean on him at this late date.

At least he seemed interested in Harriet now.

"Will you tell me about her, Pen, and how you've gone on all these years?"

What could be the harm? He *was* Harriet's father. He deserved to know something about his daughter.

"Very well. Let's sit under this tree."

Harry offered her his arm, but she pretended not to see it.

"Allow me to put my coat down for you to sit on."

She laughed. "Harry, this is the country. I've sat in the dirt in this dress more times than I can count." She settled under the tree—and frowned. There was one question she needed answered first.

"Why *are* you here? You said it was on the duke's business. Is it about the Home?"

Harry sat on her left, turned at an angle so she could see his expression. It was guarded again.

"The Home?"

"Yes. The Benevolent Home for the Maintenance and Support of Spinsters, Widows, and Abandoned Women and their Unfortunate Children."

He raised a brow.

"Jo started it—Jo is Baron Havenridge's widow—years ago after her husband killed himself. He'd lost Puddledon Manor to the Duke of Grainger—well, the previous duke—

in a card game and then promptly put a bullet through his brain. That duke let Jo stay here, and he even sent us a yearly donation to help with expenses."

Should she try to argue for the new duke's support?

Not yet.

Harry was nodding. "Um, then, yes, perhaps I am in Little Puddledon about the Home. We can discuss that later. But now I am *here*"—he gestured to where they sat— "to learn about Harriet. Why didn't you tell me about her before, Pen?"

"Because . . ."

The memories she'd locked away years ago came flooding back. She closed her eyes, but that made it worse.

She stared at the water instead.

Stupidly, all the time she'd been trysting with Harry, she'd never thought about the risk of pregnancy. She'd got her courses late, when she was sixteen—just the year before her summer with Harry—and they'd been very irregular, coming only every few months. She'd had no mother or sister or even close female friend with whom to discuss things—she certainly wasn't going to mention such a matter to her father.

When she'd finally noticed how long it had been since her last monthlies, she'd thought their absence—and the tired, draggy feeling that plagued her—were due to the dismals. She'd been in terribly low spirits after Harry left. He hadn't been just her lover. He'd been her friend and constant companion, especially those last months.

It wasn't until she noticed her breasts were tender and certain scents made her feel ill that she realized she might have conceived.

"Because I didn't know I was increasing until long after you'd left England, and then I had no idea where you were or how to reach you."

And there was something even more painful to admit. She flushed.

"And even if I had known, I . . ." She swallowed. She didn't want to say it—it just underlined how different their stations in life were. "I *couldn't* write you, Harry, because . . ." *Oh, just spit it out.* "I couldn't write. I didn't know how."

He hid his shock well, but she'd seen it flicker in his eyes.

"Now I can write—and read," she said quickly—and perhaps a bit defensively. "I learned once I moved to the Home. And you can be sure I saw to it that Harriet learned, too." She couldn't keep the pride out of her voice. "She's very bright."

"Ah." Harry nodded. "That's good."

Good? It was *wonderful*. Harriet would have no limits on what she could do.

Except the limits imposed by her birth.

"Oh, what would have been the point of writing you even if I could have?" she said more forcefully than she'd intended. "You couldn't very well have come rushing home in the middle of a war." Not that he would have even if he'd been free to do so. The only reason to hurry home would have been to marry her and thus save Harriet from the stain of illegitimacy.

That thought would never have occurred to him—and it hadn't occurred to her. She'd always understood—and accepted—her place in the world and in Harry's life.

Harry was struggling with a confusing stew of emotions. First, there was the anger, some, though not all, of it left over from his brawl with the vicar.

I have a daughter. I've had a daughter for almost a decade, and I didn't know it.

He was furious with Pen, even though the rational part of him admitted she was right. If she hadn't known she was pregnant before he left England, she would have had a hard time reaching him on the Continent, even if she'd got someone to write a letter for her. He'd been alone, behind enemy lines, most of the time. In fact, getting a missive in English when he was trying to pass as French or Spanish would have been disastrous.

But I've been back in England for a year. She knows how to write now, but she still didn't send me word.

And then there was the pain, the enormous, hollow ache in his heart—perhaps even in his soul—that threatened to swallow him. He'd missed nine years of his daughter's life—

"And my life was rather . . . complicated then," Pen said.

Lord! Ice slid through his veins. His memories widened to include more than just Pen and the time they'd spent together.

"How did your father take the news?" There was only one way Pen's father would have taken such news—with the back of his hand across Pen's face.

Mr. Barnes had had a fierce temper, especially when he was in his cups—which was most of the time.

She shot him a look and then turned back to stare at the water. "Not well."

"Ah." His stomach clenched, and his anger quickly turned against himself.

He'd brought this on her.

Zeus, he felt like a complete blackguard. *I should have kept my bloody breeches buttoned, especially when I knew I was leaving—and leaving Pen unprotected.*

"So, he beat you?" His fingers had tightened into fists, wanting to pummel a man long dead.

There was no point in that. He forced his hands to relax.

She pushed her long hair back off her face. It must have fallen out of its pins when that unholy vicar had been mauling her.

Is it still as silky as it was the summer we were lovers? Does it still smell of soap and sun and . . . Pen?

Hell, now desire was mixing with his anger and pain.

"Only once."

Bloody hell. Even though he'd expected that answer, he still felt a jolt when he heard it. If Pen's father were here right now, he'd give the man such a drubbing it would make his fight with the vicar look like a little friendly sparring.

"He wanted me to tell him who the father was. I wouldn't do it."

Years of hiding his emotions while behind enemy lines or negotiating with foreign diplomats helped him keep his voice level. "He might have guessed."

She picked a leaf off the ground and started to shred it. "Oh, he guessed all right. He just wanted to make me say it." She made a little sound—it could have been a chuckle or a sob. "No matter how well we hid our liaison, my father knew the only way the baby could be anyone's but yours is if I'd been raped. He might have been a horrid, neglectful parent, but he wasn't completely blind."

"Ah." Why the *hell* hadn't he'd thought of Pen's reputation or, more to the point, the danger that she'd conceive?

He'd been a randy lad of eighteen. He'd not been thinking of anything beyond getting his cock deep in Pen's hot, sweet body.

A surprisingly strong bolt of lust shot through him to lodge in the obvious organ.

He shifted position to make certain the organ wasn't *that* obvious.

He shouldn't be reacting this way. He wasn't a green lad any longer. He was a mature, experienced man of twenty-eight, well versed in the ways of women. He'd developed excellent self-control.

Except where Pen was concerned, apparently. Her hair had slipped forward again. He was so very tempted to push it back, to feel his fingers tangle in its smooth, soft strands again. He'd loved it when she'd been naked over him, her hair brushing his chest and his stomach. His cock.

He shifted position again.

"He went up to the house to see your father."

Oh, Lord. "Did dear Papa offer to find you a farmer to marry?" That's what his father had done when any of Walter's wild oats had taken root.

"There weren't any farmers available. He offered the blacksmith's son."

"*Felix?*"

"The blacksmith had only one son." She smiled fleetingly. "I declined."

Thank God for that. It might have seemed like a reasonable solution to Pen's problem—a home for her and her child and, since she'd have wed before the baby's birth, the veneer of legitimacy—but the cost to Pen's spirit would have been far too high. She would not have liked being married to a rakehell, rubbing elbows daily with Felix's many lovers.

"And your father accepted your decision?" Pen's father should never have given Pen the choice. He should have refused at once on her behalf. But Harry remembered the man well enough to know he would have jumped at the hefty purse his father must have dangled in front of him— the old earl had always offered the parents of Walter's pregnant paramours money to soften the blow of losing their daughters.

If I had a daughter, I'd—oh, God!

Reality slammed into him again. He *had* a daughter—had had one for almost ten years: Harriet, who might have grown up in *Felix's* household thinking *Felix* was her father.

Nausea, pain, anger, regret, shame all swirled through him.

"No, of course he didn't. We had a very, er, *lively* discussion on the matter."

Harry's stomach cramped as Pen smiled grimly.

"I'd had the foresight to arm myself with the carving knife so he didn't try to beat me again."

His hands balled into fists again. *I should have been there.*

And yet, clearly, Pen had done an excellent job of protecting herself then and her daughter and herself since.

Their daughter. Harriet. Named for him, he'd wager.

"He threatened to throw me out into the cold"—she snorted—"but I pointed out it was late summer. I made it very clear that I was not going to marry anyone, so if he wanted to be quit of me, his best option was to let me go to Aunt Margaret, my mother's sister, in Westling." She glanced at him. "That's the closest village to the west of Little Puddledon."

"I know. It was one of the many places I stopped to ask directions."

That caught her interest. "Did you see the Drunken Sheep?"

"Yes."

She smiled. "And did you have any Widow's Brew?"

He smiled back at her. "Yes, I did. I understand it's brewed here in Little Puddledon."

What looked like pride widened her smile to a grin. "It is. I grow all the hops we use. You'll see the hopyard when you visit the Home—which you'll have to do if you're here on the duke's business."

And will I see my daughter as well?

He wasn't ready to ask that question. And Pen's answer didn't matter. He was determined to see Harriet, and this time he would let her know he was her father.

Pen resumed her story. "So my father grudgingly gave me a few coins for the trip"—she smiled again—"and in the morning as I was leaving, I helped myself to a few more from the jar he thought well hidden behind a loose board in the sitting room."

Pen had always been resourceful and not shy about taking what she needed. She'd had to be. Her mother had died when she was very young, and her father spent much of his time in his cups.

"But there's no stagecoach between Darrow and Westling." Nor any good roads. It would likely take him several days riding cross-country even on Ajax to make the journey.

"I found farmers or tinkers going my way." She shrugged. "Or I walked."

A chill seized his heart. Good Lord! She'd been all alone? What if she'd encountered a highwayman or other sort of villain? As she'd learned all too well just a short time ago, even vicars couldn't be trusted to keep their hands and other organs to themselves.

He'd always been in awe of Pen's courage and determination, but sometimes her behavior bordered on the foolhardy.

Not that she'd thank him for saying so.

"Er, wasn't it a bit of a risk to set off to your aunt's unannounced?" *And unwed and pregnant.*

She shrugged. "It's not as if I had any other option. I was *not* marrying Felix. Fortunately, Aunt Margaret did take me in." She grinned. "Though she was rather shocked to find me on her doorstep."

Rather shocked. She could have been incensed. Appalled. She could have slammed her door in Pen's face.

The chill spread from his heart to his gut. *If Pen's aunt had turned her away—*

No, there was no point in worrying about the past.

"It was her idea that I become 'Mrs.' Barnes," Pen said. "We made up a story about my husband having been killed in battle. It served very well until this morning"—Pen's lips flattened into a tight, thin line—"when Rosamund—a woman who's just moved here—noticed Harriet's silver streak and told everyone it proved she was Walter's by-blow. The story went through the Home like wildfire and, apparently, the village as well. Godfrey—the vicar—heard it with his midday meal."

Harry nodded. "Bess, the innkeeper, mentioned it to me when I arrived and made the mistake of giving her my real family name." He frowned. "But you've been here for years, haven't you? It seems odd the Graham streak has just now become a problem."

Pen shrugged. "I was lucky, I guess. Harriet's streak didn't appear until this spring, after she'd been sick. I was able to persuade everyone that her fever had caused it"—she scowled—"until Rosamund showed up."

Her voice dripped with loathing.

Well, that explained the delay, at least. "But why did the woman think Walter was Harriet's father?" He took his hat off to run his fingers through his hair. "Though I suppose he had so many children born on the wrong side of the blanket, he'd be the first Graham to come to mind."

Pen shrugged. "Or perhaps she didn't do the arithmetic and assumed you were out of the country at the crucial, er, moment." Then she looked at his hair and frowned. "What happened to *your* streak?"

Right. "I darkened it. I used to do that during the war when I didn't want people to remember me. It washes out."

Pen was still frowning. "Perhaps I should have darkened Harriet's, but I didn't think of it."

His heart stilled. If Pen *had* darkened Harriet's streak, he wouldn't have known she was a Graham. She would have been just another young girl he'd met on his travels.

Would Pen have told him he had a daughter if she hadn't been forced to?

One never knew with Pen.

And would I have had the wits to figure it out?

Pen wasn't hiding the fact she was a mother. *He* was quite good at arithmetic.

Another unpleasant thought surfaced.

"Harriet doesn't think she's Walter's daughter, does she?"

Pen shook her head. "No. I told her the truth . . . finally. Up until this morning, she thought her father had been a nice, solid farmer who'd gone off to fight Napoleon." Her jaw clenched. "She's not very h-happy with me at the moment."

She blinked rapidly and sniffed several times, but despite her best efforts, one tear escaped.

"Pen—" He reached for her.

She waved his hand and his sympathy away.

"Pardon me." She cleared her throat. "It's been a hellish day."

One of the things he'd always admired about Pen—and, yes, found exciting, too—was her fierce independence, but she needed to be sensible now. There was a child involved. *His* child.

"Will you let me talk to her?"

Pen didn't answer immediately.

He could demand she let him see Harriet—*would* demand it, if he had to.

I have a child. A daughter.

He ached to see her again, this time knowing that she was his.

I have to do something for her, but what? Send Pen money for her support. . . .

That didn't feel quite right, but what else could he do?

There's a small house on the estate. . . .

Harriet could live there with Pen. They wouldn't have to live in this . . . this Benevolent Home, whatever it might be. They'd be taken care of.

And I could see them.

Pen sighed. "All right. Not that I can stop you—I do know that. And Harriet will want to meet you." She smiled—a little wistfully he thought. "She's very like you, you know."

Harry wasn't certain if Pen thought that a good thing or not.

Chapter Six

Pen walked up toward the Home through Farmer Smith's fields with Harry at her side. A few cows interrupted their grazing to watch them pass. Harry wanted to see the Home so he could report on matters to the duke, and he wanted to see Harriet.

It felt so seductively familiar to be with him like this. Their strides matched as easily as they had when she'd been seventeen and they'd explored Darrow together. They hadn't spent *every* minute of every day naked and sweaty and—

Lud! I hope I'm not blushing.

She was certain she was. She looked away, hoping Harry hadn't noticed and wishing for a breeze to cool her cheeks.

Don't be an idiot. You aren't seventeen any longer.

Very, very true. She must fight against this feeling of *rightness* with him. He wasn't the Harry she'd known. Ha! He was now the bloody Earl of Darrow. If their stations had been far removed when he was just the earl's second son, they were a universe apart now.

Except. . . . He *felt* like the same Harry. He was older, yes, but he still looked very much like the boy she'd fallen in love with. His voice was the same. He even smelled the same. And his new title hadn't made him stiff or condescending. It was as easy to talk to him now as it had been then—look at how she'd spilled the story of her father's reaction to her pregnancy.

But Harry knew Papa. He understands as no one else can.

Yes, that was true. He was her past, but he was not her future. He couldn't be.

"I'm sorry, Pen."

Yes, she was sorry about that, too—

Wait. He can't be reading my mind.

"Sorry about what?" *Harriet? He'd best not say that.*

No, she hoped he *would* say it. Those words would douse this ridiculous ember of longing before it started a fire and consumed her.

"About putting you in this situation." He looked down at her. "About seducing you."

Oh. Had he never guessed, then?

"You didn't seduce me."

"Yes, I did." He laughed. "Though I'll grant you it didn't take much work. Don't you remember?" His grin turned a bit wolfish. "I do. Lord, Pen, you were so beautiful, standing naked in that shady, secluded part of the pond, your hair loose and almost brushing your smooth white arse, your breasts—" His jaw hardened and he looked away.

She looked down to see that another part of him had hardened.

Penelope Barnes, behave yourself.

"You can be sure I thanked God—though I doubt He wished to be thanked for such a thing—that I decided to go swimming that afternoon. I thought myself very lucky."

"It wasn't luck." So, he truly had never guessed. That surprised her, but it probably shouldn't have. Young men often didn't look beyond the surface when their cocks were involved.

His brows furrowed. "What do you mean?"

"It wasn't luck or Divine Providence. You would have found me that way had you come the next day or the next."

She had his full attention now.

"I would have?"

He looked so innocently puzzled, her heart filled with— no. *I can't feel* anything *for the Earl of Darrow.*

"Yes." He really hadn't known. "I'd lo—" *No, don't use that word.* "I'd been, er, infatuated with you since I stopped thinking boys were revolting. I knew you were going to leave at the end of the summer."

She'd heard the other girls on the estate gossiping after church or in the village shops. They'd thought it very romantic that Harry was going off to fight Boney. All they could talk about was how dashing he would look in a military uniform. But all *she* could think about was that he was leaving and nothing would ever be the same. Some men died in battle or were terribly injured. And even if Harry made it through safely, he wouldn't be coming back to Darrow. The title and estate belonged to his brother. Harry would go off to make his own life, a life that would be miles—*worlds*— away from her.

The days when she could hope to catch a glimpse of him at church or in the village were ending. He would no longer come to the summer fair or the estate Boxing Day party.

And she would have to grow up. Somehow, with Harry still at Darrow, she'd felt strong enough to withstand her father's increasingly frequent talk of her marrying. She was seventeen. Even she would admit it was time. She certainly didn't want to share a house with her father a moment longer than she had to. But neither did she want to share a house— and a *bed*—with Felix or any other man she'd met to that point. No one but Harry had made her heart beat faster— or provoked the faintest twinge of interest in any of her other organs.

"I wanted to be, ah"—she could *feel* her face turning

red—"*close* to you before you left. I knew where and when you swam, so I went there a little before you arrived."

Yes, she was embarrassed. And she'd felt embarrassed and foolish and nervous at the time—but she didn't regret it. She'd do it all again and exactly the same way if she were given the chance. "So, you see, *I* seduced *you*."

She stole a glance at his face. He looked shocked.

"But you were a virgin."

"So? Virginity doesn't make one blind or deaf or an idiot."

The village matrons hadn't always watched their tongues around virgin ears, but to be honest, she could have figured things out without anyone's help. Men weren't complicated creatures.

She lifted a brow. "It worked, didn't it?"

He laughed. "All too well—as you know. But I still shouldn't have done it. I took your virginity."

There had been no taking involved. If Godfrey had prevailed back there in the clearing, *that* would have been a taking, not of her virginity, of course, but of something far more precious: her autonomy. Godfrey would have turned her from an independent person with her own desires into a female body, existing solely for his use.

"You didn't take my virginity," she said, her voice rough with the memory of Godfrey's attack. "You helped me dispose of it."

She'd thought she'd known what was going to happen that day at the pond: Harry would put his cock in the channel between her legs. It had sounded embarrassing—disgusting, really—and painful, but she'd overheard the village women sighing and giggling about it enough to hope it wouldn't be *that* unpleasant. And since marrying and submitting to a husband were, she'd thought then, a woman's only lot in life, she'd have had to endure it eventually. She'd rather her first time be with Harry. She'd felt certain if anyone could make it bearable, he could.

Well, if she were honest, she'd admit she'd hoped he could make it rather more than bearable. He'd stolen a mistletoe kiss during Christmastide that year, just a brief brush of his lips on hers followed by a laugh, and she'd liked that very much. It had stirred something hot and hungry in her that was a little frightening, but exciting, too.

So, she'd gone to the pond hoping he'd kiss her again—maybe several times. She'd thought that would be worth the rest of it. She'd never imagined what an intense, consuming experience their joining would be—and how much she'd want to do it again and again.

"All right. But still—good God, Pen, we were, er—"

Harry looked away. Pen thought *his* cheeks were a bit flushed.

"—ah, *frolicking* every day that summer, sometimes several times a day. It's unconscionable that I didn't consider you might conceive."

"You were only eighteen and going off to war."

Frolicking . . . That was one way to describe what they'd done. And it *had* been playful, joyful, satisfying—and, as each day slipped into the past, more and more desperate, at least for her. She'd felt the end rushing toward her.

And then it had arrived. They'd had one last night of wild, intense coupling—and in the morning, Harry was gone. Gone from Darrow and gone from her life forever.

Until now.

The most relevant part of her body trembled with excitement—

Oh!

She'd thought she was too old for such feelings. The only time she'd thought of coupling in years had been to cringe at the prospect of letting Godfrey into her bed.

Dare I try to seduce Harry again?

No.

Why not? I've already lost my reputation, and everyone

will probably assume I'm frolicking *with him while he's here anyway. What would one more time hurt?*

"Still, I shouldn't have done it," Harry said. "I upended your life."

She shrugged. She hadn't had much of a life to upend.

"Are you happy here, Pen?"

She hadn't expected that question. She turned it over in her mind. She knew what it meant, of course, but happiness wasn't a concept she thought much about. She was too busy looking out for Harriet and tending to the hops and her other duties. The last time she'd called what she'd felt "happy" was that summer with Harry.

Happiness was for children.

"I'm content. I'm busy. I've got my work and Harriet, of course." She glanced up at him. "Are you happy?"

He laughed, apparently surprised by her turning the question back to him. "I'm the Earl of Darrow. I must be happy."

He didn't sound happy.

She wanted to make him happy—

No! Harry's happiness is none of my concern. None at all.

"I'm certainly busy," he said. "I have many responsibilities, some of which I'm still learning about. But I can't say I'm content." He shrugged. "I'd rather be just Harry Graham again."

They'd reached the stile over the last stone fence separating the fields from the road that led up to the Home.

"Here, take my hand," Harry said.

She looked at his fingers and hesitated. She didn't need help. She was used to managing for herself.

But she put her hand in his anyway.

Oh! That was a mistake. The strength of his clasp brought more memories rushing back and in far too exquisite detail: the warm, firm pressure of his broad palm, the teasing, gentle touch of his clever fingers, the wet rasp of his tongue on her—

The relevant body part shot from trembling to throbbing. She caught her breath.

Harry's here, temptation whispered. *This is your perfect— your only—chance to see if there's still magic between you.*

"Are you all right, Pen?"

She nodded, not daring to look at him or talk for fear she'd give her feelings away. She scrambled over the stile, taking her hand back as soon as she was over the top.

There was—could be—no magic between them. Yes, Harry was here, but on business for the duke. He had no interest in dalliance, especially with a mature woman of twenty-seven.

And yet, from her observation, men were *always* interested in dalliance.

Stop. She was fooling herself. This Harry was not the boy she'd known—just as she wasn't that girl. Nine years— almost ten—was a long time. They'd both changed. They were strangers to each other now.

Strangers that shared a daughter.

Her stomach cramped. Oh, Lord, Harriet. How was she going to take care of her? She'd thought Godfrey was her answer, but look how wrong she'd been about him.

Why am I worrying about Godfrey now that the entire village knows Harriet is a bastard?

"I *am* sorry you had to face everything alone, Pen," Harry said, as soon as he'd made it over the stone fence. "I—"

She cut him off. "We both made mistakes." She must make one thing very clear, however. She looked him in the eye. "But Harriet is *not* one of them. I've never regretted having her, not once."

Harriet gave her life focus and meaning. She would do anything for her—even protect her from Harry, if necessary.

"If you think she is a mistake, then perhaps it would be best if you avoid her or at least not tell her you're her father.

Pretend you're some Graham cousin like you say Bess thinks you are."

Harry shook his head. "That won't work. The vicar knows my name. How many Harry Grahams can there be who are friends of the Duke of Grainger? Someone will figure it out—perhaps this Rosamund woman who you say recognized the Graham streak."

Lord, he was right. And when Harriet found out that her father had been here and Pen had kept his identity from her. . . .

Harriet would never forgive her.

"I don't think Harriet is a mistake, Pen. And I want to meet her. She's my only child."

Pen snorted. "As far as you know."

He scowled at her, but when he spoke, his voice was even. "I suppose I deserve that." He blew out a long breath and glanced away. "Well, of course I deserve it." When he looked back at her, his eyes were unshuttered, open and direct as they'd been when she'd known him at Darrow. "But I do think it's true. I'm not an eighteen-year-old idiot any longer, Pen. And I've never been as, ah, *abandoned* with anyone else as I was with you that summer."

She wanted to believe him, not that she cared so much whether he had other children—it wasn't her place to care or not—but because she wanted to think she could still trust him.

"And the women I've consorted with all know how to prevent conception."

Ah, yes. Whores. Lightskirts. Exactly what Godfrey had said she was—except she'd been an amateur while the others were professionals.

"I swear I won't hurt her, Pen."

She *did* trust him—but she would still be there when he met Harriet to see that he kept his word. Not that she could inflict much damage on him if he didn't, but, really, what choice did she have?

Perhaps one. She could choose where they met.

"Very well. I'd thought to take you up to the Home directly, but I think a more private place would be better for Harriet to learn you're her father."

He looked puzzled. "Is there no private sitting room we could use?"

"Nothing is private at the Home." She laughed, a touch grimly. "This is a houseful of females, Harry. Someone is certain to see you arrive or to overhear us, and the details will spread in a flash, likely heavily embroidered with speculation." And that wasn't all. "Harriet will know that, and I think it will make her nervous."

Meeting her father without an audience would give Harriet the time and freedom to decide for herself what she thought of the man.

He nodded. "So, what do you suggest?"

An excellent question. She stood in the road, considering. . . .

"I have it—the gothic cottage. It's the only folly on the property and mostly ignored. I was told it was used as a guesthouse sometime in the past. I'll take you there and then go up to the house to get Harriet." She sighed. "If I can find her. Since Verity arrived, Harriet's been playing least in sight."

Harry let Pen lead him across another field toward a line of trees, surprised at how relieved he felt that they weren't going to the main house. He'd moved easily among peasants and princes when he'd worked for the Crown. Why would visiting a houseful of women put him on edge?

Because it wasn't the women—it was the fact that he was about to meet his daughter that was jangling his nerves. And this time they would both know of their connection.

He suddenly wished he'd been able to spend more time

with his nieces. He had no notion of how to go on with a young girl.

"What is the problem with Verity?" he asked.

Silence.

He looked over. Pen's lips were pressed together. She was obviously struggling for control.

"There are always a few issues when a new girl arrives," she finally said. The words were measured. Reasonable. But her voice was tight.

Then she stopped and faced him, her expression twisted with worry and anger, control abandoned. "Verity has been *torturing* Harriet, Harry. She's eleven and has turned all the other girls against her. No one will play with Harriet any longer."

Zeus! He was shocked by the fury that exploded through him at Pen's words. He wanted to find this girl and wreak some dreadful punishment on her.

What is the matter with me? I can't attack a child. The notion's revolting.

But, *God*, in that moment he wanted to.

He schooled his emotions. Pen lived here. She must know how best to address the issue. "Tell me what you want me to do."

She looked at him, an arrested expression on her face. Didn't she expect him to want to help?

"I'm Harriet's father, Pen. It's my duty to protect her."

She blinked, and then sighed and shook her head. "Thank you. I'm so used to dealing with matters by myself, I didn't think . . ." She shrugged, smiling briefly. "I'm sure I'll come up with a solution eventually. Jo says to give it time, and she's usually right."

Pen started walking again, but Harry stood where he was for a moment. He watched her stride away. Her shoulders were back, her head high. She looked confident and determined—now.

I hate that I've caused her so much heartache.

He'd try to persuade her to move into the house at Darrow. That would solve all her problems—and his as well.

Though Pen might not agree. She could be exceedingly pigheaded.

He caught up to her as she reached the trees and started down a narrow path.

It was cooler here in the woods and quieter so that small noises were magnified. Some creature rustled through the underbrush off to their left, and birds called to each other high above their heads. He thought he heard the rush of water somewhere nearby.

And then they rounded a bend, and he got his first look at the cottage. It was larger than he'd expected, built of stone and covered in ivy, with a thatched roof and gothic arches on the porch and windows. It looked very—

"Ahhh!"

That hadn't come from Pen. He looked at her.

She'd already taken off running down the path past the building.

He ran after her, behind the cottage and up the hill, the sound of rushing water getting louder.

"What is it?" He had to shout to be heard.

She spared him a quick glance. "It sounded like Harriet."

Harriet? Zeus! He sped up—but Pen grabbed his arm before he could pass her.

"No. You'll startle her."

Startle her? That was the least of his worries. There was water up ahead. Harriet might have fallen in.

But if she hadn't . . .

Blast it, Pen was probably right. Harriet might recognize him from earlier, but having a grown man, even one that hadn't been threatening before, burst out of the trees unannounced could lead to disaster.

"And we're almost there. See?"

"Yes." They'd just rounded another curve. The trees ended about twenty yards ahead. The sound of rushing water was almost deafening.

"Stay back in the shadows."

"Very well." He'd always hated taking orders—he far preferred being in charge, which was one reason he'd usually worked alone during the war—but he forced himself to stop. He watched as Pen stepped out to the edge of a wide pool. Water splashed down from a waterfall on her left.

"Hallo, Mama!"

Harry looked up to the top of the waterfall, and his gut clenched. There was Harriet, sitting on what looked to be a very wet, very slick rock. She waved down at Pen.

Pen waved back and shouted, "Was that you I heard a few minutes ago?"

"Yes. I slipped." Harriet laughed. "I almost fell."

Good God, how could Harriet be so unconcerned? And she certainly wasn't safe now. One wrong move and she would tumble over the rocks, perhaps hit her head or break an arm or—

"Come down," Pen called. "I have someone I want you to meet."

He held his breath as Harriet got up and scampered over the wet rocks. Her foot slipped again, and his heart jumped into his throat. The relief he felt when she caught her balance made his knees weak.

What is the matter with me? My nerves aren't usually stretched so thin.

When Harriet was finally, safely standing on the ground next to Pen, Harry stepped out of the trees' concealing shade. Harriet and Pen turned to look at him—

Zeus, the girl has Pen's eyes. That's why she seemed so familiar when I met her by the stream.

"You're the man I saw with Ajax."

She was still wearing her bonnet, hiding her hair. He wished he hadn't darkened his.

He nodded. "Yes." He looked at Pen. How was he to explain the matter?

"Let's go to the cottage, Harriet," Pen said. "I—" She paused and looked at him. "*We* have something important to tell you."

Harriet frowned—and then shrugged and walked on down the path ahead of them.

This is my daughter. Mine and Pen's.

Harry felt an odd mix of wonder, pride, disbelief, and anxiety as he followed Harriet and Pen down the hill. And regret. He'd missed nine years of Harriet's life.

She's got Pen's independence and strength of will as well as her eyes.

She must have something of me, too. Something besides the silver streak.

At least the streak proclaimed her paternity. He didn't have to grapple with the question of whether or not she was his. He smiled to himself. And risk Pen neutering him as she'd likely do if he raised that issue.

He followed them into the cottage, closing the door behind him, muting the light and the birdsong.

He glanced around. They stood in a simple room—stairs off to his right led to an upper level, likely not much more than a loft. There was a stone fireplace, a wooden table, and several plain wooden chairs. Harriet went to stand by herself near the hearth.

Tension was suddenly thick in the air. It was hard to take a deep breath.

"What is it, Mama?" Her eyes flicked up to Harry's hair—he'd taken off his hat when he'd come inside—and back to her mother.

Pen hesitated a moment, and then walked across the room to close the gap between her and her—*their*—daughter.

Harriet dodged behind a chair.

Pen stopped, clearly unhappy at the barrier. "This is the Earl of Darrow, Harriet." Pen glanced at him. "Your father."

Of course, Harriet didn't exclaim with joy and rush toward him. She threw another quick glance at his hair and then looked back at Pen. "No, he's not. He doesn't have the silver streak."

"I darkened it," he said.

That brought Harriet's attention back to him, her eyes clouded with suspicion.

"I do that sometimes when I don't want people to notice me."

A frown appeared between her brows. "Why wouldn't you want people to notice you?"

"Because during the war I, er, gathered information for the Crown. I often pretended to be French or Spanish to blend into my surroundings. The silver streak would have made me stand out most inconveniently."

"You were a spy?"

"In a manner of speaking." Spying was not precisely a noble calling.

Harriet nodded as if she accepted that and then a small smile flitted across her lips, hope flickering in her eyes. "So, did Mama write to you, then?" She looked back at Pen. "Did you, Mama? Am I the reason he's here?"

"Harriet . . ." Pen looked at him.

He was tempted—*so* tempted—to lie, but he knew, even without Pen's worried eyes on him, that lying to Harriet would be a very grave mistake.

And if he *did* lie, Pen was sure to correct him.

"I wish I could say that's why I'm here, Harriet, but the truth is I didn't know about you. When I saw you by the stream, I thought you must be my brother's child. It wasn't until I talked to your mother that I realized you were mine."

Harriet's look of disappointment tore at his heart, making him add, "But if I *had* known, I would have come at once."

Her smile lit her face. He felt absurdly happy. Brilliant, in fact. He—

Oh, blast. Now she was glaring at her mother. Perhaps that had not been such a smart thing to say.

"See? You *should* have told him about me."

Pen sighed. Suddenly, she looked tired and a bit defeated. "I explained before, Harriet. I didn't know how to reach him when he was on the Continent."

She didn't mention she hadn't known how to write.

Then she looked at him, as if seeking his support. He would give it—especially as he had thoughtlessly thrown fuel on this particular fire.

"Your mother is correct, Harriet. It would have been very difficult, if not impossible, for a letter to reach me. And while I would have *wanted* to hurry home if I'd heard about you, the fact is that I probably couldn't have got free. I had superiors who were depending on me, and England is a long, time-consuming journey away when one is in Portugal, Spain, France, or Austria."

Harriet digested that. "But you came home months ago. And you're an earl now. You can do whatever you please."

That was not entirely true, but Harriet was right. He *could* have come earlier had Pen bothered to tell him he had a daughter.

Harriet glared back at her mother. "You should have written him then, Mama."

Pen's chin came up. "I wasn't going to scramble to hang on the earl's sleeve, Harriet. Imagine how that would have looked."

Harriet was not sympathetic to that argument. Her chin also came up. "Who *cares* how it would have looked! I'm his daughter. He should have known about me."

Which was true—

Oh, hell. Harriet had started to cry. She covered her face with her hands.

"And *I* didn't know about *him*. I thought my father was *d-dead*."

Pen reached for their daughter—and Harriet again dodged her.

"We didn't—we don't—need the earl, Harriet. We do fine on our own." Pen's voice shook with anger or nerves, he couldn't say.

Harriet uncovered her face long enough to hurl a few words at her mother. "*You* do f-fine. I don't. I *hate* you."

Pen flinched.

Zeus! He'd best take matters in hand. "Now see here, Harriet—"

Pen's attention snapped back to him. "Don't you *dare* use that tone with her."

No one spoke to him that way. He opened his mouth to tell Pen exactly that—and paused.

He didn't know anything about being a father—or at least anything good. His own father had ignored him—he was only the spare, after all. And Walter . . . Harry had left for the Continent around the time his second niece was born, but his brother hadn't shown any evidence to that point that he was going to be a model father.

For some reason, he remembered a bit of negotiation advice an old diplomat had given him as they'd finished the last of several mugs of ale late one night in Vienna. *Don't dig your heels in if you don't want to get stuck in the mud.*

"Harriet." He spoke softly this time as he moved closer.

Pen gave him a warning look that said she'd strangle him with his cravat the moment he took a wrong step.

"I'm sorry I wasn't here before, but I'm here now."

He waited what seemed like an eternity.

Finally, Harriet wiped her face with her hands and looked up at him. "For how long?"

Should I mention the house at Darrow?

No, not before I discuss it with Pen.

It was not at all a certain thing Pen would agree to the move. Best go slowly.

"I don't know. A few days. Perhaps a week." He looked at Pen. He didn't want to leave her right away, either.

Why?

He didn't care to contemplate the answer to that question.

"I'd like to spend some time getting to know you, if that would be all right with you"—he looked at Pen again—"and with your mother, of course."

Why is Pen frowning?

"You must be busy," Pen said.

Does she not want me to stay?

"You're an earl. You have many responsibilities." She was speaking faster than normal and looking at his cravat rather than his face. "We really do go on perfectly fine without you."

That hurt, not that it should. They'd have been in a sorry state if they'd needed him all these years.

"*I* want you to stay," Harriet said.

"Harriet!"

Harriet ignored her mother, looking at Harry instead. Her voice held a mixture of defiance and pleading. "Everyone has been so beastly since Verity got here. I want you to come up to the Home so I can show them you—" Her voice broke, but she swallowed and carried on. "So I can show them you ac-accept me." Her chin went up again. "That I'm not another discarded Graham by-blow."

He heard Pen suck in a horrified breath as anger surged through him, the depth and intensity of it taking him by surprise. The only time he could remember ever feeling this visceral a reaction was when he'd seen Pen's father hit her, when she'd been about Harriet's age. He'd been only a boy then, powerless to do anything.

Well, he was not powerless now. He was an earl and the good friend of the Home's unwitting benefactor.

But do I really want to wade into the middle of Pen's life and the lives of the Home's inhabitants?

It might not be the most sensible thing to do, but he was going to do it. He did not like the idea of anyone treating his daughter cruelly.

And he should make another point clear.

"Is that what they're saying, Harriet?" Pen was asking. She sounded as if she'd like to lop off a few heads herself.

"Yes, Mama."

"Harriet," he said, "my brother was the one who had many, er, by-blows, not me. As far as I know, you're my only child."

Pen and Harriet both looked at him doubtfully.

He was almost certain that was true, though he'd admit the risk of pregnancy had never been as much on his mind as it probably should have been. He quickly ran through the list—the relatively short list—of his paramours. None had become mothers in the time he'd, er, *known* them in the biblical sense.

"I'd be happy to go up to the Home with you. I have to go there anyway, to be honest. The Duke of Grainger asked me to have a look around for him." He smiled at Harriet. "Perhaps you and your mother can give me a tour."

Harriet grinned and gave an odd little cross between a skip and a hop. "Yes. Let's go now, Papa." She stopped, balancing on one foot. "*May* I call you Papa?"

Apparently, this was his day for surprising emotions. He couldn't quite identify the one currently swelling his chest.

He didn't trust his voice, so he just nodded.

"I don't know about today, Harriet," Pen said. "It's getting late, and the earl has been traveling."

And fighting, not that the vicar had been much of an opponent. Still, he must be looking more than a little ragged.

And he suddenly realized he was also feeling more

than a little ragged. He'd had enough emotional turmoil for one day. The thought of being inspected by a houseful of females . . .

It would be better if he were well rested and properly prepared for that ordeal. And he was here on Grainger's business, too. He should be alert so he could evaluate matters and give the duke a proper report.

Harriet had turned to him. "It's not too late, is it, Papa?"

Zeus, he hated to disappoint her. He looked at Pen—who frowned and shook her head.

All right then. He wasn't foolish enough to think he knew better than Harriet's mother, and he *was* looking forward to some time alone to consider all that had happened today— and perhaps drain a pint or two of Widow's Brew while he did so.

"I'm afraid your mother is correct, Harriet."

Harriet scowled at Pen.

Fortunately, a compromise popped into his head. "What if I walk you up to the Home now? And then I'll arrive promptly tomorrow morning"—he looked at Pen—"at what-ever the appropriate time might be."

Harriet drooped a bit, but only for a moment. "You promise?"

"I give you my word."

Luckily, the word of the Earl of Darrow was good enough for a nine-year-old girl. She headed for the door.

"You'll come early, won't you, Papa?"

A warm rush of pleasure made him smile. Would he ever tire of being called "Papa"?

He thought not.

Perhaps this is a sign I really am ready to marry and start my nursery.

"Just give me a time and I'll be there."

When he got back to London, he'd do his duty and offer for Lady Susan. There was no point in delaying any longer.

As his mother kept pointing out, he needed an heir sooner rather than later, and Lady Susan had the proper breeding to be a countess. She was the daughter of an earl, after all. She would know exactly how to manage his household. And she got on with his mother and sister-in-law. Might as well please his female relatives. Life would be simpler and more harmonious that way.

And Lady Susan *was* very beautiful.

"Mama will be up with the sun, checking the hops," Harriet said.

Pen laughed. "Well, perhaps not *that* early." She smiled up at Harry. "Shall we say nine, Lord Darrow?"

Ah. Hearing Pen use his title sent his good spirits plummeting.

He'd got used to people calling him Darrow. After all, he was indeed the earl now. He might never have wanted the title, but he had to accept it. Yet, Pen . . . She was from his past, from the time when he was just Harry, just the second son, free to go where he wished and do as he willed without having to worry about tenants and roofs and the House of Lords.

"Very well." He tried to keep his voice light. "Nine it is."

"I think you should stay at the cottage, Papa, instead of the inn," Harriet said as she skipped down the path ahead of them, "and Ajax can stay with Bumblebee."

"Er, Bumblebee?" He looked at Pen for enlightenment, but Harriet answered before Pen could.

"That's Miss Jo's horse." She looked earnestly back at him. "You'll be closer to the Home if you're at the cottage, Papa, and maybe I can visit you. Mama won't let me go to the inn by myself. She says too many of the men end up in their cups"—she grinned—"which is good for us because that means they are drinking lots of our ale."

Pen shrugged a bit helplessly. "I just don't believe inns are proper places for young children."

"I'm not young!" Harriet said. "I'm nine."

"Ancient." Pen gave Harriet a semi-stern look. "And you have no reason to go to the inn, do you?"

"I do now if Papa's there."

He would agree that an inn, even a small local inn such as the Dancing Duck, wasn't the best place for a young girl. "I assume there's a bed in the cottage?"

"Yes, in the loft," Pen said, "though I'm not certain what condition the bed is in."

"It's fine," Harriet said. "I checked before I went to the waterfall." She grinned at Harry. "I was going to move there myself, Papa, but I'll give up my plans for you."

"What?!" Pen was almost sputtering. "I would never let you stay alone at the cottage, Harriet. What were you thinking?"

Harriet stopped—they'd reached the edge of the woods—and scowled at her mother. "I was thinking I'm tired of Verity and the other girls teasing me. And pinching me. It's bad enough during the day, but at least then I can see them coming and get away. But at night, once the candles are snuffed . . ." She shuddered. "It's horrible."

Harriet's words made Harry remember the dormitories at Eton, the lack of privacy, the constant feeling of being at the older boys' mercy.

Harriet was his daughter. She should have a room of her own. He would definitely talk to Pen about moving to Darrow and taking that empty house.

"I'll have a cot put up in my room for you," Pen said. "You will stay with me until the situation is resolved."

"All right." Harriet grinned at Harry. "So, you *can* stay at the cottage, Papa!"

Chapter Seven

Pen stood with Harriet at the edge of the drive to the Home and watched Harry walk down the road to the village. In just a few minutes, his long stride had carried him around the bend and out of sight.

She felt oddly bereft.

Silly! He'll be back tomorrow.

Yes, but for how long? After tomorrow's tour, he'd have enough information to assure the duke that they had an important, thriving business here.

I cannot allow myself to feel . . . anything *for him.*

He'd been very good with Harriet, though. He hadn't talked down to her the way so many adults did when addressing children. He hadn't lied to Harriet about why he'd come to the village, though she could see he'd been tempted to do so. And he'd supported Pen, both in agreeing that it would have been difficult for a letter to have reached him on the Continent and in putting off his tour of the Home until tomorrow.

And he'd moderated his tone—and not snapped back at her—when she'd called him out for speaking sharply to

Harriet. Her own father would have given her the back of his hand for that.

Harry would be a good father to the children—the *legitimate* children—he'd have, likely with Lady Susan Palmer.

"I like him, Mama," Harriet said, giving the little skip she did when she was especially happy.

Pen's heart clenched. Oh, no. She couldn't allow Harriet to form an attachment to Harry.

"He's nice," Harriet said, doing another little hop-skip.

"Y-yes, but remember, he's leaving soon. Perhaps as early as the day after tomorrow. Or perhaps even tomorrow. I can't imagine he'll need to tour the Home for very long." She forced herself to smile. "He'll want to get back to report to the Duke of Grainger. And we do need Lord Darrow to give a good report as soon as possible. We depend on the duke's generosity to keep the Home running."

Harriet might not have been listening. "He said he might stay a week or more. He wants to get to know me." She gave Pen a sly little smile. "I think he likes you."

What was this? Surely Harriet understood the situation. "Er, yes. We were friends when we were children." And obviously *very* friendly when they were more than children or Harriet would not be here.

"No. I think he *likes* you." Harriet's smile widened into a grin. "I think he wants to marry you."

"*Harriet!*" Pen stopped and took a calming breath. She needed to nip this fantasy in the bud at once. "Lord Darrow is *not* going to marry me. I thought I explained the matter to you. Earls do not marry farmers' daughters."

Harriet shrugged as if Pen had said something completely inconsequential. "You're a hop grower now."

"They don't marry hop growers, either." Blast. That had come out more harshly than she'd intended.

She must remember Harriet had grown up in this little village. She'd never been around the nobility.

"Earls marry ladies, Harriet. Women of noble birth. According to the newspapers, Lord Darrow has been on the verge of offering for Lady Susan Palmer, the Earl of Langley's daughter, all Season. He was supposed to attend a house party with her at the Duke of Grainger's just a few days ago."

And now he's here—on the duke's business . . .

Dear God, he's probably already betrothed.

Her stomach sank.

Harriet grinned and started skipping up the drive to the house. "So, you like him, too!"

"What?" How in the world had Harriet reached that conclusion?

Harriet looked over her shoulder at Pen, her grin widening. "You wouldn't have been looking through the papers for his name if you didn't like him."

Pen caught up with her. "I was doing no such thing."

"Oh? Who else did you read about?"

Harriet was getting too smart for her own good.

"Lord Darrow is your father. He also happens to be the only peer of my acquaintance. I was simply interested to see how my old playmate—" The memory of a shockingly erotic bit of sexual play popped into her thoughts. Lud! Fortunately, Harriet was too young to know about such things—or to notice Pen blushing. "How my old friend was doing."

Perhaps Harriet *had* noticed Pen's flushed cheeks. She giggled. "*I* think you like him. You look at him the way Miss Avis looks at Billy from the butcher shop when he comes with our delivery, before she takes him back to the larder." Harriet frowned. "Miss Dorcas always laughs after Billy leaves and asks Miss Avis how she liked the sausage—and I don't think she bought any sausage. What do you suppose she means by that?"

"I have no idea." Surely the Almighty would forgive her this one small untruth. "You should not be loitering in the kitchen, Harriet. Leave Miss Avis and Miss Dorcas to do their work." She really did need to get Harriet out of the Home, but how was she to manage that now that marrying Godfrey was not an option? There were no other suitable single men in the village.

Harry's face popped into her thoughts, but she banished it immediately. She'd told Harriet the truth: earls did not marry so far beneath them, and, even more to the point, chances were good that Harry was no longer single, but betrothed to Lady Susan.

Time to focus on more practical matters. "I will talk to Miss Jo at once about moving you in with me, Harriet."

The Home was crowded. Most women had to share a room, and the girls were all housed in what had once been the Long Gallery. But Pen—and Caro—each had her own room, partly because they'd been there the longest, but also because they had no separate office and needed the extra space for a desk and shelves to keep their papers organized.

Adding a cot for Harriet would take up almost all the available floor space—she and Harriet would have to climb over each other constantly. It wasn't a permanent solution to the problem.

"Oh, I do wish we could live somewhere else," Pen said.

Harriet frowned and pulled a face. "You aren't going to marry Mr. Wright, are you?" She sounded angry and, well, frightened, too.

Pen put her arm around her and gave her a quick hug. "No! Definitely not. You were correct about him. He *is* horrible—a wolf in sheep's clothing if ever I met one." Thinking about what had happened in that clearing made her furious again.

And because she was the mother of a daughter, it also made her think. She wouldn't go into the gory details, but she did want Harriet to be prepared should she ever find herself in such an unfortunate position.

"He'd heard the story about your birth, Harriet, and, just as you predicted, he didn't think well of me. In fact, he seemed to believe it somehow gave him permission to take whatever liberties he liked with my person. He tried to force me—" She caught herself.

Remember, Harriet is only nine.

Now that her daughter was getting older and seemed so mature, Pen found herself treating her a bit too much like a confidante.

"He tried to kiss me." That was enough to get her point across. "I had to object. Vehemently."

Oh, there was no point in beating around the bush— Harriet might need the information someday. She was not a gently bred miss, protected and coddled by an army of footmen and other servants.

Pen looked Harriet in the eyes. "Harriet, it's very important to be careful around men, even at your age, but especially when you are older. Never go off alone with one. And if you find yourself having to, er, *discourage* some fellow who doesn't understand 'no' or a stinging slap to his face, a knee thrust sharply between his legs will usually do the trick. Men's Achilles heel is their male bits."

Harriet's eyes had got rather round. "Miss Webster says all men are beasts. But then she says we are all going to burn in hellfire, so I never believed her about the men."

Muriel Webster was a very plump, rosy-faced, white-haired woman who lived in the village. She looked quite jolly—until you spoke with her.

"Miss Webster does subscribe to a very dark view of the world. I don't think you need to go that far. Just be sensible and you'll be fine."

Harriet nodded and gave Pen a nervous look. "Papa doesn't seem like he's a beast."

Oh, dear. She'd never meant to give Harriet that thought. "He's not. Of course, he's not. Your father is a very fine man."

"So, he didn't . . ." Harriet looked down and drew a circle with her toe in the dirt.

"What is it, Harriet?" Anxiety started to tighten Pen's chest. Her daughter usually came right out with whatever she wanted to ask.

"Papa didn't r-rape you to get me, did he?" Harriet finally asked in a small, wavering voice.

Pen felt as if she'd been kicked in the stomach. How had they got to this? "No! Of course, he didn't. What makes you ask that?"

Harriet shrugged one shoulder as she stared at the dirt. "You said Papa wouldn't even consider marrying you, and you were shocked when I said Verity had called you a whore. And you just warned me not to be alone with a man." She looked up at Pen. "If he didn't r-rape you and you aren't a wh-whore nor married, how did you get me?"

Lord!

"Harriet, I—" Pen wished Harriet were still little enough that she could say "because I did" and be done with it. How could she explain the physical . . . hunger she'd felt for Harry?

It hadn't been just physical.

She'd loved Harry. She'd start there.

"Lord Darrow and I grew up together, Harriet. We played together as children and then, as we got older . . ." She shook her head. "I knew I wasn't his social equal, but I loved him— and I think he cared for me. I—" She looked away. She hadn't thought about this in a long time—or maybe at all.

"I didn't have much love in my life, Harriet. My mother died when I was very young and my father . . ." She swallowed. "My father was not a nice man. I don't know if he loved me. I suppose maybe he did, in his own twisted way. And I wanted to love him, but—" She shook her head sadly. "I think I mostly hated him."

She felt Harriet's fingers wrap around hers, and she smiled.

"But I did love your father—desperately. I loved him so much that I didn't care about anything else. I knew he wouldn't marry me. I knew he was leaving Darrow in just a matter of weeks. I didn't even think about the risk I was taking—that I might conceive—but if I had, I probably wouldn't have let it stop me."

She put her hands on Harriet's shoulders and looked directly into her eyes. "I'm sorry that you weren't born in a marriage, Harriet, but I'm not sorry at all—not the least little bit—that you *were* born. I love you and I'll take care of you."

And then she hugged Harriet tightly, and Harriet hugged her back. They were both a little teary-eyed when they started up the drive again.

"If you don't mind about not being married," Harriet said, "maybe you could be Papa's mistress."

Pen stumbled. "What?" She must have misheard.

But no, Harriet repeated the words. "Maybe you could be Papa's mistress. Then we would have a place to stay—mistresses have houses, don't they?—and I could see Papa." Harriet smiled. "And you could see him, too. Wouldn't that be grand?"

It would be grand—and horrible. "But the earl has to marry, Harriet. He needs an heir. I doubt Lady Susan or whoever becomes his wife would be very happy about him having a mistress nearby." That wasn't the only problem. "And I can't leave Little Puddledon. Miss Jo needs me to tend the hop plants."

Harriet smiled up at Pen. "Papa can buy us a place in the village—old Mrs. Baker's house has been empty ever since she moved away to stay with her son. We could live there. Then you could still grow hops, and we wouldn't be near Papa's wife. Papa could visit us as much as he liked."

Harriet was too young to understand the emotions—and the physical relationship—involved in such an arrangement.

"I doubt very much your papa's wife would wish to share his attentions, even without us being right under her nose."

"I don't know about that." Harriet shrugged. "I heard Miss Rosamund say that London ladies are happy when their husbands have mistresses. It means they don't have to have them in their beds so much."

Harriet frowned. "Though I would have thought London ladies could have their own beds, if they wanted them. They live in big houses, don't they? Houses even bigger than this one." They'd just reached the front steps of the manor. "We're crowded now, but before Miss Jo opened the Home here, there were separate bedrooms for the master and mistress, weren't there?"

"Well, yes." Pen sighed. She really needed to get Harriet away from Rosamund and the Home. "But it's more complicated than that." Though from what she'd read about Lady Susan, she suspected the woman was indeed more interested in being the Countess of Darrow than Harry Graham's wife.

Poor Harry. He deserves to have someone who loves him for himself, not for his title.

"It seems simple to me." Harriet grinned. "Papa's wife gets what she wants—her own bed—and we get a house." Her grin wobbled and she sounded rather wistful. "And I get to be with Papa."

Pen's heart hurt. *I'd do anything for Harriet.*

But this?

No, she couldn't be Harry's mistress, even for Harriet. If she let Harry back into her life that way, she'd lose her self-respect, her independence, her pride.

She'd lose everything.

The hard truth was *she* was the one who didn't want to share Harry.

She forced herself to smile. "Harriet, this is all beside the point. Lord Darrow hasn't shown that sort of interest in me."

Harriet opened her mouth as if to object, but Pen hurried on. "And I would not accept it if he did. It would be most inappropriate."

Harriet still looked like she would argue, so Pen put a period to the discussion.

"Now go along. I have to find Miss Jo and tell her to expect Lord Darrow's visit tomorrow."

Harriet grinned at the thought of seeing the earl again and ran off. Pen, however, stood on the steps a few more minutes before she collected herself enough to go looking for Jo.

On his way back to the village, Harry stopped by the cottage to confirm it would indeed be a suitable alternative to the inn. He hoped so. He'd like to spend as much time with Harriet as he could while he was here.

And with Pen . . .

He paused with his hand on the door latch.

Dear God, Pen. What was it about her that drew him so? It wasn't her beauty—though she *was* beautiful. It certainly wasn't her birth—she was the daughter of a drunken farmer, for God's sake. And it wasn't her brain. She might know a great deal about growing hops—he assumed she did—but he'd be shocked if she could discuss literature, art, or politics. Lord, apparently, she hadn't even been able to read until after she'd left Darrow. They had nothing but their past in common.

And Harriet.

He still found it difficult to believe he had a daughter.

He stepped through the cottage's door—the place seemed sadly empty without Pen and Harriet there—and went over to the hearth. Someone—Harriet?—had left a tinderbox on the mantel as well as a candle. There was even coal in the coal box, though it was August. He likely wouldn't need a fire.

It had been August when he and Pen had been lovers.

The years had changed her. The soft curves of her cheeks had hollowed a bit, making her cheekbones more prominent. There were lines on her face that hadn't been there before, on her forehead, between her brows, bracketing her mouth. She seemed . . . tighter. Less carefree.

Of course, she was less carefree. She was a mother. She'd had to raise Harriet on her own.

And he was older, too. That had been part of the problem with shopping for a wife on the London Marriage Mart. Girls of seventeen now seemed like children, yet the older women, those who hadn't been snapped up already, were often squint-eyed or snaggle-toothed, vapid little mice or brash, overbearing battle-axes.

At least Lady Susan was none of those things. She was a paragon, really—especially when she managed to keep her tongue behind her teeth. He couldn't choose a better female to be his countess.

He just wished he felt a bit more enthusiastic about marrying her.

Or enthusiastic at all.

He climbed the narrow stairs to inspect the bedroom. As he'd thought, it was small—far smaller than the main room below. He had to duck to navigate the doorway and then he couldn't stand upright except in the very center of the room. The bed looked to be a good size though—

He had a vivid image of Pen, sprawled naked on the sheets.

Bloody hell, what's the matter with me? I should be imagining my bride-to-be.

He sat down on the mattress. Try as he might, he could

not picture the proper Lady Susan without her expensive, carefully chosen clothing.

Perhaps it's because I haven't kissed her yet.

Though he wasn't precisely eager to do that, either.

Nonsense. It was just that Lady Susan was a well-bred virgin. She'd yet to be awakened to the delights of the marriage bed. He would coax her to passion. He had plenty of experience with women, though not, of course, with timid virgins.

Mmm. Pen might have been a virgin, but she'd not been a timid one. He grinned. No, not timid at all. She'd been curious, fearless, and responsive. Zounds, they'd had some splendid tuppings.

He lay back to test the mattress. It felt sturdy enough to support some exuberant bed play.

He closed his eyes, remembering Pen's lithe, strong body with its long limbs, narrow waist, and lovely rose-tipped breasts. Her skin had been so soft, her mouth, eager.

His cock ached to visit her warm, narrow channel once more.

The experience would not be the same.

It might be better . . .

Enough. He sat up and rearranged his swollen, misbehaving organ. He'd take a quick dip in the pool by the waterfall to wash the blacking out of his hair and the lust from his cock.

He stood—and slammed his head into the ceiling. Ow! He collapsed in a stream of curses back onto the bed, gripping his head in his hands.

At least the pain in his head distracted him from the ache lower down.

He was very likely making too much of his affair with Pen. He'd been scarcely more than a boy when he'd consorted with her. He'd had very little experience with women.

Chances were if he took her to bed now, the tupping wouldn't be anything out of the ordinary.

I'd like to find out.

No. That was his cock talking. Even if Pen was willing, Little Puddledon was a small village. Word would get out almost immediately and Pen's reputation would be ruined.

It's already ruined thanks to that gossipy Rosamund woman.

That was unfortunate, but Pen could bring herself about, especially if she continued to live a careful, prudent life. She'd been here for years. Once the villagers got over the initial titillation, they'd revert to their original good opinion of her. Which was all the more reason not to seduce her.

He smiled. *Or let her seduce me. Had she really been the instigator that first time?*

He stood—cautiously—and made his way safely out of the room and down the stairs without acquiring any more bumps or bruises. He looked up when he stepped outside. The sun was low in the sky, but there was still enough light for a bath as long as he was quick about it.

He took the path up to the pool. A cautious finger dipped in the water told him it was cold, but not frigid, so he shed his clothes and stepped in before he could think any more about it.

Brr! The cold didn't encourage him to linger, but it had the definite advantage of shrinking his cock to its proper—well, its shriveled—size.

He dunked his head and rubbed away the concoction he'd used to darken his streak. Then he climbed out, shook himself like a dog to get some of the water off, and, wishing he had the towel that was back in his saddlebag at the inn, used his hands to get rid of the rest. Then he stood in the sun, naked, arms outstretched, letting its rays dry him a little more. It was late enough in the day that all the women must be back in the Home—at least that's what he hoped—so he shouldn't shock anyone.

Of course, females living in a place called the Benevolent Home for the Maintenance and Support of Spinsters, Widows, and Abandoned Women and their Unfortunate Children might not be easily shocked. At least the ones with children must have seen the male form before.

Zeus, it felt good to be alone again. He'd spent days alone when he'd been on the Continent, but here in England some-one was always just a step away, be it other members of the *ton* squeezed into a ball, his estate manager wishing to discuss drainage ditches, or any of the army of servants he employed. He hated to think he'd never again have more than a few stolen moments to himself.

He wouldn't mind Pen's company though—and not just to admire the scenery.

When he'd offered her his hand to help her over the stile, she hadn't seemed completely indifferent to him.

She'd had such a lusty nature as a girl. Living among women, in a small village, with a daughter to raise, she'd likely not had much opportunity for carnal pleasure. He'd be doing her a favor—and himself one—to see if she'd like one last tupping. Then she could go back to being a model citizen.

Blast! His cock was growing again—and the sun was sinking below the horizon. He pulled on his clothing and hurried down to the inn.

He had the thread of a hope that he'd somehow be able to slide through the tavern and up the stairs to his room without being noticed, but that was snapped the moment he stepped through the door.

"There he is! That's the man who attacked me!"

Oh, Lord, the vicar's here.

If there had been a single pair of eyes that hadn't noted Harry's arrival, that situation was now rectified. Everyone turned to stare at him, and a low, threatening murmur began to fill the room.

He surveyed the vicar's swollen face with a certain amount of relish. It had to hurt to talk, though perhaps the man had imbibed enough ale that he wasn't feeling too much pain.

Bess, clearly sensing trouble, hurried over to him. "Mr. Graham, I'm sorry, but the vicar says—oh!"

She'd noticed his hair.

He gave her a smile, the one he'd developed for use in just these situations where he wished to appear pleasant, but not approachable. "I'm afraid I wasn't completely forthcoming when I arrived. I gave you my name, but not my title."

Bess's eyes widened. "You mean you're the new . . ."

"Earl of Darrow." He looked back at the vicar, his lip curling. "I regret to say I came upon this"—he let disgust fill his voice—"*person* attacking Mrs. Barnes, my childhood friend and the mother of my daughter."

It was a wonder all the air wasn't sucked out of the room as everyone drew in an audible breath at the same time. The vicar's eyes started from their sockets, the color draining from his face, making his purpling bruises even more pronounced.

"I-I d-didn't," the vicar sputtered. "S-she—"

Harry moved quickly, grabbing the man by his cravat and hauling him up so their noses almost touched. His voice was colder than the pool by the cottage. It was a tone that had caused braver men than this fellow to soil their breeches.

"Do. Not. Say. It."

"Auggh. Augh. Aurgh."

Harry let the vicar go and watched as the worm scuttled backward, clutching his neck and swallowing visibly. He pinned the man with a narrowed gaze. "If I hear you've uttered one word against Mrs. Barnes, sirrah, things will go very badly for you indeed. Do I make myself clear?"

"Augh." The vicar nodded. "Urgh."

"And as I believe I mentioned to you before, I do think you should consider other employment opportunities. I know beyond any doubt that the Duke of Grainger will not be pleased when I tell him how you insulted Mrs. Barnes."

The vicar leaned against the bar as if he needed the support and finally managed to get his voice to obey him. "But, my lord, you must understand, I didn't mean . . . That is, it was all in good, er, ah, f-fun."

"Odsbodikins, vicar," one of the other men said. "Do ye *want* the earl to kill ye?"

The vicar looked back at Harry, as if expecting him to deny murder was his intent.

He obliged. "I won't kill you." He smiled grimly. "I'll just make you wish I had."

The last remaining color—except for the bruises—drained from the man's face. Harry half expected him to collapse completely, but he managed to keep his hold on the bar and his body upright.

"Go home, Godfrey," another man said. "Bess doesn't want to have to clean yer blood off the floor."

"Aye," said another. "Look in the mirror, man. The earl's done enough damage to ye today."

"And it was well deserved if ye treated Mrs. Barnes poorly." That came from the far corner, but it started a dark rumbling.

"Right. She's always behaved like a lady."

"Devoted to her daughter, me wife says."

"Knows more about hops than I'll wager ye know about Christian charity, vicar."

"Aye!"

"Hear, hear!"

"And if it weren't for her hops, we'd not have our brew!"

The men lifted their mugs. The rumbling was getting louder.

"All ye give us, vicar, is callouses on our arses from sitting in those bloody hard pews on Sunday, listening to ye flap yer jaws."

The vicar must have finally decided retreat was in order. He straightened, though still keeping a firm hold on the bar. "Very well, gentlemen. I can see my presence is not wanted here."

Lord, that was an invitation for abuse. Someone behind Harry hooted and the rest of the men added to the din, stamping their feet and banging their glasses on the table.

The vicar sniffed and made as dignified an exit as he could, head held high, eyes straight ahead, walking, but not running, across the room.

"Don't let the door hit ye in the arse, vicar," someone shouted.

He must have had the room's derisive laughter echoing in his ears as he finally disappeared out into the evening.

Harry was quite pleased with the way things had gone. He grinned at Bess. "Another round of Widow's Brew on me."

The men roared their approval.

Chapter Eight

Monday

Harry rode up the drive to the old brick building that housed the Benevolent Home for the Maintenance and Support of Spinsters, Widows, and Abandoned Women and their Unfortunate Children. It was not a particularly large or impressive edifice.

He smothered a yawn. He'd been up very late last night, staying in the tavern until the last few men left, drinking with them and buying them drinks. He'd done the same in any number of taverns on the Continent. He'd found it an excellent way to build rapport, and had hoped as the men got to know him, they'd be more inclined to take his—and thus Pen's—side if the vicar turned nasty.

To his surprise, he hadn't had to do any persuading, at least with regard to Pen. The men all heartily despised the vicar, who'd been in Little Puddledon only a few months, so they were more than willing to believe the worst of him. But more to the point, they held Pen in high esteem—and not for the things the *ton* prized in women. They didn't care about her birth or beauty. They didn't even care that she'd had a child out of wedlock. What they valued were her good sense and her insights on fertilizer, soil, and pest control.

"Papa!"

His heart did a little reel around his chest when he heard Harriet's voice. She and Pen had just come out of the Home's door.

"Papa!" Harriet called again and left Pen to run down the steps toward him. "I was watching for you."

He swung down from Ajax's back, grinning. It was definitely time for him to settle down and start his nursery if being called Papa made him feel this happy.

"Are you going to greet Ajax, too?" he asked as Harriet came up.

She carefully patted his horse. "Hallo, Ajax."

Ajax turned his head to look at her, and she giggled.

"Would you like to ride him down to the stables?"

Harriet's eyes got very large—and then she frowned. "I-I don't know how to ride, Papa. I've never been on a horse." She glanced at Ajax a bit nervously. "And this one is very large. Much larger than Bumblebee."

Pen came up then, having walked rather than run down the steps. "Good morning, Lord Darrow. How nice of you to be so prompt."

He laughed. "Good try, Pen, but I'm not going to let you treat me as some stranger that's stopped by to discuss hop growing—though I will tell you the village men were singing your horticultural praises last night."

"Oh." She looked equal parts annoyed and pleased. "And of course you aren't a stranger,"—she looked at Harriet and blushed—"Lord Darrow."

Harriet ignored their stilted interaction. Her thoughts were still on Ajax. "Mama, Papa asked me if I wanted to ride his horse down to the stables." She definitely sounded nervous—but excited, too.

Pen frowned. "You don't know how to ride, Harriet."

"You won't really be riding," Harry said. It was clear to him that Harriet needed a little encouragement to get over her fears. "I'll lead Ajax. You'll just sit in the saddle."

"Oh." Harriet looked up—way up—at Ajax's back.

"Really, Lord Darrow, are you sure that's wise?"

What was this? "Pen! You used to be so fearless."

Pen blushed, likely thinking of the same fearless things he was, things that involved riding—but not horses.

He took the opportunity her tongue-tied silence provided to turn back to Harriet.

"I'll lift you up so you can see how you like it, shall I? And I promise if you aren't comfortable, I'll get you down straightaway."

Harriet looked again at Ajax's saddle. He thought she was torn, but leaning toward trying. She just needed a slight nudge.

"You really don't have to worry. Ajax is extremely well behaved, I promise you."

"I don't know, Harry." Pen had found her voice. "That's a very large horse."

He smiled at hearing Pen say his Christian name, but his focus was all on his daughter. "Large, but well trained. He was with me on the Continent, so has seen conditions far more unsettling than a young girl and a quiet, country house." This was why children needed two parents—one to coddle and one to challenge.

Challenge, but not push. He wouldn't force Harriet, but he also wouldn't give up until he was certain she truly wasn't ready to try. "Shall I lift you up? I'll keep a hand on you until you're comfortable."

He could feel Pen fluttering with worry next to him, but was pleased she didn't urge Harriet to be cautious and safe—even though she must want desperately to do so. He could almost feel the words fighting to make their way out of her mouth.

Ajax swung his head back toward Harriet as if to see what the delay was and snuffled his own form of encouragement.

Harriet laughed. "All right," she said. "I'll try." She gave Harry a worried look. "You won't let go of me, will you, Papa?"

"Not until you're ready. Now up you go." Harry put his hands around Harriet's waist. "It will be better if you sit astride, so swing your right leg over the saddle, all right?"

Harriet nodded, and then, not giving her more time to fret, he lifted her. She couldn't weigh even five stone.

"Oh!" she said once she was settled. "Oh! I'm up so high."

"She *is* very far from the ground." Pen wasn't completely successful at keeping the worry out of her voice.

He laughed. "You're a foot taller than I am, Harriet. Do you like the view from up there?"

She nodded. He could tell her nerves were settling.

"Excellent. Now sit tall. Hold Ajax with your legs. Get your balance."

He waited. He could see Harriet concentrating.

"Good?"

She nodded and he let go. "You can hold onto the saddle if you need to, but learning to balance is better."

"I'm fine." Harriet grinned. "I like it. Will you teach me to ride Ajax, Papa?"

He laughed as he pulled the reins over his horse's head—better to have a hold of him just in case. "No. Ajax is too much horse for you to ride by yourself. You should start on a pony."

"Oh." Harriet looked crestfallen.

Hell, she doesn't have a pony—or anyone to teach her to ride here.

"The stables are this way," Pen said.

But if I can persuade Pen to move to Darrow, I can teach Harriet myself.

He would mull that idea over later. Now he had to keep an eye on Harriet.

"You're doing very well," he told her, genuine pride in his voice. "I'd say you have a natural seat." Which would be only right. She *was* his daughter, after all.

He followed Pen several hundred yards around to the side of the house, aware as he went of all the eyes watching him. Not all were in plain sight, though a few girls and women managed to find a reason to be in the yard. But from the corner of his eye, he saw curtains twitch or shapes duck quickly back from windows as he passed.

He'd spent too many years when a keen awareness of his surroundings meant the difference between success or capture not to have a sixth sense about such matters.

"Here we are," Pen said.

He helped Harriet down from Ajax's back as a tall, stout woman with a broad face and short, gray hair came out of the low stone building they'd stopped by.

"Ohh," she said, a note of reverence in her voice as she caught sight of Ajax. "An Arabian."

Harry felt a welcome sense of relief. This woman knew her horses. Ajax would be fine here.

"Lord Darrow, this is Miss Winifred Williams," Pen said. "Winifred, the Earl of Darrow."

"Mmm. What a handsome fellow you are, sir."

Miss Williams was not addressing Harry. She'd dropped him a quick curtsy, but had hardly spared him a glance. Her attention was all for Ajax—and Ajax was eating it up, twitching his ears to listen more closely.

Pen gave Harry a rather helpless, amused look.

"I rode Ajax all the way from the front of the house, Miss Winifred," Harriet said.

Miss Williams's brows rose. "Did you now?"

"Well, I rode on his back while my papa led him. He's going to stay with Bumblebee while Papa stays at the cottage."

"If that won't be too much trouble," Harry said. "I could keep him at the Dancing Duck, if you'd rather."

That earned him Miss Williams's full attention. "There's no need of that. Thomas is a good ostler, but I can do as well by this fine fellow as he can. Come along and see for yourself." She turned back to Ajax. "You'll like Bumblebee. She's a very calm, quiet girl. She'll be a restful stablemate for you."

Once he saw that Ajax would be well cared for, Harry walked with Pen—and Harriet, who'd wrapped her fingers around his—across the yard to another building.

"Jo's waiting for us in her office," Pen said. "She wants to be the one to show you around and answer your questions, so you can give the duke a full report." Pen's brows knitted. "We *do* depend on his annual donation. We are trying to be self-supporting—and the success of the brewery has helped immensely—but as you must know, the last two growing seasons were dreadful."

He didn't know, but, fortunately, Pen didn't require him to reply and reveal his ignorance. Not that there wasn't a perfectly good, even obvious, reason for his lack of knowledge. He'd still been on the Continent two years ago, thinking he'd eventually have a career in the Home Office. Last year he'd been juggling so many new responsibilities, he'd trusted his estate manager to do whatever was needed with the fields.

This year would be different. Once he got his most pressing duty attended to—offering for and marrying Lady Susan—he could concentrate on learning more about running Darrow and his other properties.

Pen paused before opening the door and looked down at their daughter. "You don't have to come with us, Harriet."

Harriet's grip on his fingers tightened. "I want to, Mama."

Pen frowned. "You'll be terribly bored."

"No, I won't." Harriet edged closer to him. "And I won't get in the way, either. I promise."

Pen hesitated, but must have concluded, as he had, that Harriet wanted everyone to see them together, because she finally nodded and opened the door.

An older woman, dressed in a high-necked, gray gown and a lace cap that covered most of her dark blond hair, looked up from where she was working at a scarred, wooden desk. A brown and white spaniel, lying at her feet, lifted its head, too, took one look at Harry, and started growling.

"Freddie!" the woman said sharply. "That's no way to greet our guest." She looked at Harry a little nervously as she stood and came around to greet him. "Please accept my apologies for my dog's bad behavior, my lord—" She looked at Pen. "At least I assume you are Lord Darrow."

Pen laughed. "I'm not likely to be bringing some other strange man into your office, Jo." Pen turned to Harry. "Lord Darrow, this is Lady Havenridge, Lord Havenridge's widow and the woman behind the Benevolent Home for the Maintenance and Support of Spinsters, Widows, and Abandoned Women and their Unfortunate Children."

The woman smiled—and Harry realized she was likely only a few years older than he. "I am so glad you are here, my lord. Pen tells me that you have come on the Duke of Grainger's behalf."

Lady Havenridge might be glad he was here, but her dog certainly wasn't. It was still growling.

"Stop it, Freddie," Harriet said, going over to sit down on the floor and pat the dog's head. "Lord Darrow is my papa. He's nice."

Freddie did not agree. He was happy enough when Harriet stroked his ears, but the moment his gaze turned Harry's way, the growling started again—this time complete with a show of teeth.

"Freddie!" Lady Havenridge smiled apologetically.

"Please don't take Freddie personally, my lord. He just doesn't care for men."

"He even growls at poor old Albert, don't you, silly?" Harriet asked, getting rather too close to the beast's face—and teeth—for Harry's comfort.

Freddie licked Harriet's face.

"Well, then," Lady Havenridge said, "shall we get started? I don't want to take more of your time than necessary, Lord Darrow."

"I'm in no rush, Lady Havenridge." Harry nodded at Harriet and didn't even try to suppress his grin. "I'm sure you must know that I've just discovered I have a daughter."

Lady Havenridge smiled back at him. "Oh, yes. Pen told us—and said you'd be staying at the cottage. I hope you find it comfortable." She took a step toward the door. "Now, shall we get started?"

They made quite the parade as they walked back around to the front of the house. Lady Havenridge led the way, Harry at her side so he could hear her commentary. He'd much prefer to be walking with Pen and Harriet, who were a step or two behind, but Freddie was with them and he didn't want to provoke the dog into taking a bite out of his breeches.

"I do have a preliminary question for you, Lady Havenridge," Harry said. "The duke's donation is entered in his books as going to a JSW. Do you know who or what that might be?"

Lady Havenridge's brows rose. "JSW? Oh. How odd. I assume those must be my initials—my family name is Smythe-Waters. Josephine Smythe-Waters."

"Ah. Yes. I suppose you must have the right of it."

They climbed the steps to the front door, and Lady Havenridge launched into her tour.

"At the moment, we have fourteen women—including

myself, Pen, and Caroline Anderson, our brewster—living here as well as ten girls and five infants."

"No boys?" Harry asked. They had just stepped into the moderately sized entry. His boots clacked on the marble floor, but the sound was overwhelmed by a babel of female voices spilling out of the neighboring rooms.

"No one wants boys, Papa!" Harriet said, coming up next to him. He glanced around—Freddie was busy sniffing a potted tree. "They are loud and messy."

"Your papa was a boy once, Harriet," Pen said—and blushed.

Splendid. This was going to be very entertaining if Pen changed colors every time she said anything that recalled their youth.

I'd like to do *something to recall our youth—*

No. He must remember he was sent here by the duke. He needed to pay attention—and not to Pen.

"Two of the infants are boys," Lady Havenridge said, "but we've found we can't keep boys much past the age of five." She smiled regretfully. "It really is too bad. We are squeezed in here cheek by jowl, as you will see. Boys tend to be especially, er, *exuberant* and so require more space." She shook her head. "And we don't have enough room to have a separate dormitory for them."

"We also don't tend to get that many mothers with boys," Pen said.

"Right. I'm not certain why that is. And those we do get seem to find husbands quickly." Lady Havenridge shrugged. "Perhaps they think their sons need a father or perhaps men see them as 'proven breeders' since they've already produced a boy."

Lady Havenridge said "proven breeders" with obvious distaste, but Harry had some sympathy for those anonymous men. Sons could work in the fields and manage the animals better then daughters. And in his case, only a son could succeed to the title.

Lady Havenridge led him around the main floor, pointing out the long gallery that had been turned into a dormitory—Harriet showed him which bed was hers—and the smaller chambers where the women shared two or three to a room. He saw the schoolroom while a reading lesson was in progress—an unsettling number of young female eyes turned to examine him until Lady Havenridge blessedly moved the tour along—and the dining room with two long wooden tables crammed into a space meant for one.

Sadly, he did not see Pen's bedroom.

He did see the brewhouse, which was interesting, though Miss Caroline Anderson, the woman in charge, was a bit . . . *intense*. At one point, he'd thought she wasn't going to let him leave unless he swore to personally carry bottles of Widow's Brew to every tavern in London. Even Harriet deserted him then, going off with Freddie to visit Ajax.

He did hope Freddie didn't have an aversion to male horses, because he suspected Ajax would not appreciate being growled at.

"How do you manage living among all these women?" he murmured to Albert, the only other male he'd met at the Home—besides Freddie—as they waited for Pen, Miss Anderson, and Lady Havenridge to finish discussing some brewing issue. Albert had to be seventy if he was a day, but he was clearly in excellent shape as, if Harry understood matters, he—along with two of the female residents, Bathsheba and Esther—did most of the manual labor involved in the brewing process.

Albert chuckled. "I have my own room in the brewhouse so I can get away by myself, and I go down to the inn when I need to be with my mates. I was there last night when ye laid into the vicar." He grinned, showing off the gaps where two of his teeth were missing. "Well done!"

Albert leaned closer. "No one ever liked that jumped-up buffoon. We couldn't understand why a smart woman like Mrs. Barnes tolerated him at all."

"Has he been, er, *annoying* her for long, then?" Harry asked. Though he couldn't very well seek the man out to beat him again. That wouldn't be sporting.

Albert shook his head. "He's only been here since just afore Easter. The old vicar was a far better man, but it turned out he was tupping the butcher's wife. They ran off together—in Lent!—and so we needed a new man of the cloth at once." He made a dismissive sound. "They were scraping the barrel when they found old Godfrey. We'll all be right pleased if the duke does send him packing."

"I have no doubt he will."

The women's discussion ended just in time for all three to hear those words.

"Continue his support?" Miss Anderson asked rather forcefully, though Harry thought he heard a thread of anxiety in her voice as well.

He smiled. Best not mention what he and Albert had actually been discussing. There was no need to drag the disreputable vicar into the conversation, though he assumed the women knew everything there was to know about the fellow. Gossip in a small village brewed faster and was ready for enthusiastic consumption far more quickly than ale.

And, in any event, it was easy to give the answer the women must be hoping for.

"I can't speak for the duke obviously, but I promise to recommend he do so. You've a very impressive operation here."

The women's relief and pride were almost tangible—but

it didn't take the determined Miss Anderson long to recover. She was clearly the primary saleswoman of the trio.

"That's excellent news." She smiled in a persuasive, almost flirtatious, way. "You know, my lord, we can always use more benefactors. If you would like to—"

"Caro!" Pen said, sharply and in an appalled tone. "You can't be meaning to pick the earl's pocket!"

Miss Anderson frowned at Pen. "I'm only inviting him to add his support to the duke's." And then she turned the full force of her smile on Harry. "Surely, you would like to help needy women and children, my lord?"

I would like to help one *needy woman and her child—Pen and Harriet.*

And on the heels of that thought, another hit him: He was completely unmoved by Miss Anderson's striking beauty. His cock didn't twitch even slightly in appreciation. He might think that organ dead, except that it sprung— literally—to life whenever his eyes strayed to Pen.

"Pen is right," Lady Havenridge said. "You are putting the earl in an uncomfortable position, Caro."

Which brought Miss Anderson back to him. "*Are* you uncomfortable, my lord?"

He laughed. "No. But I also am not going to commit to anything before I know Grainger's position on the matter." *And not before discussing it with Pen.* "I believe he owns the estate, does he not?"

Lady Havenridge turned pale. "Surely, you don't think he'll evict us, do you?!" she said, horror and worry in her voice.

He hadn't meant to set the cat among the pigeons and get them all in a fluster. "No, not at all."

"He'd better not be thinking of evicting us," Miss Anderson said darkly. "If he *is* considering such a move, I would like to speak to him first. Once I explain my—*our*— plans for the brewery, I'm sure he'll be persuaded the

Home is a good investment as well as a suitable recipient of his charity."

"Of course," Harry said in what he hoped was a reassuring tone. "I really don't think you need to worry, though."

Miss Anderson opened her mouth as if to argue further, but Pen spoke before she could.

"Would you like to see the hopyard, Lord Darrow? I need to check on the plants, and would be happy to show it to you."

Miss Anderson's mouth opened again, but this time Lady Havenridge swooped in. "A brilliant idea, Pen." She started toward the door, thus bringing them along with her. "And the earl might wish to see our oast house as well, don't you think?"

They stepped out into the late-morning sun as Pen laughed. "I suspect Lord Darrow has had his fill of tours, haven't you, my lord?"

He had, but he didn't want to seem ungrateful or disinterested. "May I reserve my decision on the oast house until after I've seen the hopyard?"

Lady Havenridge chuckled. "Spoken like a true diplomat." She extended her hand. "If you have any further questions, Lord Darrow, please do not hesitate to ask one of us. Or if you need anything at the cottage." She smiled. "You are more than welcome to take your meals at the Home, but I must warn you you will be the only male present. Albert usually does for himself or goes down to the Dancing Duck."

His face must have shown his reaction—he really was losing his touch—because Miss Anderson laughed. "It might be a bit overwhelming at first."

"Or we could pack you a basket, if you'd rather eat at the cottage," Pen said.

He was not anxious to break bread with the females at the Home or the men at the inn. "Thank you. A basket sounds like just the thing, if it's not too much trouble."

"Of course it's not. I'll stop by the kitchen and tell Dorcas on my way back to my office." Lady Havenridge smiled. "I suspect she'll be delighted to make something up for you. She used to cook for a family with five sons and often seems disappointed our girls don't eat more."

"Thank you. I hope I won't disappoint her." He looked at Pen. "Shall we be off?"

Pen led the way past the other buildings and down a path through the fields. "I'm sorry about Caro asking you for money like that."

"No need to apologize. She saw an opportunity and took it, as any good businesswoman would. And I *am* interested in helping the Home." *Even if you and Harriet aren't living there any longer*, he thought, but knew better than to say.

"However, I do need to discuss the situation with Grainger before I commit to anything myself. Not that I think he will stop his support—I meant it when I said I'd encourage him to continue his donations—but I can't presume to speak for him."

She nodded. "I understand. And you're right, Caro *is* the best businesswoman of the three of us. Jo says she was bumbling from one project to another, trying to find something that would put the Home on a better financial footing, until Caro arrived. Caro was the main force behind the idea to go into brewing."

"An inspired decision." He grinned. "Widow's Brew is one of the best ales I've ever tasted."

"Don't let Caro hear you say that or she'll have your name and that quote on a handbill all over London." Pen sighed. "I often wish I was more like her. She doesn't let anything stand in her way—and more often than not, she gets what she wants." She shook her head, but he heard the admiration in her voice. "She's bold and fearless."

Surely, Pen knew herself better than this? "I would say the same about you, Pen."

She looked up at him, her face blank with surprise—and

then she laughed. "Oh, I was only ever bold and fearless where you were concerned. In everything else I was—and am—a mouse."

He stopped her with a hand on her arm. "No, Pen. That's not true. Look how you stood up to your father."

She frowned. "I never stood up to him." She looked away, her cheeks suddenly flushed. "Well, except when I wouldn't tell him you were my baby's father."

He touched her cheek and she turned her face back to meet his gaze. "You stood up to him every day of your life, Pen, the only way you could. You didn't let him break your spirit."

She shook her head, but he could tell she was listening.

"A mouse wouldn't have refused to marry Felix. A mouse wouldn't have set off, alone and pregnant, to travel miles with only a hope—a prayer—that at the end of the journey she'd find safety. And then, when that safety fell apart, a mouse wouldn't have taken her young daughter and found a new refuge among strangers."

Pen's color was still high. "You give me too much credit. I hadn't any choice in the matter."

"Yes, you did. You *could* have married Felix."

Pen looked ill. "No, I couldn't have."

"I grant you it would have been unpleasant"—that was putting it mildly!—"but in many ways, it was the path of least resistance. Your father would have been happy, you would have stayed in familiar surroundings with people you'd known from birth, *and* you would not have had to undertake a perilous and uncertain journey. Not to mention Harriet would have been born legitimate." *With that blackguard Felix in a position of power over her.*

The thought turned his stomach.

"But I knew Harriet would have the Graham streak," Pen said. "I thought it would show up when she was two or three.

Once people saw it, they'd think she was just one more of Walter's whelps. I couldn't bear that."

His stomach turned again.

"They might have guessed she was mine," he said, "if they'd been paying attention that summer. We weren't *that* discreet." And yet . . .

He was afraid the people of Darrow *would* have made the same mistake the villagers here had.

He liked that idea almost as little as he did the notion of Harriet living in Felix's house.

"No one would expect a solitary mouse like me to capture your interest, Harry." Pen snorted. "Walter was so indiscriminate, he'd climb into any woman's bed as long as she had a pulse."

"Pen, for the last time, you are *not* a mouse. Give yourself some credit." He frowned at her. "Or if you won't do that, give *me* some credit." He waggled his brows. "I've been told I have excellent taste in women."

Oh, blast, that makes me sound like a bloody rake.

Pen didn't appear to take offense. She just laughed and started walking down the path again. In a few minutes, she stopped. "Here we are."

"Where?" He looked around. All he could see was a welter of green leaves.

"The hopyard, of course." Pen disappeared into the greenery.

He followed her. Once he was in among the plants, he began to see some order to the tangle.

"They're vines." He was reminded of the vineyards he'd seen in France, but these plants were far taller—they grew up poles that must be fifteen feet high.

Pen was inspecting a leaf. "Bines, not vines. I train the plants to grow up these poles every spring and then we cut them down at harvesttime. Now I have to check them several times a day for bugs and blight. I could lose the entire harvest if I don't keep a sharp eye out."

"I see." The space between the rows of plants was very weedy. "Aren't you afraid your skirt will get stained?"

Pen gaped at him as if he were an escapee from Bedlam—and then she laughed. "No. As I told you on the stream bank, I am not one of your London ladies, Harry. I don't have time to worry about my clothes."

Of course, she wasn't a London lady. The London ladies—well, Lady Susan—would be discussing fashion not foliage. And to think they'd go looking for bugs in the bushes—

He laughed.

"What's so funny? Ah, got you!" Pen picked some insectile invader off a leaf and squashed it between her fingers.

"I was just imagining those London ladies here."

"Lady Susan Palmer?" Pen flushed. "Forget I said that," she mumbled and moved farther down the line of hop plants.

Ah, so Pen's been reading the gossip columns, has she? Interesting.

He looked around. They were quite alone here. The tall plants hid them from any observers. It was rather . . . intimate.

He caught up to Pen.

"These are the hop flowers," she said, "or cones, if you prefer."

The thing she was touching did look very much like a miniature pinecone.

"In a week or so, when they are ready to harvest, we'll have everyone in the Home and anyone in the village who's willing come pick them. We aren't big enough to have to use itinerant pickers, though if Caro gets her way, we'll get to that point."

"How do you know when they're ready?" There was something very compelling about Pen now. The hesitancy he'd heard when she'd compared herself to Miss Anderson was gone. She sounded self-assured and . . . powerful.

"I can tell by the feel of the cone and the scent. Here." She held her fingers up to his nose. "It smells grassy. When the cones are ready, they smell of . . ." She laughed. "Well, they smell of hops."

"Mmm." He took her fingers in his hand, cupped them, and held them close to his nose . . . and mouth. He drew in a deep breath. Yes, there was a scent of grass—but there was also the sweet, spicy scent of Pen. His fingers stroked the back of her hand—it was so soft. His thumb stroked her palm. It was slightly rough. A working hand. Strong.

He wanted to feel it on his chest. His stomach. His cock. He used to love how Pen would cradle his ballocks as her clever mouth—

"H-Harry?" Pen tugged on her hand, but not hard as if she really wished to get free.

He pressed a kiss to her wrist, to her pulse that fluttered beneath his lips. "I've missed you, Pen."

"Harry, I . . ."

He cupped her face. "What?"

"I—"

"Papa! Mama! Look, I've got a picnic basket."

He wanted to curse, but instead he—and Pen—laughed as Harriet came crashing down their weedy aisle.

Chapter Nine

Pen finished rummaging through the picnic basket Harriet had brought down from the house. There had been no good place to eat in the hopyard, so they'd brought the basket to the orchard.

She spread the plates and cups and food out on the blanket she'd found in the basket. Dorcas must think Harry ate like ten men—she'd packed far too much food.

Then she sat back on her heels and looked over to where Harry was showing their daughter how to bat fallen apples with a stick.

Thank God *Harriet had arrived in the hopyard at precisely the moment she had. A second later . . .*

She closed her eyes. Oh, dear God. A second later and she would have let Harry kiss her. He'd been *so* close. She'd seen his intention in his face.

She squeezed her eyes more tightly shut as a wave of agonizing embarrassment rolled through her. Oh, who was she trying to fool? A moment later and *she* would have kissed *Harry*. The touch of his lips on her wrist had gone straight to her head—and her feminine parts—and, like a spark to tinder, had ignited a raging need, even more consuming than what she remembered from when they were young. All sense, all restraint, all *sanity* had turned to ash. She'd been a hair's breadth from plastering herself to his hard body, pulling his head down, and pushing her tongue—

She shook her head as if that would dislodge the mortifying image.

"I did it!"

Pen's eyes flew open to see Harriet grinning at her father—and Harry grinning back at her.

"Well done!" he said.

Harriet turned to Pen. "Did you see me, Mama? Did you see how I hit the apple and how far it went?"

For a split second, she considered lying, but she'd promised herself never to lie to Harriet—well, beyond the story she'd spun about the fictitious Mr. Barnes. "I'm afraid I missed it."

Harriet's face fell. "Mama!"

"I'm sorry." Pen always hated to disappoint her daughter, but she felt especially bad—well, guilty—this time because her failure was due to the lustful, *sinful* thoughts she'd been having about the man she was carefully not looking at now.

"You'll just have to do it again, Harriet," Harry said. He laughed at Pen. "Pay attention this time."

Oh, God. He's so bloody handsome when he laughs. "I will."

Harriet gave her a hard look. "You promise?"

"Yes, I promise."

Harriet picked up an apple, raised her stick—and then looked at Pen again. "Are you watching now, Mama?"

"Yes, I'm watching."

Harriet tossed her apple up in the air, swung . . . and missed.

She stomped her foot in frustration and glared at Pen as

if it was Pen's fault. "You should have watched last time, Mama."

"Try again, Harriet," Harry said encouragingly. "You can do it."

Harry had batted drops when they'd been children. He'd tried to teach Pen how to do it, but she'd been hopeless and he'd quickly lost patience with her.

He had far more patience with Harriet.

Of course, he did. He was no longer a boy—he was a man. *Mmm, yes, indeed.*

He'd taken off his hat and coat, waistcoat, and cravat to give himself more freedom of movement, leaving them on the blanket next to Pen. She could see the strong column of his neck, the fluid way his broad back and shoulders and hips moved as he tossed another small, misshapen apple into the air and whacked it, sending it flying so far into the distance she lost sight of it.

If only he'd discard his shirt as well. I'd like to see the muscles in his arms and touch the soft hair that dusts his chest and trails in a narrow path over his flat belly to his . . .

Dear *God*. She fanned her face. She couldn't very well fan under her skirts, though that was where the hottest part of her was. Hot and achy. Empty.

She suddenly and far too vividly remembered how it had felt to have Harry fill her, again and again until she—

She *had* to pay attention to Harriet. If she missed the next time her daughter hit an apple—if there *was* a next time—Harriet would be extremely displeased. And Harry would wonder what she'd been thinking of—

Focus!

She stared at the two of them. Harry was explaining, and Harriet was listening. They were both so intent, their expressions mirroring each other's. Even without their black hair and silver streak, they were so obviously father and daughter.

"It's all in the timing," Harry was saying. "You're swinging after it's gone past. Swing a little earlier. Just keep your eye on the apple. You can do it."

He sounded relaxed, confident, encouraging. He'd been so good with Harriet earlier, too, when he'd got her to overcome her—and Pen's—fears and sit on his horse while he led it. He would make a wonderful father. Lady Susan Palmer was a very lucky woman.

I wish—

No, there was no point in wasting time with silly wishes. Planning was what she needed. She'd thought to marry Godfrey to give Harriet a home, but she saw now that what Harriet really needed was a father, a man who would encourage her to challenge herself.

But who could Pen choose that would do that? Not Godfrey. And not a man like her own father. That man should never have had children, though perhaps things might have been different if her mother had lived. Maybe then her father would have been happy and wouldn't have tried to drown himself in whiskey each night.

Lud, she couldn't think of a single likely candidate in the village. Perhaps the new vicar—surely the duke would follow Harry's recommendation and get rid of Godfrey— perhaps he would prove to be a good, kind man who she could marry and who would treat Harriet like his own daughter.

Harriet tried again, and this time her stick connected. The apple flew several yards.

"I did it, I did it!" She jumped up and down, and then turned to Harry and threw her arms around him. "I did it, Papa."

"You did, indeed. Well done," Harry said, hugging her back, warm enthusiasm in his voice.

Then Harriet looked at Pen. "Were you watching that time, Mama? Did you see it?"

"Yes, I did. I'm very impressed. You did much better than I ever did."

Harriet's eyes grew round. "You used to hit apples, Mama?"

"I used to *try*. I was once a girl, you know. And your papa tried to teach me, but without success. You are a much better pupil than I was."

Harry laughed. "Or perhaps I'm a much better teacher now than I was then."

Harriet looked from Pen to Harry and back again. Then she held out her stick. "Come try now, Mama. Papa will show you how. It's fun."

"Yes, do come try, Pen," Harry said. "I want to right my past failures."

He paused, frowned, and cleared his throat. She'd wager the failure he was thinking of now had nothing to do with trying to teach her to hit apples.

You didn't fail me, Harry. You gave me my greatest gift.

"That is, any good teacher must want *all* his pupils to master their lessons," he finally said.

Pen smiled. "That may be true, but this pupil declines your generous invitation." She had no desire to flail about with a stick in front of Harry and Harriet. "Now come over and have your luncheon. I hope you're hungry. There's enough here for an army."

"Dorcas put in extra for Papa," Harriet said as she flopped down diagonally from Pen—which left the only space open for Harry *next* to Pen.

Hmm. Pen looked at her daughter as Harry easily folded his long legs to sit. Surely, a nine-year-old was too young to engage in any sort of matchmaking?

Harriet grinned back at her, a suspiciously matchmaking gleam in her eye.

No, it must be my imagination.

And in any event, the only appetite Harry appeared to

have was for food. He was busy examining the luncheon offerings.

"What do we have? Meat pie. That looks good. May I cut you a piece, Pen?"

He'd stretched in front of her to reach the pie, which brought him far too close for her comfort. She should lean back.

No, he would move in just a moment. Best not give any hint he was affecting her.

He was so close she could see each dark hair in the faint stubble that limned his jaw. She'd used to trace its rough path with the tip of her finger—and then move on to outline his lips.

Oh. A few strands of his hair had fallen out of place. She would just—

She clenched her hands to keep from reaching out. She remembered all too well how soft and silky it was, how she used to comb her fingers through it—

Oh, God, I can smell him.

One would think—or at least she had hoped—that he would smell sweaty and stale after exerting himself, but he didn't. He smelled like Harry, spicy and male—

And just like that she was seventeen again, naked, on her back with Harry over her, resting his weight on his forearms, his hair falling forward to brush against her, face so close she felt his breath on her cheek, panting—they were both panting—as he slid in and out, in and out, faster and harder, each stroke taking her higher, drawing her tighter. She'd breathed him in, filling her lungs with his scent as he filled her with his body and then his seed, and she'd shattered, convulsing around his hard length that pulsed deep, deep in her—

"Is this too much?"

Yes. It had been too much. It had always been too much, and yet she'd always wanted more.

"Pen? Is this too much pie?"

Oh. She blinked. Harry was looking at her, laughter—and heat—in his gaze. *Bugger it!* He knew exactly what she'd been thinking.

"No. It's fine. Thank you."

She took the plate without looking at the serving he'd given her. She'd eat the whole bloody thing, even if she had to choke it down.

"How old were you when you met Mama, Papa?" Harriet asked before taking a bite of her meat pie.

"I think I was seven or so, which would have made your mother six when we met." He poured Harriet a glass of lemonade and then filled Pen's glass and his own with— what else?—Widow's Brew. "Isn't that right, Pen?"

She nodded as she took a sip. She usually drank tea or lemonade in the middle of the day, but perhaps the ale would relax her. "It was early September, and you and the other boys were playing hide-and-seek." She smiled at Harriet. "Your father thought he'd discovered the perfect hiding place and was quite taken aback when I showed up."

It *had* been the perfect hiding place. She'd used it often that summer and for the same reason she had that particular day: her father had been in another of his drunken rages. But this time when she'd crawled into the green cave made from a tangle of tree limbs, leaves, and vines, she'd found Harry.

She'd seen him before, of course, but always at a distance: in the earl's pew at church or at the open houses the earl and countess held for the estate at harvesttime, Christmas, and Walter's birthday. But she'd never approached him, even on the rare occasions when she'd had the opportunity. Her father had warned her, in ominous if cryptic terms, to stay away—*far* away—from the earl's son.

In retrospect, she realized he, like many people, had forgotten about Harry. He'd meant she should stay clear of the earl's heir, Walter. Even then, Walter had a reputation for stealing kisses. She'd been far too young to be at risk, but she hadn't understood that.

So, when she'd found herself alone with Harry in a tight, secluded place, she'd been terrified.

And then he'd grinned, just as he was grinning now, and had told her not to be a ninny but to come all the way in and be quiet so they wouldn't be found out.

And just like that, he'd won her over.

"And then I convinced you to play, too."

"Yes." She hadn't wanted to. She was a solitary creature, both at heart and due to her father's temper, and she was afraid of the noisy, boisterous boys, but Harry gave her courage. He always had.

"You knew the best hiding places." Harry's grin slid into a more lecherous expression. He must be remembering all the spots she'd found for them to, er, *frolic* in that last summer. He'd forgotten—no, she'd likely never told him—how she knew so many secret places. Avoiding her father, hiding from him at times, had been the only way she'd kept her sanity—and, perhaps, her life. He'd had a strong right arm.

Harry knew that. He'd seen him hit her once, just a cuff across the face, when she'd been Harriet's age. Harry had been furious—and Papa had laughed at him.

She'd got much better at dodging after that, and especially that summer. She didn't want Harry to find bruises on her body. She wanted that time with him to be magical, separate from her real life.

Harry was telling Harriet stories of their childhood now, and Harriet was hanging on every word. Pen took another sip of ale.

There must be a man I can marry who would make a good father for Harriet.

She would hope for the best with regard to the new vicar.

No, she had a better option than passively hoping and praying. She'd talk to Harry. Harry was the duke's friend. Perhaps he could persuade the man to send the village a young, kind, *unmarried* vicar. Harry, too, would want the best for Harriet.

But when and where could they discuss it? Not here or now. She didn't want Harriet listening in. And in any event, she should be getting back. It must be . . . She consulted her watch and gasped.

That got Harry's attention. "What is it, Pen?"

"It's almost three o'clock. I had no idea it was so late. I need to go. I have to check the hops again. But don't let me hurry"—she looked at Harry's and Harriet's empty plates— "you."

Harry laughed. "We've been waiting for you. You were woolgathering."

"Oh." She looked in the basket. "Oh, dear. It seems we've managed to eat almost all of the food Dorcas packed. You won't have any leftovers for your supper, Lord Darrow."

"Miss Dorcas will give Papa more, Mama."

"Harriet is of the opinion that all I need do is compliment Miss Dorcas on her cooking—which I will have no trouble doing—and she'll refill the basket."

All Harry need do was smile at Dorcas and she'd empty the larder into the basket for him. "Harriet is likely correct."

"Of course, I am, Mama!" She hopped up. "Let's go, Papa."

They gathered up the plates and cups. Harry reached for his waistcoat as Pen tried to stand—oh!

Her foot had fallen asleep. Well, or perhaps she shouldn't have had that Widow's Brew. She lurched, tried to catch her balance—

Harry caught her, hauling her up against his chest. His almost-naked chest. There was only a thin linen shirt between her cheek and his hard muscles. His arms came round her, holding her close.

And once again, she was surrounded by his smell. Oh, God. She drew in a deep breath. Her heart—and other organs—softened, wanting to let him in.

Stupid!

"Are you all right, Pen?" he murmured by her ear.

Think about something else. Greenflies! Mildew!

"Yes." *Move away from the man.* "I'm f-fine." She put her hands on his chest . . . *Push!*

It was the hardest thing she'd ever done, but she managed to put some space between them. She stepped back farther.

"It was just that my foot fell asleep." She raised her skirt slightly and twisted the relevant body part right and left. "See? It's fine now."

"Very fine." His voice was a bit thick with—

He's staring at my ankle!

She dropped her skirt at once. "Yes. Well. We'd better be going."

"Yes," Harriet said. "What's taking you so long?"

Harry laughed and picked up his waistcoat. "Nothing."

Harriet had done far better than Pen batting apples, Harry thought as he watched his coltish daughter skip on ahead. It was true that he was a better teacher now—he *hoped* he had more patience and skill than he'd had as a young boy— but Harriet might also have more innate talent.

He felt an absurd bubble of pride. He'd always been good at any sort of sport. Perhaps Harriet *had* got something more than a silver streak from him.

I wish I could teach her to ride. I could if I can persuade Pen to move to that empty house at Darrow.

It would not be easy. Most women would jump at the chance to live a life of leisure in a pleasant, sturdy home, but Pen wasn't most women. She was very independent. Ridiculously so.

Perhaps if I present it as an opportunity for Harriet . . .

Pen would do anything for Harriet. Look at how she'd been willing to marry that bloody vicar.

"I have something I wish to discuss with you, Lord Darrow."

"Oh? And what would that be?" He looked over at Pen. She'd refused to take his arm, of course, and was keeping a good couple feet between them.

Just as well. Every time she touched him—or he touched her—he felt as if he was going to burst into flames. No, worse. He felt as if his ballocks were going to explode. He wanted—*painfully* wanted—to bury himself in her hot, sweet body.

His randy cock swelled with enthusiasm.

"I, er . . ." The color rose in her cheeks and she looked away.

Interesting. Hmm. Perhaps I can seduce her into moving to Darrow.

Pen had had strong physical needs the summer they'd been together, needs she'd not been shy about letting him satisfy. Lord, she'd been so wonderfully lusty every time they'd coupled. He'd never before or since bedded a woman who'd shown such pure enjoyment in tupping.

"It's a matter of some delicacy."

"Oh?"

She must have had other lovers—a woman of such strong appetites couldn't live like a nun—and yet . . .

How would she have managed it? She'd had sole responsibility for Harriet, a duty he could see she took very seriously. And she'd lived at the Home for years. He thought himself a brave man, but he wouldn't have the courage to enter those female-ruled halls with carnal intentions.

If it *had* been almost ten years since she'd had a man between her thighs, she must be going mad with frustrated desire. It would only be charitable of him to relieve her distress.

Yes! His cock was one hundred percent behind that plan.

She was still attracted to him. He was certain of it, just as he was certain she would have let him kiss her in the hop-yard if Harriet hadn't arrived at that precise moment. He'd recognized the intent, focused look in her eyes. He'd seen that look so many times that last summer at Darrow. And when she'd stumbled getting up just now and he'd caught her, she hadn't pushed away from him at once but had stilled, pressing her cheek against his chest.

But even more telling was the moment he'd asked her about the meat pie. Her eyes had been much more than intent then—they'd been burning with passion. He'd been close enough to feel—and hear—her breath coming in little pants just as it had when she'd been seventeen, naked and desperate under him, straining for her release.

If Harriet hadn't been on the blanket with them, he would have kissed Pen, laid her back, and come into her in one long, glorious thrust, lodging his cock so deeply inside her, he couldn't tell where he ended and she began.

And now his cock was so thick and his balls so hard, he could barely walk.

"Yes." She bit her lip. "I, er—"

This got more and more interesting. What could she—

"Can I spend the rest of the afternoon with you, Papa?" Harriet had skipped back to them.

Whatever Pen wished to discuss, she wasn't going to be able to do it now with Harriet here.

"Certainly." Wait. This wasn't completely his decision to

make. "If it's all right with your mother, that is. I don't want to take you away from any important chores or lessons."

Harriet turned to Pen. "May I, Mama?" She hopped from foot to foot as if her feelings were so intense they'd taken control of her body. "Papa won't be here long. Only a few more days."

Her words slammed into his gut like a fist. "Only a few more days" wasn't long enough.

"Pleeeeease?" Harriet drew the word out until she ran out of breath. "I promise I'll be back in time for supper."

Should I mention the house at Darrow now?

It was on the tip of his tongue to do so. This was the perfect setup. He'd dangled prizes of all sorts in front of men and women in countless negotiations over the years, and the tactic that worked best was to persuade someone else to latch on to the scheme, too. Pen might be able to turn him down, but she'd be hard-pressed to withstand her—*their*—daughter's entreaties.

Right. Their daughter.

This wasn't a matter of national interest or even just an intellectual game he was playing. There was a child involved. *His* child. Harriet would be crushed if Pen refused to consider moving, which she might do.

He'd have to deal with Pen directly.

Very directly.

His randy cock thought that was an excellent idea.

Pen sighed. "Very well. But after supper you must do your reading and arithmetic problems."

Harriet leaped into the air and then did a little jig before saying, "I promise, Mama." She turned to Harry. "What shall we do, Papa?"

Harry laughed. "You tell me. I'm the visitor." He grinned. "You can show me some of your favorite places. How's that?"

"Oh, yes." She took his hand—the one on Pen's side since

it wasn't holding the empty picnic basket—and skipped along beside him. "I'll show you the barn—and the barn cats! There's the sweetest little gray one I named Mist, and an orange one I think I'll call Pumpkin. Or maybe Tiger. I haven't decided yet. And a black one I was going to name Night, but then I saw he had a little white streak between his ears so now I think I'll call him Earl instead. Or Darrow." She smiled up at him. "For you, Papa."

"Ah." There was something touching and ridiculous about having a barn cat named for him, but his main emotion was an odd, painful . . . wistfulness?

It wasn't a feeling he ever remembered having before.

He'd been happy living by his wits during his years working for the Crown. He'd never minded the constantly changing scenery, both of land and people. He'd thrived on the variety—it was one of the things he missed most now that he was tied down with all the responsibilities that came with the title.

But perhaps there was something to be said for family. For having children and a plot of land to call your own.

Not that the Earl of Darrow's holdings could be called "a plot" of land.

He should be happy he felt this way. It was one more sign that it was time to stop stalling and marry Lady Susan.

Harriet frowned. "Though I don't know if it's a boy cat or a girl cat. I asked Miss Winifred—she knows about lots of things besides horses—and she said the kittens are still too little to tell." She looked up at him hopefully. "Can *you* tell?"

He knew next to nothing about cats. If a reputed expert on the matter wouldn't venture an opinion on the creatures' gender, he certainly was not going to. "I'm happy to meet the kittens, Harriet, but I can't presume to know more than Miss Winifred."

"Oh." Harriet looked crestfallen. That would never do.

"You could still name the cat Darrow, you know. Darrow isn't a girl's or a boy's name—it's a title."

Harriet frowned. "It sounds like a boy's name to me."

"Well, how about this? Once you know if the kitten is a boy or a girl, you can call it Lord or Lady Darrow, as the case may be."

Harriet thought about that a moment and then beamed at him. "I like it! That's what I'll do."

He felt absurdly pleased with himself—more pleased than when he'd helped negotiate the stickiest point in an international agreement.

He looked over Harriet's head at Pen—she was clearly trying not to laugh.

"I see you have an exciting afternoon ahead of you, Lord Darrow," she said, snickering.

All right, it *was* ridiculous. He'd laugh, too, if anyone told him he'd be spending an afternoon with barn cats and a nine-year-old girl.

He grinned. "Indeed, I do."

They'd reached the manor, and Pen stopped. "This is where I must leave you, Lord Darrow. Unfortunately, we're too close to harvesttime for me to be able to take an entire afternoon off." She frowned. "Though I did hope to discuss that, er, matter with you."

He smiled. Perfect. "And I have something I wish to discuss with you. Perhaps you could come down to the cottage after supper, when all your duties are attended to, of course."

She smiled. "Yes. That would be splendid." She frowned again. "It might be a bit late, if that's all right."

"Any time is fine. I can begin work on my report to the duke while I wait for you." He grinned. "You might even have some suggestions of additional things I should bring to his attention."

Her face lit up, whatever matter that was concerning her momentarily forgotten. "Yes, indeed. I would be happy to do that." Then she turned to their daughter. "Don't run the poor earl ragged, Harriet, and do be sure to get back in time for supper."

"Yes, Mama."

Harry believed he saw Harriet roll her eyes, but thought it best not to comment on the matter.

"Let's take this basket to Miss Dorcas, Harriet," he said instead, "and see if she'll be kind enough to refill it while we are busy with the kittens and whatever other treats you have in store for me."

Chapter Ten

Pen hurried across the field toward the woods. She'd meant to leave for the cottage earlier, but one thing after another had delayed her. First, there'd been supper, and then she'd had to see that Harriet did her schoolwork.

She felt the little hum of pride she always did when she thought about Harriet and her studies. Her daughter was very bright—even Iris, the Home's teacher, said so, and she should know. She'd taught for years at a girls' boarding school before she'd come to Puddledon Manor. Harriet should do very well for herself when it came time for her to make her own way in the world, especially if she was given the right opportunities.

Which Pen was determined to see that she was. Pen's marrying a vicar—though obviously not Godfrey—would be a good step toward that goal. It would give Harriet respectability as well as a home. By the time she was ready to marry or to fend for herself, no one would remember the story of her connection to the Earl of Darrow. They would think of her as Vicar Somebody's daughter.

Well, unless the Earl of Darrow insisted on being part of her life. But surely having Harry's support could only help Harriet, especially if Harry managed to do all his supporting behind the scenes. He would want what was best for his daughter.

Except he'll have other daughters—and sons—by then.

She felt a momentary stab of . . . discomfort.

Ridiculous! The whole point of him marrying Lady Susan—or whichever well-bred woman he ultimately chose—was to have children. To get an heir and a spare.

She must be realistic. He'd been very good with Harriet today and had seemed to really care about her, but it was simply human nature to focus on what—or who—was right under your nose, especially when they lived in your house and carried your name. Once Harry left Little Puddledon, Harriet would be, as the proverb said, "out of sight, out of mind."

Perhaps I can get him to set up some sort of financial arrangement for her.

No. That felt too much like begging. She'd managed perfectly well without him for the last decade. She'd manage just as well for the next. And if things *did* get difficult, then she could ask. But chances were, if he helped her with the vicar issue now, she'd not have to come hat in hand to his door later. She must remember to point that out.

Should I try to hint around about it or should I just be blunt?

Blunt might be best. She wasn't terribly good at hinting.

She reached the path to the cottage, started down it—and promptly stumbled over a tree root. Blast! She managed to catch her balance before she went sprawling in the dirt.

It was very difficult to see. The sun was low in the sky, and there were deep shadows under the trees. She should have come earlier.

She started walking again, paying more attention to where she put her feet. It had been hard to get away even after Harriet had finished her schoolwork. Harriet had been so excited and happy, she'd wanted to tell Pen every detail of the few hours she'd spent with her father.

Pen had never seen the point of fathers—beyond the moment of conception—until today. Her own father had been horrible: bigger and stronger than she, easy to anger, often drunk. She flinched, remembering how she used to hold her breath and lurk in the shadows so as not to set him off. It had been such a huge relief to finally get free of him and be in control of her life. She *never* wanted to go back to living in the constant anxiety she'd lived in at Darrow.

But after seeing how Harry had encouraged Harriet both to ride his horse and to keep trying to hit those apples . . . Perhaps there *were* some positive things a proper father could contribute.

Ah, there was the cottage. It looked dark. She hoped Harry hadn't gone to sleep already.

A shocking image of Harry spread naked on the cottage bed burst uninvited into her thoughts.

She shoved it back out. No good could come from letting her imagination travel *that* treacherous path.

Except that was exactly the path her blasted imagination most wished to travel.

She lifted her hand to knock—and paused.

When she'd left Harriet just now, she'd told her she was going to the cottage and would try not to wake her when she got back—and Harriet had grinned. Dear Lord! She'd thought her daughter too young to see a romance under every bush, but perhaps she was mistaken. There *had* been that suspiciously matchmaking-like maneuvering she'd done on the blanket at luncheon.

Ha! Harriet doesn't need to look under *any vegetation for a romance. She saw you clearly in the hopyard and the apple orchard.*

There had been nothing to see. Harriet couldn't have discerned—or understood—the . . . *need* Pen had felt.

She'd just been happy her mother was talking to her father. Anything else was Pen's imagination.

She frowned at the door. *But if I go inside . . .*

Excitement fluttered in her . . . chest.

She squashed it. She was in control of herself. She was only coming here as Harriet's mother. She had no interest in Harry beyond his role as Harriet's father—well, and perhaps as the duke's emissary.

Right. She'd never been a good liar.

She lifted her hand again to knock just as the door swung open.

"Eep!" She jumped back, caught her heel on her skirt's hem, and started to fall. *At least I'll land on my rump rather than my—oh!*

Harry was quick. He lunged forward, grabbed her by her upper arms, and pulled her against his hard chest.

His hard, *naked* chest. This time there was no linen between her cheek and his skin. She listened to the strong, steady beat of his heart.

Lord! Her own heart stuttered and then started again in slow, expectant thuds. Her breasts felt swollen and her womb heavy. The channel between her legs ached for Harry to fill it.

"Hallo, Pen," he said softly.

The words whispered past her cheek. If she tilted her head just a little, his lips would—

Stop! You are not *seventeen any longer. You are a mature woman—a* mother!—*of twenty-seven. You came here to discuss the possibility of marriage—to the new vicar.*

She pushed and Harry let her go.

She would ignore the fact that he was half naked—

He *was* only half naked, wasn't he?

She looked down over his lovely muscled chest—it was even lovelier than she remembered—and was disappointed— no, *happy*—to see that he was, indeed, wearing breeches, though only a few of the buttons were fastened as if he'd scrambled into them.

And could scramble out again . . .

"Want to help me finish dressing?" His voice was teasing, but she heard an undercurrent of heat. He must be thinking what she was—that it would be far more fun to help him undress.

If she were still seventeen, she'd tease him back—or just run her hands down the narrow path of soft hair over his flat belly to his fall, work the few buttoned buttons free, and release his lovely, long—

Her eyes had followed her thoughts. Now she watched as a bulge grew, straining against the cloth, begging her to—

"You're blushing."

And he must know why. She kept her unruly fingers busy untying and removing her bonnet. "Why aren't you wearing a shirt?"

The words came out a bit sharply, but that was better than the alternative—breathlessly.

She thought he looked disappointed that she hadn't played along with him, but he didn't pursue the matter. He shrugged—and she studied how his muscles shifted.

Was she panting?

Of course not.

"I was feeling in need of a bath after exploring the barn and fields. Besides the kittens, I made the acquaintance of several hopefully-not-flea-bitten dogs, a cow named Bessie and another named Veronica, and a pair of inquisitive goats. I'd barely got back from the pool by the waterfall when I heard you at the door." His grin returned. "Too bad you didn't arrive just a few minutes earlier. You'd have got quite an eyeful."

She was already getting quite an eyeful and could imagine—in far too much detail—exactly what else she would have seen.

I'm here to discuss the new vicar, not to lust after Harry's body.

At the moment she had zero interest in the new vicar.

Harry moved to pick his shirt off the back of a chair— *Good!*—but stopped. *Bad!*

"Do you mind if I leave it off for now? I'm still a bit damp."

Damp. Exactly. That's what she was.

No, that's what he'd said *he* was.

She should insist he put on his shirt. It was the only proper thing to do. Their days of lounging in the sun together, half—or completely—naked were long over.

Unfortunately.

He's only here for a few days. When he leaves, I may never see him again. I might as well see as, er, much of him as I can now.

She spoke before her better sense could prevail. "It makes no difference to me."

Idiot! You're playing with fire.

Nonsense. She was old enough to look without touching.

You don't need to touch the man to go up in flames.

"I'm afraid I can't offer you a cup of tea." He smiled. "I've neither tea nor a cup. But I do have some brandy. Only one glass, though, so we will have to share. Would you like some?"

She should say no and get right down to business. The sooner she did, the sooner she could leave—and the less chance she'd have to do something really, really stupid.

On the other hand, brandy might make Harry more mellow and willing to consider her requirements for a vicar.

She ignored her better sense again.

"Yes, thank you." She sat in one of the less-than-comfortable wooden chairs and watched Harry get the brandy bottle. He had a lovely, broad back.

Focus on business. "Have you had an opportunity to write that letter to the duke?"

"I have. I did that before I bathed."

She did wish he'd stop talking about that blasted bath. It made her imagine him completely naked, wet and slick, water running down his body, hands—

Business. The Home. The letter.

Harry poured some brandy and then handed the glass to her. "I'll get it. And let me light a candle. It's getting dark in here."

She took a sip and watched him pad over to the hearth— his feet were bare!—and bend over to light a spill in the fire. Mmm. His arse was covered by his breeches now, but she remembered how tight and muscled it had been, especially when he was thrusting—

She took another sip of brandy.

He lit a candle and brought it over with his letter. "Here you go. You can see I've left room at the bottom if you think I need to add a postscript." He leaned over to point that out and to pick up the brandy glass.

Oh, Lord. She was enveloped in his scent again.

"Yes." She cleared her throat. "I see. Thank you." She swallowed. She needed more space. "You can take the glass." She was never going to be able to concentrate unless he moved away.

He sat in the chair across from her, the width of the table safely between them—until he put his muscled forearms on it and leaned forward.

She forced her eyes to focus on the letter. She hadn't seen Harry's handwriting before—of course, she hadn't. She couldn't read when she'd been seventeen. His hand was bolder and, well, messier than the neat, precise script Jo and Caro favored. She leaned closer.

"Careful you don't set your hair on fire," he said, moving the candle back.

"Thank you." She had to read the first paragraph over several times before she began to decipher it. It wasn't just that his writing was difficult to read—Harry's presence was a constant distraction.

"Having trouble with my infernal scrawl, are you? It was the bane of my tutor's existence, I assure you." He leaned closer to look at the letter, putting his face within inches of hers. "Can I help you puzzle it out? And here, have some more brandy." He handed her the glass.

She took another sip. The brandy slid down her throat, warming her and easing some of her tension.

"I believe I have the gist of it, though I'm certain Caro would say you should have covered our brewing operation in far more detail and with more enthusiasm." She turned her head to smile at him—and almost brushed his cheek with her mouth.

She sat back quickly. *Talk about the vicar. Harry doesn't mention the need for a new vicar. That is something he should add.*

Yes, but first she must be certain he made the strongest possible case for the Home.

"And Caro would have a point. We *are* working to become self-sufficient. We aren't there yet, but we are much closer than we were. Not that we could ever buy Puddledon Manor—there's little hope of that. But I do think the duke's monetary support can eventually be decreased. We might even be able to pay him rent at some point, and so add to his income."

She leaned forward again, but remembered in time to stop before she got too close to Harry.

It was vital he understood the seriousness of the situation. "I don't know what we'll do if he doesn't let us stay. We have nowhere else to g-go."

Panic she hadn't felt since Aunt Margaret died blinded

her. If the duke ordered them out of the Home, where *would* they go?

She felt a comforting warmth and realized Harry had covered her ice-cold hands with his own large, warm ones.

"Don't worry, Pen. Everything will be all right."

She took a deep breath. She wanted to believe him.

"Grainger is a good man. He's a widower with a young son of his own. He'll wish to protect women and children."

She frowned at him. "Then why did he hold up our funds and send you here?"

"He wanted to find out exactly what it was he was supporting. The estate books didn't say." He shrugged. "The only possibility that occurred to us was that the old duke or perhaps his son had hidden away a bastard here."

"Oh." She felt herself flush. She pulled her hands back from his. "And instead you discovered *you* were the one with the b-bastard."

He frowned. "Yes. Pen, you know—"

She cut him off. "Harriet and I are fine, Harry. We'll be fine as long as you can persuade the duke to keep supporting the Home."

He looked as if he was going to argue, but then changed his mind and took a sip of brandy. He offered the glass to her.

Oh, why the hell not? "You're going to have to pour more if we keep this up."

He shrugged. "There's plenty."

And he would have to carry her up to the house. But not yet. She wasn't even tipsy yet.

She noticed his eyes follow her tongue as she licked a drop of brandy off her upper lip, and her temperature shot up.

Now is the time to mention the new vicar before I do something I shouldn't.

But Harry spoke first. "You've done a wonderful job raising Harriet, Pen. I thoroughly enjoyed my afternoon with her"—he grinned—"even given all the animals I had to meet. She's a delightful girl—bright and charming."

Oh. The anonymous vicar vanished from her thoughts like a puff of smoke as she felt herself . . . *glow* with pleasure. That was the only way she could describe it. No one else had ever appreciated Harriet the way she did.

She smiled back at Harry. "She is, isn't she?"

"Yes." He took another sip of brandy and then reached for her hand. "I'm so sorry I wasn't there when she was born, Pen, and that I've missed so many years of her life, but I'm very happy to have discovered her now." His thumb stroked slowly over the back of her hand. "And to have found you again."

"Mmm." Oh, God. She'd let down her guard when Harry had mentioned Harriet, and now the need she'd felt in the hopyard and the orchard came roaring back a thousandfold—a gale-force wind compared to a summer breeze. Her self-control shattered into a million pieces.

The weight of Harry's hand on hers, the slight friction of his thumb moving over her skin, brought back so many memories.

It's been over nine years since I've felt a man's touch. Nine long years.

Had she groaned?

No, that had been Harry.

"Lord, Pen."

He was staring at her, but there wasn't much for him to see, just a high-necked serviceable gown and her hair pinned primly up on her head. What *she* could see, however . . .

She wanted to run her hands over the muscles in his shoulders, his arms, his chest.

"I've missed you." His voice was low and husky and tight. His thumb moved to stroke her palm.

She closed her eyes briefly, biting her lip.

"You were always so responsive. So focused. So . . . so *alive*." His hand moved to her cheek.

I want to be alive again. To be more than Harriet's mother.

She turned her face, pressed her lips to his palm, and then let the tip of her tongue touch his skin.

She heard his sharp inhalation and her body—her breasts, her womb—trembled in anticipation.

Zeus! The rasp of Pen's tongue shot straight to his cock, which had already been pleasantly interested in the proceedings. Now it was desperate, demanding to be freed to find the dark, warm home it knew was under Pen's skirt.

Think with your head, *man—the thing your hat sits on. You haven't seen Pen for close to ten years. She was almost raped yesterday. She does not want to be mauled again.*

Pen's tongue stroked lightly over his skin and the few thoughts he'd dragged into his brain spun away. Not surprising. Every drop of blood in his body had suddenly rushed to his cock.

It had always been this way with Pen. With other women, sexual congress was a delightful, satisfying diversion. With Pen, it was as vital as breathing. He literally felt he'd die if he didn't sheath himself in her soon.

He took his hand back, gripping his knee instead. "Make love with me, will you, Pen?"

So much for his vaunted skills of seduction, but then Pen had never been one to play games. And he didn't want to seduce her, if that meant somehow tricking her or over-powering her better sense. He wanted her to choose this freely because she wanted it. "Please?"

He wanted it, too, of course, more than he could remember wanting anything in a long, long time. He held his breath. If she said "no" . . .

And she might well do that. He could see the indecision in her eyes.

His stomach knotted. If she said "no," he'd tell her he was sorry, but they'd talk another day about . . . whatever it was she had come here to discuss. He wouldn't mention the house at Darrow. He'd thought—*hoped*—he could offer it to her with only the purest of intentions—to save her from having to worry about the future and to keep Harriet near him so he could be a part of her life—but he'd been fooling himself. He had an ulterior motive that was as far from pure as one could get.

He wanted Harriet close, yes, but he wanted Pen closer.

She bit her lip.

It would be so easy to—

No. This has to be her free choice.

The water in the pool had been cold when he'd had his bath. If Pen said "no," he'd see her to the door, say good-bye, and go back there in the hopes it was cold enough to extinguish this fire she'd kindled.

Or you could visit Bess at the inn.

No. The notion was revolting. And it wouldn't work. In fact, he might embarrass himself and disappoint Bess if he tried. His need wasn't only physical. It was . . . something more.

It would be better to pleasure himself than—

"Yes."

His thoughts stilled, and he focused again on Pen. She was smiling just the way she used to that summer, the corners of her lips barely turned up, her eyes wide and dark with desire and need.

Thank God!

"I—" His throat was so thick with lust he had to clear it. "I think we'd better go upstairs." His randy cock was about to explode. "Where the"—he swallowed—"bed is."

They'd hardly ever made love in a bed, he realized with

a bit of shock, or even indoors. They hadn't wanted to be discovered—though from the benefit of hindsight, it was a minor miracle no one had stumbled on them by the pond or in the woods and fields.

Or perhaps someone did see us and thought it not worth mentioning that one of the earl's sons was swiving a tenant farmer's daughter.

He pushed that unpleasant thought aside. He had more important—more immediate—things to focus on.

"All right." Pen made a nervous little noise, part giggle, part gulp as she started for the loft. "I suppose we're too old to, er, *frolic* on the table or against the wall."

That's right. Many of their couplings had been shockingly quick.

"No, not too old, but I'd rather be comfortable and not have to worry about falling down."

And he did not intend to be quick. He was going to take his time and savor the experience—assuming his swollen cock would allow him to. At the moment, he wasn't entirely certain it would let him climb the stairs.

He wanted to make love to Pen slowly on a bed like a twenty-eight-year-old man with some skill—not like a fumbling, lust-crazed eighteen-year-old boy.

That summer at Darrow had been a time apart, his last days of childhood—though at eighteen, he wasn't a child obviously. But he'd been unencumbered by duty or responsibility, a freedom he'd never know again.

Of course, he hadn't appreciated it. He'd been too anxious to get on with his life, to shake Darrow's dirt from his boots and have adventures. But he'd appreciated Pen. And whenever he looked back at that time, she was there, the brightest, warmest, happiest part of his memory.

Except she hadn't been there. She'd been exiled, on her own, raising their daughter.

Right. He should have been a bit more encumbered by responsibility that summer.

He would be responsible now. He'd move Pen and Harriet to Darrow. They'd have no more worries—and they'd be close to him. He could watch Harriet grow up, and he could *frolic* with Pen as often as he wanted.

Unless his cock exploded. Climbing these infernal steps was painful.

"Watch your head," Pen said, ducking to get through the bedroom's doorway. "The ceiling is very low." She laughed. "Though I suppose you know that."

"Yes," he said, ducking as well. "I have the knot on my head to prove it." The room was so small and the roof so steeply pitched, he had to crowd close to Pen to stand up straight.

He breathed in her scent, a light mix of lemon and . . . and something uniquely Pen. Ah.

In the last ten years, he'd been here—in the charged moments before the first amorous move was made—any number of times with any number of beautiful, eager women, but he had never before felt such intense anticipation. This was *Pen*.

Memories of young love and, before that, friendship, mixed in with his desire.

You are expecting too much.

Perhaps he was, but he couldn't help himself.

"Oh?" Pen had to tilt her head to meet his gaze. She looked concerned—and then grinned. "I'll kiss it and make it better, shall I?"

His cock twitched. It wanted so badly for her lips to touch it now, but if they went that route, the encounter would be over before it began. He was very afraid it was going to be over too quickly no matter how much he tried to control himself.

I shouldn't be this randy. I'm not a lad any longer.

"Do you remember when you said that before?" He pulled the first pin from her hair. Ah! It was as silky as he remembered.

She closed her eyes and gave a little hum of pleasure—and his cock twitched again.

"Yes. That night we were"—she smiled—"playing in the bathhouse pool."

He pulled out the next pin.

They had indeed been playing, naked in the water, the bathhouse lit only by moonlight. They hadn't wanted to light a candle for fear someone from the house would see it and come investigate.

"You were chasing me," she said, "and bumped your hip against that statue of a water nymph."

Yes, his hip. It had almost been a much more sensitive body part.

Her tongue peeked out to moisten her lips. Lord! With any other woman, he'd know the gesture was carefully calculated to scramble his wits, but with Pen, it was completely natural.

"And I kissed it better, didn't I?"

She'd done more than that. Her mouth had slid easily from his hip to his cock, her clever fingers stroking and petting. She'd had a wonderful instinct for pleasure.

He pulled out the last pin, and Pen's lovely, rich brown hair tumbled free.

"You did." His fingers combed through the silky strands. He leaned closer, so only a breath separated their mouths. "Much, much better."

And then he closed the gap.

Her skin was so soft, and she smelled so good. His lips teased a corner of her mouth, brushed her temple, nuzzled the sensitive spot on her neck just below her ear—and were rewarded with a breathy moan that shot straight to his groin.

She tilted her head, inviting him to explore further, while

her hands moved, sliding up to his shoulders and then down again, stopping on his buttocks, tugging him closer even as she arched her hips to meet him.

"Harry. Oh, God, Harry."

This time he was the one who moaned. "Pen." He needed her in a way he'd never needed any other woman.

He stepped back and reached for her buttons, but her fingers moved faster. In a blink, her dress dropped to the floor, and she stepped out of it.

His face must have given away his surprise, because she smiled a little tightly. "I'm not a Society miss, Harry. I don't have a maid to dress and undress me like a doll." She loosened her stays just as quickly. "Don't you remember?"

He did remember. They'd never made a performance out of shedding their clothes—they'd always been too eager, or too desperate, to draw out that part of the mating ritual.

Her stays joined her dress on the floor, leaving her in just her shoes and stockings.

Ah! Her body was so familiar—and yet different, too. It was fuller, softer than it had been, and there were faint, pearly lines where her skin had stretched with her pregnancy.

She lifted her chin. "I can put my clothes back on, and we can pretend this never happened."

He heard the slight waver in her voice. "Pen." He touched one of the lines, tracing it gently down to where it disappeared into the curly thatch that hid her entrance—and the path Harriet had taken into the world. "Each mark is beautiful."

"Beautiful?" Her laugh was a little high and thin. "You should have seen me. I was as big as a house at the end."

"Yes, I *should* have seen you. I wish I had. I wish I'd been there to see you grow big and heavy with our daughter. I wish I'd been with you as you struggled to push her into the world and when you held her for the first time." He moved his finger to her breast, circling her nipple. "And I wish I'd been there to watch her suckle."

Her eyes were wide and . . . wet? *His* eyes felt damp.

She blinked, and the tears, if there had been any, were gone, but her voice quavered. "I wish you'd been there, too, Harry."

But he hadn't been. He hadn't even known they'd made a child. What a shallow, irresponsible boy he'd been. He wished . . .

Regret was pointless. There was no going back, only forward. He would be responsible now. He would move her to the Darrow house where he could take care of her and Harriet and any other children they might have. She would never have to worry again.

Words crowded his throat, but his body was done with words. Actions spoke louder, and lust and need and some other deep emotion he couldn't identify urged him to action. He would show her with his body how he would care for her.

"Pen." He brushed his lips over hers as his fingers stroked the sides of her breasts. "Let's go to bed."

Chapter Eleven

"Yes." And just like that, she went from melancholy to desire—desperate, consuming, urgent desire. Her body had waited nine long years for a man's touch—for *this* man's touch. It could not wait one moment longer.

She wrapped her arms around his back, flattening her breasts against his warm, naked chest.

That wasn't enough. She slid her hands down to pull his arse—unfortunately still cloth-covered—against her. Oh! The long ridge of his cock, trapped behind his fall, pressed into her belly.

"To bed, Pen."

Yes!

She was delighted to hear the lust in his voice.

Fortunately, the room was so tiny, the bed was only half a step away. She collapsed onto it and reached for him. "*Hurry.*"

He did not hurry. Instead, he stood there and *looked* at her.

"God, Pen, you are so beautiful."

She hadn't thought she could feel any more desperate, but she did. "Harry, I'm going to die. I need you *now.*"

He smiled, though his expression *was* a bit strained. He must be feeling at least some of the need she felt.

"Soon." He pulled off one of her shoes and then carefully untied her garter.

She arched up, wanting his fingers higher, but he laughed and slid his hands away, pulling her stocking down over her knee and calf and ankle and off her foot.

She was panting, her body open to him, begging him to come inside. "Harry, you're torturing me."

He grinned. "Yes, but it's a good sort of torture." He blew on her damp nether curls as he untied her other garter.

"Nooo." She moaned and arched up again, but again he moved back, his hands sliding the other stocking off.

"I promise the reward will be worth it." He carefully laid her second stocking next to her first.

"I'll be dead by then."

"No, you won't." He sat on the edge of the bed. He still had his breeches on.

All right, she would help him. She reached for his fall—and he caught her hands before they could touch the fabric.

"Harry!" She pulled back, but he wouldn't release her.

"Patience, Pen."

How could he talk of patience?

Ha! *He* hadn't spent all these years alone. He'd likely had any number of lovers.

"You don't understand. It's been Nine. Long. Years." Not that she'd thought much about carnal relations during that time. She'd had no interest in such matters when she was pregnant and a new mother, and then later she'd been too busy—and tired and worried—to care about bed play.

She closed her eyes briefly. No, that wasn't it. The painful truth was no man had ever moved her to passion the way Harry did. When he'd left Darrow, he'd taken her desire with him.

Now that he was here, it came flooding back, threatening to drown her.

"I'm begging you, Harry. I need you. Now." She tried to lean closer to him, but he wouldn't let her. "Hard and fast."

Ah, she saw the heat spark in his eyes. He was going to— No, he wasn't.

"Trust me, Pen."

She wasn't good at trust. Trust meant giving someone else control. That was too risky. It was better to rely only on herself.

She'd never been able to rely on anyone else. Not her father. Not Harry, though that hadn't been Harry's fault. She'd known from the moment she decided to seduce him that he was leaving.

Just as he'll leave this time . . .

Stop! This is only a bit of bed sport. Nothing more. It might even cure me so I can find happiness with the new vicar.

Ugh! She didn't want to think about any other man when she was with Harry.

"Trust me," Harry said again, and then he leaned forward so his mouth just brushed hers. "It will be good, I promise."

And just like that, she surrendered. She *would* trust him—or at least she would try. She had no other choice.

"All right."

The intensity in his eyes grew, and he leaned forward again. This time his mouth was open when it came down on hers.

Oh! Yes. It felt so good, so very, very good to be kissed like this again, deep and hot and wet.

He pressed her back into the mattress as he slowly explored her mouth and then moved to her jaw, her throat, her collarbone.

"Oh. Oh, Harry." She was panting and whimpering, her

hips twisting on the bed, her legs spread wide in the hopes that the air would cool her and keep her from going up in flames.

Harry's lips moved slowly up the slope of her breast. Too slowly. She threaded her fingers through his hair and pulled, hoping to get him to move faster.

"Stop trying to be in charge," he murmured against her skin.

"Stop trying to drive me m-mad. Oh!" His lips brushed against her, so very, very close to—

And then she felt the wet rasp of his tongue on her nipple. Lightning shot through her to lodge between her legs. "Oh! Oh, oh, *ohhh*."

His tongue and mouth kept teasing, circling, stroking, while his fingers played with her other nipple.

"Harry. Please." He should take off his breeches, but at this point, she'd not complain if he just opened his fall. As long as his lovely coc—

His mouth moved lower, kissing the undersides of her breasts, her ribs, her belly.

"H-Harry?" What was he doing? She flushed, squirming—but with embarrassment this time. He shouldn't be looking at—

"Trust me," he said yet again. His tongue traced one of the pearly lines from her pregnancy. His breath stirred her nether curls. He was so close he must be able to *smell* her desire.

She no longer cared. Need so intense it obliterated all embarrassment, all sense of decorum, even all rational thought, was building in her again.

"Please, Harry. Please." She didn't know what she was asking for, but she knew whatever it was he could give it to her.

She felt his fingers part her folds, felt the tip of his tongue lightly trace her opening.

"Harry!" She grabbed the bedclothes so she wouldn't fly apart.

"You're beautiful, Pen."

"Uh. Um."

And then his tongue touched her small, hard nub, slid around it, over it—

"Harry!"

Exquisite, almost painful pleasure exploded through her. She half sat up, and then collapsed back onto the mattress.

He kissed her inner thigh before lifting himself over her, grinning, clearly pleased with himself. "It was good, wasn't it?"

"Y-yes." It *had* been good, but it hadn't been . . . complete. "But now I want—*need*—you in me." She reached for his fall.

His face tightened, his eyes turning hot as she worked the first button loose. Then he sat up, jerked off his shoes and stockings, and tore off his breeches.

Oh! He was so beautiful. He'd been handsome at eighteen, but the years had chiseled away any trace of youth's softness, leaving him leaner, more muscled. She let her eyes travel slowly from his shoulders across his chest and belly down to the nest of curls above his thighs where his long, swollen cock stood out.

Her inner muscles shivered in anticipation.

This time when she reached for him, he came into her arms at once.

She buried her face in his neck and breathed in his scent. She loved having his weight on her.

"Oh, Harry."

"*This* time it will be hard and fast," he said.

"Mmm." She ran her hands down his back to his lovely, naked arse. "Mmm."

It wasn't hard and fast, but it was perfect.

He teased her at first, pushing in just a little and then almost pulling out. She closed her eyes to concentrate on the sensation. In and out, shallow and deeper, stretching and filling, stoking her need again. "Harry. Oh. Harry. Yes."

And then he was sliding into her, deeper and deeper, his weight pushing her into the mattress. *This* was what she had missed. Not the excitement or the physical satisfaction—or not just those things. She'd missed this connection, this closeness.

She'd been so alone for so long. She wrapped her arms around him to hold him even closer.

For nine years she'd been a mother. A farmer. A businesswoman. But not a *woman*, not like this.

It's not love, she cautioned herself. *It's only lust. Only physical.*

But it felt like love.

And then pleasure washed through her once more, but this time Harry's body anchored hers—both inside and out.

And as her pleasure ebbed, she felt the warm pulse of his seed.

Have I conceived again?

She should feel panic, but all she felt was a deep contentment.

Harry collapsed onto her. She could barely breathe—and it was wonderful. She slid her hands down his back to his arse, holding him, trying to keep him with her a moment longer.

And then he lifted himself away, leaving her damp flesh chilled and her arms empty, bereft—until he stretched out next to her, gathered her close, and pulled the coverlet over them.

She buried her face in his chest, too drugged by their lovemaking to feel anything but a lazy, bone-deep happiness.

"I should have pulled out, Pen." He smoothed her hair

back from her face. "I meant to do it, but then . . ." He kissed her forehead. "You overwhelmed me just as you always did when we were young."

"It's all right." She *should* be worried, but she still couldn't manage it, not when she was skin to skin in a warm bed with Harry. "It's not the right time."

She hoped. Her courses were still irregular, so it was hard to say when the right and the wrong times were. Still, it had taken three months of almost constant tupping to get Harriet and she'd been years younger then.

"I'll be more careful next time." He grinned. "Or, at least I'll try to be more careful."

"Mmm." All she cared about was that there would be a next time.

I should ask Avis how to avoid getting pregnant. She must know. She's been coupling with the boy from the butcher shop for months.

Harry's hand was stroking her arse. "What did you want to discuss?" he asked.

It felt so good, she wanted to purr like one of Harriet's barn cats. "Hmm?"

He laughed and slapped her lightly on her rump. "Focus, Pen. Why did you come down here? You said you had a matter to discuss, remember? It wasn't just to go over my letter to Grainger."

"Oh." Yes. The new vicar. She shifted position. She was not going to list the attributes she'd like a potential husband to have when she was lying naked in Harry's arms. "It's nothing. We can talk about it some other time."

Harry frowned at her. "It must have been something to bring you down to the cottage."

The lie—well, no, it was also the truth, now that she thought about it—came easily. "Some*one*." She leaned up on her elbow to press her mouth to his. "I've missed you."

He kissed her back, slowly and thoroughly. "And I've missed you, too, as I believe I've just demonstrated—and will be happy to demonstrate again once I recover."

She sighed. She wished she could stay here that long, but she couldn't.

For once it was a very good thing she was a mother.

"I'm afraid I have to get back. I've moved Harriet into my room." She untangled herself from Harry, got up, and started dressing. "I don't want her to wake up and wonder where I am."

Worse, she didn't want Harriet to imagine . . . Well, she hoped Harriet was still too young to imagine what precisely had occurred here, but she wasn't too young to start building happily-ever-after air castles.

Harry pulled on his breeches and shirt. "I'll walk you back."

"No need." She put on her shoes. "I know my way, and there's a full moon."

"That may be, but I'm still coming with you. I wish to discuss a few matters"—he grinned—"that for some reason slipped my mind earlier."

Her heart turned over at his smile, but she resisted the pull he exerted on her. Well, she *tried* to resist. She knew it would be better—at least wiser—to nip this . . . whatever it was, in the bud now. If she kept visiting his bed, she *would* be no better than a whore, just as Godfrey had labeled her.

No, if she kept visiting his bed, she'd lose her heart to him. *Ha! It's already lost.*

She followed Harry down the narrow stairs and out into the cloudless night. The full moon had risen above the trees, lighting the path through the woods enough that they could pick their way without stumbling. He offered her his arm, but she ignored it. The temptation to lean on him—in all things—was too great at the moment. She needed to rebuild her wall of independence.

An owl hooted off in the distance and another owl answered.

"You really don't have to come with me."

He ignored her. "I'd meant to raise the subject of Harriet's future, before I got"—he grinned at her—"distracted."

"Oh." It was on the tip of her tongue to tell him not to concern himself, that she had things well in hand, but she swallowed the words. She did not wish to be Harry's charity case, but this wasn't just about her. She had to consider Harriet's welfare. If Harry took a personal interest in their daughter, it could only improve Harriet's prospects.

"I want to see more of her, Pen."

Her silly heart leaped. If Harry came to Little Puddledon to see Harriet, he'd see her, too. She could have many more wonderfully thorough tuppings.

Her womb shivered in anticipation, but her heart stilled. Each time she welcomed him into her body, she'd lose another piece of herself.

Was that too high a price to pay for Harriet's future?

Her womb said no. Her heart said maybe.

And her brain said, *Are you a bloody idiot?!*

"If you move back to Darrow," Harry was saying, "I can visit her—and you—every day."

She stumbled. Move back to Darrow? "What?"

He'd caught her elbow to steady her, but she stepped back out of his grasp almost immediately. His touch scrambled her wits, and she needed to concentrate.

"Don't you see, Pen? It's the perfect solution. Old Mrs. Fisher's place is empty. You remember the house, don't you? It's set a bit apart from the others and has—or had—a lovely garden. It's a little rundown now, but I'll have it set to rights before you arrive."

She remembered the house—and old Mrs. Fisher, except she now realized the woman likely hadn't been much older than Pen was now when last Pen had seen her. And of course the house had been set apart. Had Harry forgotten the woman had been the village lightskirt?

How appropriate—

No! I'm not a lightskirt.

Everyone will think you are.

Living back among the people she'd grown up with, being Harry's mistress . . .

Her stomach twisted in a way that didn't feel like excitement or anticipation.

She couldn't do it.

Don't be hasty. Think of Harriet.

She'd do anything for Harriet, wouldn't she?

Perhaps not this.

"It'll be just the thing." Harry smiled, but the moonlight made his face look a little cold.

"I don't know . . ." She hadn't worried that anyone would find out what she'd been doing with Harry when they were young. She hadn't cared. But this was different. This time she'd be completely dependent on him—a kept woman, in truth. She'd have to give up her independence, her job here, her position in the community.

And she was a mother now. Rosamund and Verity had shown her just how cruel people could be. Harriet might benefit from being near Harry, but what if everyone else shunned her?

And there's another major difference between now and then.

"I've read that you're going to marry." She looked ahead rather than at Harry. She could see the dark bulk of the manor. They didn't have much farther to walk. "If the newspapers are to be believed, you'll offer for the Earl of Langley's daughter very soon." *If you haven't already.* "Is that right?"

"Yes." He let out a long breath.

She glanced at him. He was frowning at some point in the distance.

"Ever since I got back to England, my mother has been trotting eligible young misses by me, Pen. We made a pact—she would stop hounding me and I'd pick one of the girls by the end of the Season—and I'm already past that deadline. I don't have forever, she said, and she's right. Walter died young and unexpectedly."

He looked back at her—the shadows made his frown darker. "I picked Lady Susan. I almost managed to pop the question the last night I was at Grainger's, before I came down here. If it hadn't been for a sudden rainstorm, I'd be betrothed now." He shrugged. "I'll attend to the matter once I get back."

He might as well be saying he'd attend to getting his hair cut.

"It doesn't sound as if you love her." She'd been just as unenthusiastic when she'd considered trying to get Godfrey to propose, but he'd been her only option. Harry had a much wider selection of women to choose from.

Harry snorted. "Of course, I don't love her, Pen. That's not how these things work. It will be a marriage of convenience. Most *ton* marriages are."

"But it sounds as if you don't even like her much." She didn't want Harry to chain himself to someone who would make him miserable. "I know you need an heir, but surely your mother would rather you wait a little longer to find a woman you can care for. Why pick Lady Susan?"

"I *tried* to find a better candidate, Pen," Harry said. "You might think the selection on the Marriage Mart is extensive, but it's not. The girls in their first Season are just too young." He grinned at her briefly, his teeth flashing white in the moonlight. "Consorting with a seventeen-year-old was fine when I was eighteen, but it's not very appealing now that I'm twenty-eight—even though my mother keeps pointing out that younger girls have more breeding years." He shook his head. "They all seem like complete ninnyhammers."

She'd not thought herself a ninnyhammer at seventeen, but then she'd not grown up in a cocoon of wealth, with servants and governesses and dancing masters. Yet it was also true that she was more aware of the world—and Society's rules—now. She was more . . . Not wiser, precisely. More realistic. Perhaps that was it. She'd had some of her foolish dreams knocked out of her.

"So that left the others," Harry continued, "the ones who didn't take their first Season . . ." He shook his head. "Let's just say it was often painfully clear why they were still on the shelf."

She felt a momentary pang of sympathy for those girls. It must be extremely mortifying—and perhaps more than a little frightening—to be in that position, especially if your entire upbringing had been focused on achieving the one goal you'd failed at—bagging a noble husband.

"I'm sure Lady Susan and I will rub along tolerably well," Harry said. "She's an earl's daughter. She's been trained to supervise servants and manage an earl's household. And she *is* very beautiful, so it won't be a chore looking at her"— he smiled briefly—"or doing other things with her."

Of course, that made Pen think of the "other things" they'd just done at the cottage. Harry must be thinking of them, too, because his face was suddenly stark with need.

"Is she passionate, Harry?" *Why am I asking this question? I don't really want to know the answer.* But her foolish tongue kept going. "I can't think you'd like to be married to a cold fish."

"I don't know if she's passionate or not, but it doesn't matter. She'll just lie back and think of England, I imagine, and I'll do my best to get the business done without offending her modesty or inconveniencing her too much."

She stared at him.

"Not all women are as lusty as you, Pen, especially Society virgins." He grimaced. "I do hope she doesn't chatter in the bedroom the way she does in the ballroom."

"Oh."

Harry must have heard the doubt in her voice, because his tone became a bit defensive.

"It's not as if we'll live in each other's pockets, after all. I'll spend most of my time at my club when we're in London, and Darrow Hall is such a huge pile, we could go days without seeing each other."

What he was describing . . . It sounded terribly lonely—worse than actually being alone.

Harry touched her cheek lightly. "Don't fret. I assure you, Lady Susan's not looking for a love match, either. She wants a secure, respected position, and I have one on offer. It will all work out."

Harry must know best. It didn't make any sense to her, but then she'd never had much contact with the *ton*—except for Harry, of course.

"Well, I hope it does. Still, I can't think she'd be happy to have your mistress living right under her nose."

That made him grin. "On the contrary, I think she'd be delighted. Having you nearby means I won't be in her bed any more than the minimum necessary to get an heir."

So Rosamund is right . . .

"But if it makes *you* uncomfortable, I do have houses you could live in on my other estates." He frowned suddenly, as if a new, unpleasant thought had occurred to him. "Perhaps it *would* be best to set you and Harriet up at one of those other places, at least while my mother, sister-in-law, and nieces are still at Darrow Hall."

Ah. She hadn't considered his family. Her memory of Harry's mother was of an elegant but pale, older woman sitting in the family's pew at church or smiling somewhat woodenly at estate celebrations. And she hardly knew Letitia at all. She'd married Walter a few years before Pen left Darrow, but had spent most of her time in London.

"Your nieces are around Harriet's age, aren't they?" She had to swallow to overcome a sudden lump in her throat. "I c-can't see your mother or sister-in-law liking them rubbing elbows with your b-bastard."

Because that's what Harriet is.

Best be brutally honest—Harry's family was sure to be.

His brows angled down into a scowl. "Harriet is my daughter—my mother's granddaughter."

"And illegitimate. I know how the world works, Harry."

He didn't argue. Instead he looked away, jaw clenched. He knew what she said was true.

It was a full minute before he spoke again, and then his voice sounded tired. Discouraged.

"I might be able to persuade them to move to the London house, though London isn't the best place for the girls. The air is filthy, and there's the never-ending din of carriages and horses and people."

They'd almost reached the house. She stopped in the shadows of an oak tree in case anyone was still awake and looking out the window.

Whether his family would welcome her and Harriet or spurn them didn't matter.

"I can't leave Little Puddledon, Harry. I'm needed here, especially now. It's almost harvesttime. I have a job to do."

Harry frowned down at her. "But I need you too, Pen. And I need Harriet. I'm her father. I want to spend time with her—to get to know her—and I can't move to Little Puddledon." He stepped closer, but he didn't touch her.

"Let me make things easier for you, Pen. I'm serious about the house at Darrow or at one of my other properties, if you prefer. Come live there. You won't have to worry about anything. I'll see to your expenses and Harriet's education. And I won't insist you be my mistress, if you don't want to be." He grinned. "Though I can't say I won't try very hard to seduce you."

That made her laugh. He could still manage a mischievous little boy look rather well.

But it was no laughing matter. She desperately wanted what he offered—and yet she didn't want it, too.

"I don't know, Harry. I should say no and be done with this, but seeing you again . . . I need time to think. And Harriet needs time, too."

"That's fair. I'll stay a few more days, shall I? That will give Harriet more time to get to know me"—he grinned—"and me more time to, ah, *persuade* you."

"No." She blurted the word out before she could stop herself.

"No?"

"No *persuasion* of that sort. I need to make this decision with my head"—she pointed to that part of her anatomy—"and not my—" She'd been going to say heart, but lost courage at the last moment and just fluttered her fingers.

I can't let myself fall further in love with Harry.

Harry grinned rather salaciously. "Are you certain I can't persuade your"—he fluttered his fingers lower, at the part of her anatomy he'd been persuading so thoroughly just a short while ago.

That made her laugh. "You are not to try."

"No? Hmm. I can promise to try not to try." He gave her that little boy look again. "I can't guarantee I'll succeed."

"Harry . . ."

"I promise not to touch you first. How's that?"

She laughed. It was impossible to say no to him. "Very well."

If she decided—as she likely should—to stay here in Little Puddledon, he'd be gone in just a few days. She might as well enjoy—though not *too* much—the last little bit of time she had with him.

"Now good night."

He held up his hand—but abided by the new rules and didn't touch her. "Will I see you in the morning? I'm sure your"—he fluttered his fingers at her lower body again—"needs to be around me to make up its mind."

"Harry . . ." She was trying not to laugh. He looked so disarmingly—and, she was quite certain, cunningly—hopeful.

"We could spend the day with Harriet—when you aren't tending to your hops, of course. Surely, our daughter will be a suitable chaperone and keep us from misbehaving."

"Keep *you* from misbehaving."

He grinned. "So even Harriet's presence won't constrain you?"

"*I* am not going to misbehave." She tried to sound haughty, but failed miserably, especially when she giggled at Harry's absurdly dramatic expression of disappointment. "All right. We will come down to the cottage in the morning. This time be certain you're dressed."

"I promise." His eyes brightened—though perhaps that was just the reflection of a stray moonbeam. "Do I get a good-night kiss?"

She should say no, but he knew her too well. She'd heard the challenge in his voice. "All right."

He reached for her, but she stepped back quickly.

"Remember, you promised not to touch me first."

"True." He leaned over rather theatrically and extended his cheek.

This is easy. She pressed her lips to his skin, felt the roughness of his beard against her mouth—and then the touch of his hand, stroking through her hair.

She stepped back. "Good night."

She walked briskly—well, yes, she ran—for the front door, hearing Harry chuckle behind her.

Chapter Twelve

Pen stepped over the threshold and then looked back to see if Harry was still under the tree.

He was. The white of his shirt—he hadn't bothered with waistcoat or coat—was bright in the shadows. He waved.

She waved back and started to close the door, but stopped once he turned away. She watched him until he vanished in the darkness.

I'll see him tomorrow.

She felt an uncomfortable churn of delight and dread as she finally shut the door, turned, and—

"Eek!"

Caro was standing in the middle of the entry.

Pen caught her breath—and frowned. "Were you spying on me?"

Caro didn't deny it. "I saw figures lurking in the shadows under the tree. Of course, I kept an eye out. You could have been villains preparing to break in."

Pen snorted. "In Little Puddledon?"

"Yes. Don't think you are safe from rogues just because you live in this little backwater." Caro looked significantly at the door. "Especially when London sharks come swimming in."

"If you mean Har—" Pen caught herself when she saw Caro's brows shoot up. "Lord Darrow is not a shark."

Caro's brows stayed up.

"And there's only one of him." Might as well split hairs.

Caro rolled her eyes.

"And if you saw it was Lord Darrow, then you knew no one was going to break into the house. You were just sticking your nose into matters that don't concern you."

Caro's eyes narrowed. "I don't know that they don't concern me. What *were* you doing in the shadows with the earl so late at night?"

"Talking." Which is all she had been doing . . . in the shadows. "And it's not that late."

"It's almost midnight."

Pen nodded at the longcase clock in the entry. "It's only a little after eleven."

"No, it's not." Caro didn't even bother glancing that way. "You know as well as I do that clock runs slow. And even if it were correct, it would still be late—you're always in bed by ten."

This was one of the many problems with living in a houseful of women. They noticed far too much.

"What? Are you my mother now?"

"No, of course not. But I saw how you gazed in rapture at the earl when he toured the brewhouse."

Pen's mouth dropped open. "I did no such thing. I may have smiled at him occasionally—he's an old friend—but I never 'gazed in rapture' at him. What a ridiculous—and revolting—notion."

Caro rolled her eyes again.

I didn't *look at Harry that way, did I?*

Her heart sank. Caro was infernally accurate at reading people. It was one of the things that made her such a good saleswoman.

"And then when I saw how distracted you were at supper,

I knew something was afoot. So I kept my eyes open and . . ." Caro flushed and looked away.

Oh, Lord, this was bad. Pen waited for the rest of it.

"And I saw you go out," Caro told the portrait of some dead Havenridge, hanging on the wall by the door, "so I . . ."

"You what, Caro?" Pen clenched her hands into fists.

Caro looked back at her, her expression a mix of anger and worry. "I followed you to the cottage."

"What?!" *Did she see Harry—a naked-from-the-waist-up Harry—catch me?*

"I didn't follow you *all* the way to the cottage."

Thank God for that.

"So, if he threw your skirts over your head and took you on the lawn, I didn't see it."

"Caro!!"

"Is everything all right down there?" Jo had appeared at the top of the stairs, dressed in her nightgown and wrapper, Freddie by her side.

"No," Caro said.

"Yes," Pen said at exactly the same moment.

"Oh, dear." Jo started down the stairs, Freddie's nails clicking on the marble as he followed her. "Let's go into the sitting room so we don't wake anyone."

"Actually, I was just going to bed," Pen said, starting to edge toward the stairs, hoping to dash—no, walk sedately— past Jo. "It's been a long day. If you'll excuse me?"

"No, I'm afraid I won't." Jo smiled. That is, her lips formed a smile. Her eyes were dark with concern. "I'm worried about you, too, Pen." She stopped on the last step, a hand on the banister. Freddie planted his rump on her other side. Pen was trapped unless she wanted to force her way past them.

She blew out a long breath. "All right. I do hope this won't take long. I *am* very tired."

"I bet you are."

Caro's insinuation was embarrassingly clear—at least to Pen's guilty conscience.

"Caro," Jo said sharply, "you are not helping matters."

Caro frowned. She looked as if she wished to say more, but pressed her lips together instead and went off to the sitting room.

"After you," Jo said pleasantly enough, but Pen could tell she wasn't moving until Pen did. She was not going to let Pen escape.

Oh, what did it matter? One way or another, the story would come out. Such stories always did.

Pen shrugged and, somewhat gracelessly, followed Caro into the sitting room. She wanted to take a seat in the farthest, darkest corner, but she knew she wouldn't get away with that either, so she flopped into one of the chairs closest to the hearth, directly across from Caro, and glared at her. Caro glared back.

"Isn't this cozy?" Jo said with false gaiety as she went over to poke the fire awake. She looked from Pen to Caro. "I think we might need a little brandy."

Pen had already had a little brandy, but she wasn't going to say that. And her . . . exercise seemed to have burned off any of its drugging effects. "That sounds splendid."

Caro just grunted.

Jo fished the key to the spirits cabinet out of her pocket. She'd learned, after dealing with more than one drunken resident over the years, to keep the brandy locked away. Escorted by Freddie, she fetched the decanter and brought it and three glasses over to the table.

"Not too much," Pen said—and then watched Jo fill her glass.

Perhaps it was just as well. The brandy would blunt her emotions and give her a welcome, if false, feeling of contentment.

"Let's start with a toast, shall we?" Jo said. "To the Home."

"To getting Widow's Brew in every London tavern." Caro looked at Pen and pulled a face. "Or in *some* London taverns."

Pen smiled back at her. Caro could be overly ambitious and extremely annoying, but no one worked harder than she did. Her doggedness and enterprising spirit were responsible for much, if not all, of their financial success. Pen just wished Caro would be less busy about Pen's personal business.

Pen lifted her glass. "To a good harvest."

They clinked glasses and drank. The brandy's warmth loosened the knot in Pen's stomach a little. She took another sip and felt the tension in her neck ease, too. She settled back in her chair and looked at the other women.

As much as Caro might annoy her, Pen knew she—and Jo—cared about her. They were her friends, deeply committed, each in her own way, to a common goal: seeing the Home succeed. She'd never felt this sort of shared purpose before.

If I go with Harry, I'll have to leave all this behind.

Worse, if she went with Harry, she'd be neither fish nor fowl. His noble friends would look down their long noses at her, both for being Harry's mistress and for her common roots. As a farmer's daughter, she was as common a commoner as they came. Yet the common people among whom she'd live would give her the side-eye as well. They'd see her as a fallen woman, but too close to the master to treat with all the scorn and disparagement they felt.

As to how they'd treat Harriet, the master's bastard . . .

No. Free from Harry's seductive presence, she could see that agreeing to go off with him was a very bad idea.

But what about love? Must I give up all hope of love?

She could not imagine ever loving anyone the way she loved Harry.

"So," Jo said, "what were you two, er, discussing so intensely—and *loudly*—in the entry just now?"

Good God! "Did you hear it all, then?" Pen asked, appalled at the thought she'd so lost awareness of her surroundings that she might have aired her dirty laundry for the entire Home to inspect. She didn't feel a bond of friendship with any of the other residents—especially not with Rosamund.

"No," Jo said calmly. "If I had, I wouldn't need to ask." She smiled. "And don't worry. There was no one else within earshot, but as your volume was rising, you did risk attracting an audience."

Well, thank God for that, at least.

"Pen was down at the cottage with the earl, Jo"—Caro sent Pen a dark look—"for almost two hours."

Lud, had it really been that long?

"Oh." Jo frowned slightly, the way she always did when she was concerned, and stroked Freddie's ears. "I knew you'd gone out, but I'd assumed I'd just missed your return. And I didn't know you'd gone to the cottage." Her frown deepened. "Was that wise, Pen?"

"It would be if she'd spent her time persuading the earl to open his wallet for us," Caro said sharply, "but if she got any money from him at all, it wasn't for the Home."

"Caro!" Pen and Jo said in unison.

Caro had the grace to blush. "I'm sorry. I know you didn't get paid for what you did, Pen."

Pen opened her mouth to deny Caro's insinuation—

No. It's safer not to pursue the matter.

"Pen." Jo put her hand gently on Pen's knee. "You're a grown woman and a mother, responsible and sensible. I'm not about to tell you what you should or shouldn't do, but do be careful. The earl may not have your best interests at heart."

Caro snorted rather elegantly.

"No, he . . ." They didn't know Harry. "You misunderstand."

Jo's brows shot up at that, and Caro snorted again, less elegantly.

Well, yes. Pen would admit she'd sounded defensive.

"Har—that is, the Earl of Darrow, ah—" She couldn't discuss what she felt about Harry, at least with Caro there. What could she . . .

They *had* discussed business. That's what she needed to concentrate on, not all the other. "He invited me to look over the letter he'd written to the duke in support of the Home, in case I had anything to add."

Caro sat up straighter. "Really? What did he say? Was it a strong letter?"

Clearly, she should have taken this approach the moment she'd encountered Caro in the entry.

"Yes, it was." Pen grinned. "Though I did tell him you'd like to see him dwell even more than he did on the brew-house operations."

"Of course." Caro's brows knitted. "I'd like to have a look at it myself to be certain he got things right. We don't want the duke cutting off our funds if an extra sentence or two—another detail—could have persuaded him."

"I don't think you have to worry, Caro." Pen looked at Jo, too. "Har—Lord Darrow seems certain the duke will continue his support."

"But if that's the case, why didn't he send his donation this year?" Jo asked. "That's what I don't understand."

"Apparently, the duke truly didn't know what it was he was supporting. He thought perhaps there was a bastard involved." She flushed. "The previous duke's bastard, that is."

"I see." Jo chewed on her bottom lip as she considered that. "The earl did tell me that the relevant entry in the duke's books was labeled quite mysteriously as *JSW*. My initials, I presume."

Caro grunted suspiciously. "I, for one, won't breathe easier until the funds show up," she said. "But I suppose there's nothing to be done right now." She finished her brandy and stood. "I'm off. I've got a few accounts I need to update before I go to bed." She gave Pen a speaking look. "I had meant to get to them earlier."

I didn't ask you to spy on me.

Pen managed to swallow those words and just give Caro a tight smile.

"Sleep well, Caro." Jo picked up the decanter as Caro headed for the door. "Let me pour you a little more, Pen."

"No, thank you." She'd finished what was in her glass and was now feeling a pleasant sense of detachment. She saw her opportunity to escape and was going to take it. "I'm tired. I believe I'll go up now, too."

Jo caught her hand. "Stay a little longer. We still have things to discuss."

"We do?" Pen's heart sank as she looked longingly at Caro's departing back.

The door opened—and closed, leaving her alone with Jo.

"Yes." Jo lifted the decanter again. "Are you certain I can't give you some more?"

"Er . . ." If she drank enough, she'd become so bosky, Jo wouldn't be able to get anything out of her. "Oh, very well."

Jo concentrated on pouring as she said, "I congratulate you on distracting Caro. Very wise to bring up the earl's letter. That—as I'm sure you were hoping—took all of her attention." She glanced at Pen. "It did not, however, take all of mine."

"Oh." Pen shifted in her chair and took an incautious sip. The brandy went up her nose and set her to coughing.

"Careful. Are you all right?"

Pen nodded, trying to think quickly, though she'd already had enough brandy to make that difficult. How much did she want to tell Jo? Not all the details, of course. Those were private. But should she admit she'd been in Harry's bed?

Blast! She felt a hot flush sweep over her face. Hopefully the light was too dim for Jo to notice.

She glanced at Jo.

Jo had noticed. "I don't believe you spent almost two hours going over the earl's letter, Pen."

"N-no. We also talked about Harriet. Har-Lord Darrow *is* her father."

"Oh, just call him Harry. I'm not going to rip up at you for the familiarity." Jo's right eyebrow rose. "You've done far more familiar things with him than referring to him by his Christian name."

"Yes. Well. Er, of course." *I don't have to admit I did anything recently.* "He *is* Harriet's father, so I suppose that goes without saying." And now she was babbling. Babbling was never good. Jo wasn't as direct as Caro, but she was nobody's fool. She'd had years of experience drawing confessions out of people.

But I have no need to confess! I didn't break into the liquor cabinet or do anything else to hurt the Home.

On the heels of that thought came the question: *But what if I decide to leave?*

"He's very interested in Harriet, of course," she said, pushing aside that question for now. "He didn't know about her until he came upon her down by the stream and saw her silver streak. At first he thought, as everyone else did, that she was Walter's. Until he saw me. We were, er, *friendly* right before he left for the war."

Jo just sat there, letting Pen blather on until she ran out of words.

"What's really bothering you, Pen?"

"I—" All at once, the wall of independence and strength she'd built over the years—perhaps starting even when she was a child, growing up with an erratic, drunken father—cracked. "I l-love him, Jo."

And then, to her horror, she started to cry, great gulping wails and noisy, ugly snuffling.

Jo didn't say a word—she just moved to crouch next to Pen's chair. She opened her arms, and Pen threw herself into them, burying her face in Jo's shoulder and clinging to her as if she were the one solid thing in her world.

They stayed that way for several minutes—Jo holding Pen, patting her back, murmuring soothing platitudes, and Pen sobbing—until the storm finally passed. Then Pen gave a great shudder and sat back, fished her handkerchief out of her pocket, and blew her nose with an inelegant honk.

"Better?" Jo asked.

"N-no!" The tears threatened to flow again. She pressed her eyelids tightly together as if that would dam them. "What am I going to *do*?"

The last came out as a wail.

She felt Jo pat her hand.

"I don't know. Why don't we talk about it? They say two heads are better than one, don't they?"

"Y-yes." Perhaps Jo *could* offer some good advice. She'd once loved a man enough to throw her lot in with his, though in her case that had involved marriage.

Freddie, now that the worst of the waterworks had subsided, came over to lean against her leg. She stroked his head and felt a bit calmer.

"Harry offered to set me and Harriet up in a house on one of his estates, Jo. He wants to be closer to Harriet, to be a real father to her." She looked down into Freddie's expressive brown eyes before looking back at Jo. "My father was dreadful, so I never put much stock in the role, but I think— I *know*—Harry will be different. Harriet is already very taken with him."

Jo frowned. "She's not imagining he'll marry you, is she? Because he won't. I hate to be so blunt, but facts are facts. The peerage does not marry down, except in very rare situations."

"I know that." Pen stroked Freddie's ears. "I explained the matter to Harriet, but I'm not entirely certain she believes me. She's young and fanciful and thinks hoping and wishing hard enough will make the impossible happen."

Jo nodded. "If she lived around the nobility, she'd understand, but Little Puddledon is so far removed from the *ton* and Society, she hasn't fully experienced our class distinctions."

"Very true. But here's the thing, Jo. Even before Harry arrived in the village, I'd determined to do something to make Harriet's life more secure. Remember, I told you Verity was bullying her."

Jo sighed. "Yes. And I think I asked you to give it time. It hasn't been that long, but is it any better?"

"Perhaps a little. You know I've moved Harriet into my room. A lot of the problems were happening at night when the girls were unsupervised, so I'm hoping having her sleep with me will address that"—she smiled—"though it does make my room difficult to navigate. And having Harry acknowledge her helped, too, I think, if for no other reason that it seems to have given her a bit of pride and a little swagger."

Jo grunted in a noncommittal way. At any other time, Pen might have taken that as an invitation to argue, but she had other things to worry about now, so she let it pass.

"It's also given her something to focus on, rather than the way the other girls are treating her. So, I don't want to disparage Harry or break that connection."

"Of course not. He seems to be a fine man." Jo smiled. "And I'm enough like Caro to hope that he *does* take an interest in the Home and decide to add his donation to the duke's." She put her hand on Pen's and squeezed it supportively. "But your welfare and Harriet's come first."

Pen knew Jo meant that. Caro—if she were here—might not agree. Nothing seemed to come before her precious Widow's Brew in Caro's mind.

"In any event, I'd decided that I could improve Harriet's situation by marrying. I had thought to see if I could persuade Mr. Wright to offer for me."

"Oh." Jo's face went carefully blank.

Of course Jo must have heard. "Godfrey didn't spread the story, did he?" Though it was just the sort of thing that rodent would do.

"Er, not precisely. Bess told Dorcas who told Avis who told everyone else that Godfrey came into the tavern last night with his face a bloody mess and told everyone a man had assaulted him. When the earl walked in later, Godfrey accused him. Things were about to get ugly, but Lord Darrow explained why he'd hit the vicar. I believe he just said Godfrey had attacked you, but everyone filled in the blanks—and sided with you against Godfrey, of course." Jo smiled tightly. "Godfrey is not well liked, you know."

"I know now." She should have given the whole thing far more thought—and paid far more attention to gossip.

Jo leaned forward to put her hand on Pen's knee. "Are you all right? Godfrey didn't injure you, did he?"

"No, he didn't." Pen appreciated her concern, but so much had happened since that unfortunate experience, she was surprised to realize the memory of it didn't really trouble her.

"But he would have injured me—he would have raped me—if Harry hadn't come along." She shuddered. *That* would have been a nightmare. "Harriet told me Sunday after we left church that Godfrey was horrible. I should have listened to her."

She was glad Harriet had been able to see through Godfrey's pious façade. That was a skill that would serve her well over the years.

"Harry is going to recommend that the duke replace him."

Jo nodded. "I would hope so!"

"So that was why I went down to the cottage—to discuss the new vicar. I was going to ask Harry . . . That is, I wanted to . . ." She addressed Freddie. "I was going to explain—or at least hint—that there were certain attributes the new vicar should have."

"Oh? And what would those be?"

Pen flushed. "That he be unmarried. Not old, but not too young."

Jo's brows shot up and it looked as if she was trying not to laugh. Her voice did waver a little when she asked, "And how did that conversation go?"

"We never got to it, because . . ." No, she wasn't going to tell Jo what they'd done. She didn't need to. Jo must already have surmised what had happened.

"I love Harry, Jo. I think I always will. But he is going to marry soon, likely Lady Susan Palmer." Pen swallowed. "It makes perfect sense."

"Yes." Jo nodded. "It would be a good match."

Pen wanted to throw the rest of her brandy in Jo's face, but she took another sip instead. Jo was only saying what Pen had told herself. It *would* be a good match.

Oh, God, life is so unpleasant sometimes.

And then she spilled the rest of her story.

"Harry wants me to be his mistress, Jo—and, God help me, I really, really want to be. But I'd have to leave Little Puddledon and all we've built together here. I'd be totally dependent on him. And, well, I think sharing him with his wife would kill me." Her voice had got a little shrill.

She took a deep breath and tried to regain some calm. "I swore I would do anything for Harriet, but I don't think I can do this."

"Are you certain your becoming the earl's mistress *would* be best for Harriet, Pen?" Jo asked gently, clearly choosing her words. "Have you thought the matter through? It might be very . . . uncomfortable for her to be the master's bastard. People might not accept her."

"I *know*." People had joked about Walter's whelps, and those children had had at least the veneer of legitimacy.

"And how would you feel when the earl's legitimate children are born? They would be treated much differently than Harriet."

"Not by Harry!" Though could she swear to that? She didn't know the future—nor did Harry. He might say truthfully now that he would always care for Harriet—not just with food and shelter, but with his time and interest—but once he had other children, his priorities might—no, *would*—change.

"Perhaps not, but by everyone else. It's inevitable. The children of his marriage would live in the big house, ride in the earl's carriage, sit in his pew at church services while Harriet . . ." Jo shrugged.

Pen felt anger build in her at each scene Jo called up in her imagination. She'd been upset at how Verity had treated Harriet, but now she was positively livid—at something that hadn't happened.

Clearly, she should reject Harry's offer, and yet . . .

She leaned forward. Jo might have an answer for her. She had experience with love.

"I would hate that, but when I think of telling Harry no, of watching him leave . . ." She pressed her lips together, struggling to maintain her composure. "I feel like my heart will break."

Jo made a warm, commiserating sound. "I'm so sorry."

"You loved your husband, didn't you, Jo? Do you think it's possible to love again?"

Jo sat back as if she hadn't been expecting that question. "I . . ." She took a sip of brandy—a very slow sip. The silence stretched out long enough that Pen gave up hope of an answer. She started to get up—

"I did love Freddie—no, not you, you silly dog," Jo said as Freddie the dog barked and wagged his tail. Jo took Freddie's face in her hands, dodging his wet tongue to kiss the top of his head. "Well, of course I love you, but you're not the Freddie I'm talking about."

Freddie barked and put his head in Jo's lap. She stroked his ears and looked back at Pen.

"I loved Fr—" She caught herself as her dog's tail beat a muffled tattoo against the carpet. "I loved my husband madly when I married him. I was young—only seventeen. The age you were when you conceived Harriet." She smiled briefly. "You know how passionate young girls can be."

"Yes." Though she'd felt just as passionate at the cottage a few hours ago.

"But as the months passed . . ." Jo shook her head. "I'd thought the flowers, the sweet words, the courtesy he'd treated me with during our courtship would continue, but I was wrong. Once I had his ring on my finger, I became just another of his possessions, there for his pleasure whenever the urge took him. I think he cared more for his horse than he did for me."

"Oh." Perhaps Jo had not been the best person to ask. Pen couldn't imagine Harry being that way.

Or maybe you are fooling yourself. Harry's been gone for years. Do you really know what he would or wouldn't do?

"And, of course, I soon discovered the extent of his gambling problem. All—or almost all—men gamble, but Freddie"—she patted her dog again—"Freddie couldn't control himself." She smiled. "Which is how I ended up here."

"Oh. Yes. I'm sorry. I didn't realize." Oh, why had she brought this up at all? "I thought your marriage had been happier."

Jo shrugged. "It wasn't *un*happy, once I adjusted. And I

had to marry sometime. I was a vicar's daughter—it was expected I would wed. My father was the third son of a baronet, and my two older sisters had married vicars, so my snagging a baron was quite the feather in my cap." She looked down at Freddie. "My parents were delighted, my sisters were envious, and I was quite proud of myself."

Jo leaned forward to look Pen directly in the eye. "Here's my advice to you, Pen. Be cautious. Love doesn't fare well in the real—the day-to-day—world. You think you love the earl." She shook her head. "No, that's patronizing, isn't it? I suppose you *do* love him. But can you be certain your love will last, especially given all the challenges you'll face? Or that his will?"

Jo sat back. "Think about it. I don't mean to be discouraging, but do weigh matters. You would be giving up everything you have, everything you've worked so hard for, and for what? To be the earl's toy? His hobby?"

"Harry's not like that." Even Pen heard the uncertainty in her voice.

Jo kindly did not point it out. "Perhaps he's not, but the fact remains that you're sacrificing your life and he's giving up exactly nothing."

She wanted to argue the point, but she couldn't. Jo was right.

"I would wait until after Lord Darrow marries to commit yourself, Pen. Have him come here if he wants to continue the connection while you decide. He can stay at the cottage. Your place here is secure, and I'll help you address the problems with Verity and Rosamund, if they persist."

Pen nodded. This wasn't the advice she'd been hoping for, but it was precisely the advice she needed to hear.

"A rushed decision is never a good decision," Jo said gently.

"Yes. You're right." It didn't feel rushed—it wasn't as if

she'd just met Harry. That was part of the problem. It felt so right—when it didn't feel terribly wrong.

Jo touched her lightly on the arm. "I don't want to see you hurt, Pen, but I also don't want to lose you—I'm not completely unbiased here. The fact is I need you. The Home needs you. Caro can't brew a drop of Widow's Brew without your hops. At least stay through the harvest, no matter what you ultimately decide."

Right. She couldn't leave everyone in the lurch. "I promise to stay at least that long." She let out a dispirited breath. "And I'm not a silly, lovestruck girl, blind to the facts. I doubt I'll be leaving at all."

"I really *am* sorry to be the voice of unpleasant reason." Jo stood and shook out her skirts. "And now Freddie and I should go up to bed. Are you coming?"

"No. I think I'll sit here a little while longer."

"Should I leave the decanter out?"

Pen laughed, though it came out more as a croak. "No. I know drowning my sorrows won't really help."

Jo nodded. Then she bent over and hugged Pen tightly, before locking away the rest of the brandy and leaving, Freddie trotting at her heels.

Pen sat in front of the fire an hour longer, tossing one mental "if only" after another into the flames.

Chapter Thirteen

Tuesday

Harry grinned as he pulled on his shirt. He couldn't remember waking up this happy in a long, long time. The dark, heavy cloud that had hung over him since he'd learned of Walter's death was finally lifting. He had a plan. He'd do his duty and offer for Lady Susan as soon as he left Little Puddledon. No point in putting that off. The sooner they married, the sooner he could get an heir on her, and the sooner they could go their separate ways.

But before he did that, he'd spend today and tomorrow and the next day wooing Pen, persuading her to take his offer and move to Darrow or one of his other estates.

He closed his eyes briefly. Zeus, it was wonderful to have Pen back in his life. Beyond wonderful. Far, far beyond. He'd woken several times during the night, hard and ready to bury himself deep in her sweet body.

He grinned again. Soon he'd able to do that.

Ah! Someone was knocking on the door.

He bounded over and threw it open, his grin widening further when he saw Pen and Harriet.

"We brought you breakfast, Papa," Harriet said, pointing to the big basket Pen was holding.

"Thank you. I'm very hungry." He smiled at her, and then he smiled at Pen as he took the basket from her.

Pen did not smile back.

That wasn't good.

"Have you eaten?" he asked.

"Yes," Pen said.

"Yes, but I can eat more," Harriet said with a little hop skip. "Dorcas packed lots of food." She grinned. "And Avis put in a blanket and told Mama to be sure we went somewhere private so you could—"

"Harriet!" Pen said sharply. "Don't tease the earl with Avis's silly chatter."

He and Harriet both gaped at Pen.

She flushed. "Excuse me. I didn't sleep well."

Right. Now that he looked more closely, he saw the shadows under her eyes—and *in* her eyes.

Hell.

When he'd left her last night, he'd known she'd been leaning toward refusing his offer, but he'd also sensed her wavering. She'd given him that kiss, staid and virginal as it had been, and he'd seen how she'd run from him, not, he was *quite* certain, in fear of what *he* would do, but of what *she* would do if she stayed a moment longer.

He'd have sworn she'd left the door open for seduction. How could she not? She was the lustiest, most deeply passionate woman he'd ever encountered, both here in England and on the Continent. She needed tupping like a plant needed water—and he was willing and eager—very, *very* eager—to tend to her needs.

But this morning, the door was shut tight, if not locked and bolted. What had happened between the time he'd seen her wave good-bye from the safety of the Home's entry and now?

He intended to find out.

"Well, it's a beautiful morning," he said with false heartiness. "Let's have a picnic. Do you have a suitably private place in mind—" He saw Pen open her mouth, but he finished his sentence before she could speak. "—Harriet?"

Pen scowled at him and he smiled blandly back at her while Harriet hop-skipped in front of him.

"Yes! There's a pond with ducks on the other side of the stream," Harriet said.

Harry lifted a brow. "And do we have to swim across the water to get there?"

"No, Papa! There's a bridge."

That was a relief. "And a nice place to spread a blanket?" Harry kept his eyes on Harriet rather than the prickly woman next to her.

She nodded. "Yes. I'll show you." And she was off running.

"Shall we?" He offered Pen his arm, but she ignored it.

"I've been thinking about your proposition, Harry."

He was not ready to discuss the matter. "That sounds a bit dire. Let me break my fast before you serve me any bad news."

She opened her mouth—and then closed it again with a frown. "Very well."

They followed Harriet around past the cottage and up the path to the waterfall, but veered off on a trail he'd not taken before.

"Come on, Papa!" Harriet called from a good thirty yards away.

He smiled down at Pen. "It seems we are not moving quickly enough for our daughter." *Their* daughter. They were permanently, inalterably tied to each other through this person they had made together.

He liked that thought.

Pen smiled back at him and shook her head bemusedly.

"Harriet was so excited this morning, she wanted to come down to the cottage two hours ago."

He chuckled. "Thank you for keeping her from doing that. You would have found me sound asleep." He waggled his brows. "Our activities of last night exhausted me."

Damnation! That had been the wrong thing to say. Pen's brows snapped down. She opened her mouth—

"Come *on,* Papa."

Harriet had come back and grabbed hold of his hand, tugging on him to hurry along—and saving him from what Pen had been about to say.

He knew his reprieve was only temporary.

They crossed over the bridge—he could see and hear the waterfall off to the right—and then the path widened, the trees on either side forming a green tunnel. Soon they came out on a field which sloped down to a pond.

Harriet dragged him closer to the water. "See, Papa? Ducks!"

"I see."

Several of the ducks chose that moment to plunge their heads into the water, forming a line of feathered bottoms and making Harriet giggle.

"It looks as if they are having their breakfasts," Harry said. "I'm hungry for mine. Let's go find out what's in this basket."

"There's plum cake!" Harriet skipped up the slope next to him. "Dorcas makes the best plum cake."

"Does she? That's excellent news as I'm quite partial to plum cake."

Harriet grinned up at him. "So am I!"

He stopped when he judged they were well out of reach of wandering ducks—and the unsavory deposits they left behind—and put the basket down.

"Will this do?" he asked Pen. She'd stayed at the mouth of the path while he and Harriet inspected the ducks.

"Yes." She managed a smile, an exceedingly fleeting one that didn't reach her eyes.

This just got worse and worse.

They spread out the blanket and sat down, Harriet so close to Harry she was almost in his lap, and Pen as far from him as she could be and still be on the blanket. The contrast between this picnic and the one at the apple orchard could not have been greater.

What happened after she left me last night?

He was determined to find out.

"Give Papa some plum cake, Mama!"

"And you some, too?" Pen smiled warmly at Harriet as she handed Harry some cake, but when she glanced at him, all the warmth vanished, leaving her eyes bleak.

"Yes!"

She gave Harriet her cake and then looked down, sorting through the basket far more intently than necessary. "We have bread and butter and jam as well, my lord. And it looks as if Dorcas has put in a bit of cold beef for you, if you should like it."

He was back to "my lord."

"No, thank you." He suddenly wasn't hungry any longer.

At least Harriet seemed unaffected. She chatted away happily as she ate her plum cake.

"Isn't the cake good, Papa?"

"Yes. Very good," he lied. The plum cake could be the best ever baked this side of heaven, but it would still taste like sawdust to him at the moment. He *had* to get Pen alone and find out what was amiss.

"May I have some more, Mama?"

"You can have the rest of mine."

Ah. So, his wasn't the only appetite affected.

Harriet was too happy at her good fortune to ask questions—or perhaps it was just that she was nine years old and happy to be with her father and mother.

He frowned. How could Pen not see that? Harriet *needed* him in her life. And if Pen's reaction to him last night was any indication, Pen needed him, too.

And he needed them, blast it.

He put down his cake. He couldn't choke down another bite.

Pen sighed. "Harriet, why don't you go look at the ducks? I have something I need to say to your papa."

Harriet grinned. "Like Avis meant?"

Pen shook her head. "Not quite."

"Oh." Harriet gave him a worried look. "You aren't going to leave now, are you, Papa? You won't go without saying good-bye?"

"I'm not leaving, Harriet." He tried to smile reassuringly. "Don't worry."

Harriet clearly *was* worried. She looked back at Pen, and then got up slowly and walked down to the pond, not one hop or skip in her step.

Zeus! He glared at Pen. He wanted to lash out. Why was she being so difficult and upsetting their daughter? But he managed to keep a rein on his temper. He knew from long experience that words needed to be used carefully.

"My lord—"

"Pen!"

He saw, out of the corner of his eye, Harriet stop and look back, so he lowered his voice, struggling to modulate its tone. "I understand that you are upset with me—though I don't know why—but don't diminish what's between us by 'my lording' me."

He saw her flinch and was sorry for it, but if she was going to drive a knife into his heart, she was going to have to do it honestly, with her eyes open.

She nodded. "You're right, Harry. I suppose I was trying to make this easier for myself, but that's not fair." She took a breath and then another. She looked away. "I—"

She stopped again, and his heart spasmed. He hated to see her so clearly struggling to—

To what? Remember that knife.

Right. He waited in silence.

She tried again. "I talked to Jo last night. She's a widow. I thought she might help me think some things through."

Lord, this sounded bad—and confusing. "Pen, I'm not dead."

"And I'm not your wife, nor will I be."

She said it matter-of-factly, but . . . Did she think he should offer for her?

No. She couldn't think that.

Do you *think you should offer for her?*

He froze, taken aback by the notion.

Zeus! If he wasn't the Earl of Darrow, he *might* ask her to marry him. But he *was* the earl. Earls did not marry farmers' daughters, at least not in England.

"I kept going over things in my mind all night, Harry, and I just can't agree to come with you. Not now and maybe not ever."

No. That couldn't be her decision. "Pen—"

She held up her hand. "Don't. I know—well, I'm afraid—you could persuade me to change my mind, but I think that would be a mistake." She looked down at the blanket and took a deep breath. When she looked back up, her expression was set. Determined. "Let me tell you why."

"Very well. I'll listen, but I won't promise to agree with you." Did she not understand? "It's not just your life at issue here, Pen. It's Harriet's and mine."

He looked over at his—*their*—daughter. She was tossing something—crab apples?—into the water. The ducks had paddled off to one side and were watching—and quacking. He looked back at Pen.

She was looking at Harriet, too. "Yes, I know." Then she focused on him.

"I love you, Harry. I think I always have and I always will." She said it slowly, sadly. Despairingly.

Anger, sparked by a touch of panic, flickered in his gut, making his tone sharp. "And I love you, Pen."

She flinched.

Blast. That hadn't helped matters. He thought very briefly of making a salacious comment, but stopped himself. This was not the time for that sort of talk.

He tried to gentle his voice. "So, what is the problem?"

She met his gaze directly and said calmly but no less emphatically, "Love isn't enough." She frowned. "Don't you see that?"

"No, I don't." Love *was* enough. It was everything. How could *she* not see that?

Desperation begat anger. He'd—

Keep hold of your temper. Nothing will be helped by brangling.

Pen's frown deepened, a thread of annoyance in her tone now. "That's because you aren't opening your eyes and looking. We wouldn't be living in some fairyland, Harry. We'd be here in England, at Darrow or one of your other estates."

"So?" Where was she going with this?

"So, think how people will treat me and Harriet and any other children we might have."

Anger flickered again. "They will treat you properly or answer to me."

"No, they won't. They'll whisper and point and avoid us—and that's if we are fortunate." She glanced at Harriet again. "I don't mind it for myself—"

She stopped and sighed. "No, that's not true. I *would* mind it, but what would *kill* me is seeing people treat our children cruelly. I know how I've reacted to Verity torturing

Harriet for just a little while. It would be much, much worse if I had to live in a village of Verities."

"No. You're wrong." Of course, she was wrong. She knew nothing about the *ton*. He would explain matters and then she would see. "Many members of the nobility have children born on the wrong side of the blanket. They—"

Pen cut him off. "Did you listen to yourself, Harry? Did you hear the words you used? Would *you* wish to be born on the 'wrong' side of something?"

He frowned, opened his mouth—and then closed it. He could not truthfully say yes.

"Poor Harriet is already illegitimate," Pen said. "There's nothing I can do about that. I tried. I made up a husband who died in the war—and then that lie blew up in my face. I can't honorably put other children in that position."

Aha! That was the crucial point. "But this is different. This time I'll be there to support you. You won't be alone."

He leaned forward, as if he could magically pull her agreement from her by force of will. "I'm a powerful man, Pen. I made my fortune on the Continent, and now I've also got the wealth and influence of the title. I can and I will protect you. And support you. You and our children will want for nothing. And when it comes time for Harriet—and any other daughters we might have—to marry, I'll provide dowries for them."

Pen did not look persuaded. "And if we have sons?"

He blinked. He hadn't thought of sons. "Then I'll find them trades."

"What if our first son is born before you have a son with Lady Susan, or whomever you marry? Will our son care that his younger half brother gets what would have been his, if only he hadn't had the misfortune of being my son, too?"

"Of course n—" He stopped. Perhaps that *would* be a

bitter pill to swallow. He'd never envied Walter the earldom, but then he'd never had any sort of claim to it.

Just as his illegitimate son would have no claim to the title in law, but setting younger brother above older brother . . .

"Precisely." Pen shook her head. "I truly don't know the answer to that question. Will your legitimate and illegitimate children grow up together? Will they be friends? Or will my children feel—or be made to feel—inferior?"

He sat back. "I said I was powerful, Pen. I am. I won't let our children be made to feel inferior to anyone."

Pen's right brow winged up. "Even the Prince Regent can't command people's emotions. You may be able to force people to *pretend* to accept them, but that is not the same thing."

He wanted to argue the point, but he couldn't.

"And what of your wife? Are you going to force *her* to accept Harriet and her siblings?"

He frowned. "I don't know. I mean, I won't try to compel Lady Susan to be kind to them, but I *can*—and will—compel her not to be cruel."

"My, that sounds like a harmonious union."

"Sarcasm does not become you." He shifted on the blanket. "You may have a point, but I suspect in Lady Susan's case, she couldn't be bothered to notice her own children, let alone yours."

Pen didn't reply to that. She just gave him a look that he was afraid was a mixture of horror and pity.

He shifted position again. *It doesn't matter. I only need Lady Susan to get an heir. That's all.*

"The advice Jo gave me last night," Pen finally said, "was to not act in haste but to wait until after you wed. Then, I could base my decision on observable facts, not mere wishes and dreams."

She paused, pressed her lips together—and then shook her head as if dismissing some thought or, worse, some dream.

"And waiting to decide would be good for the Home, too. It's almost harvesttime, Harry. If I leave now, before the hops are safely picked and drying in the oast house, we might lose the crop. I'm the only one who knows precisely what to look for to keep the plants healthy."

She leaned toward him, frowning. "And if we lose this harvest, we'll have to cut—perhaps drastically—our Widow's Brew production. That will put us back on shaky financial ground, even with the duke's support."

He didn't like what she was saying, but he did have to admit it made some sense. .

"Very well. I can wait until—what?—September or October to have you with me. In the meantime, I'll offer for and marry Lady Susan." *And hopefully get her with child— with my heir.*

Pen went on as if she hadn't heard him. "It was good advice, but . . ."

His stomach knotted. "But you aren't going to take it?"

He didn't need to ask. Her tone made her position clear— and he could tell it wasn't a position he was going to like.

"I thought I would at first, but the more I considered it, the more I realized I didn't need to wait. I've already decided. I can't go off with you, Harry. I'd be giving up too much. I've made a place for myself here. I'm needed and I'm respected."

Panic was making him short-tempered. "*I* need you."

"Do you?" Pen sighed. "Maybe you do, and if so, I'm sorry for it. But as I tossed and turned last night, trying to imagine all the arguments, I realized there were more important reasons I have to say no." She looked at him. "I don't want to share you, Harry. And it's not fair or honorable of me to ask your wife to do so."

"I assure you, Lady Susan won't care." He forced his lips into a grin. "Once she's given me my heir and spare, she'll happily hand me over to you to have all to yourself."

Pen shrugged. She didn't look at all persuaded.

"It's true."

"Oh, I believe you." She looked away, down at the pond.

He followed her gaze. Harriet had taken off her bonnet and was using it as a basket to carry a growing collection of crab apples.

Harriet waved.

Pen waved back. "When I first heard the rumor that Harriet was Walter's, I felt physically sick."

He'd felt sick, too. He felt sick now.

"But it wasn't just the notion of Walter touching me that made me ill, it was the thought that people believed I had lain with a married man. That made me feel like a whore."

"What?!"

"Shh!" She looked down at Harriet again—as did he. Fortunately, Harriet hadn't heard them—or was very good at pretending she hadn't.

He lowered his voice. "You aren't a whore."

"Why? Because I don't charge for my services?"

"That's not it, and you know it."

She nodded. "Yes, I do know it. And I actually don't fault women who must earn their keep on their backs. I was close to doing that myself after Aunt Margaret died. I likely would have, if I hadn't found the Home. There aren't many jobs open to women, Harry. And Harriet and I had to eat."

Pen said this all so matter-of-factly, he was simultaneously appalled and impressed.

And angry. He should have been there to help her. He should have considered something—some*one*—could have come from all the swiving he and Pen had done that summer. It would have been astounding if Pen hadn't conceived.

"By the time the sun rose, I'd concluded that, for me,

marriage changes things. When you marry, you take a vow before God, don't you, to 'forsake all others'?"

He shifted on the blanket again. "Er, yes. I suppose so. But no one actually keeps those vows, Pen, at least not among the *ton*."

He should have expected Pen to think this way. She was, well, from the lower orders, who were more pious than their noble brethren. Zeus, he could just imagine the reaction he'd get if he said such a thing in White's or any of the other gentlemen's clubs. There would be shocked silence, followed by uproarious laughter—and perhaps an escorted journey to Bedlam.

Pen scowled. "Well, perhaps they should. Or at least they should try. Promising something you have no intention of doing is lying."

"Technically, yes." He thought about trying to explain what everyone in the *ton* knew the vow *really* meant: a man would be discreet in his extramarital adventures, and a woman would wait until she'd produced an heir and spare before embarking on her own assignations.

"*Literally* yes." Pen held his gaze. "Harry, if you can't imagine loving Lady Susan, don't marry her. You deserve—and the children you have with your wife deserve—that your union start off in love." She looked down for a moment. "During the night, I—I tried to put myself in Lady Susan's place. I felt pity for her, Harry."

"Misplaced, Pen. Trust me on that. Lady Susan Palmer is more likely to be annoyed if not appalled should I profess undying love. She wants a marriage of convenience as much as I do."

Pen stared at him and then frowned. "I suppose I must believe you, if you say it is so. But if I agreed to be your mistress, I would feel I was in the wrong. I would be contributing to the failure of your marriage and betraying a fellow female."

He was equal parts impressed with and frustrated by her position. "Pen, my marriage will only fail if I don't get an heir. Everything else is unimportant."

Pen scowled at him. "No. Love is important. You must know that, if you truly love me." She shook her head. "Why can't you hope for an heir *and* love, Harry? Lady Susan is not the only well-bred female in England. Look some more. There must be someone who has the proper pedigree *and* whom you could come to care for."

Good God! "I already told you. I looked all Season and didn't find such a paragon." Did he sound a bit tetchy? He knew Pen meant well, but she just didn't understand.

"So then look longer." She sat back. "All I know is that I will not be the person who comes between you and your wife."

His hands balled into fists. God give him patience. He wanted to shake some sense into her. Or, better, kiss her until she agreed to be his mistress.

Well, he could wait a little longer. He'd come back to Little Puddledon from time to time to visit Harriet. After a month or two or three of celibacy, Pen's tune would change. Such a passionate woman must require regular, vigorous tupping to keep her humors in balance. He could—

No, he could not. Pen had gone years without a man. She was not going to be seduced into changing her mind. And it would be wrong of him to try.

She'd always had her own strict code of honor. It had been one of the things—besides her face, her figure, and her lusty sexual appetite—that had drawn him to her.

"Very well." His mouth tasted like ashes and he felt as if he'd lost that brawl with the vicar. "But I will still wish to see Harriet, you know. I plan to visit Little Puddledon regularly."

Pen nodded. "But not *too* regularly. I don't want Harriet expecting something you can't sustain once you have a family."

Was she *trying* to infuriate him? If so, she was succeeding brilliantly. "Harriet *is* part of my family."

"I know. It's just once you marry—"

"For the love of God, Pen, will you stop? Give me some credit, if you please. I am not going to crush my daughter's feelings."

Pen's mouth hung open a moment, and then she flushed. "Yes. Of course. I'm sorry."

"As well you should be." He struggled to control his temper. Nothing would be served by ripping up at Pen. And his ire couldn't be laid at her door completely—he was quite aware that sexual frustration played a role, too. "I would hope you know me better than that."

"I do." Pen's posture stiffened, as if she suddenly had a rod up her back. "But I'm Harriet's mother, Harry. My first duty is to protect her."

"From her father?! What sort of a monster do you take me for?"

Pen's eyes widened, but then she stiffened another inch. "I know you'd never intentionally hurt Harriet, but I also know you can't really say what your marriage will be like until you're in the midst of it."

That was true, but it was also immaterial.

"Pen, it doesn't matter." Perhaps she could be forgiven for her doubts. He'd not been here for Harriet's first nine years. She might well have persuaded herself he didn't care. "I'll agree that I can't know how marriage will change my life, but I give you my word that I will never abandon Harriet." He held Pen's gaze. "No matter what happens between us, no matter whom I marry or how many other children I have, Harriet will always be my daughter, my firstborn, and I will always be her father."

Pen studied his expression, and then she nodded.

"Mama. Papa," Harriet called from the pond. She'd found a log to sit on. "Are you finished talking yet?"

"Almost," Pen called back. "Just a little longer." She turned back to him. "I had one other matter I wished to raise with you."

"All right. What is it?" Any topic must be better than the one they'd just got through.

Or maybe not. Pen was taking an infernally long time to say anything.

"Pen, Harriet won't wait forever. What did you wish to discuss?"

She sighed. "You won't like it."

His stomach tightened. "Well, then, tell me it straightaway before the anticipation does me in."

She took a deep breath. "I never told you why I came down to the cottage last night."

He forced a grin in the hopes of lightening the atmosphere. "What? It wasn't to seduce me?"

She frowned at him, but she laughed, too. "This time I didn't seduce you. You seduced me."

He dropped his voice. "We seduced each other. And it was good, wasn't it, Pen?"

"Yes, it was good. It was always good with you, Harry."

Then why won't you be my mistress?

He had heard all her arguments, but none of them cured the need throbbing in his cock.

And in his heart.

If only it were Pen, rather than Lady Susan, who was an earl's daughter.

"I wanted to talk to you about the new vicar," Pen said.

"What?" How had they got to the new vicar?

Her brows furrowed. "The duke *will* replace Godfrey, won't he? It could be very uncomfortable if he doesn't."

For a brief moment, Harry wondered if Godfrey staying on would be the push he needed to get Pen to come live at Darrow, but he rejected the thought almost as soon as it formed. It was beneath him. And even if Pen wasn't so directly involved, he couldn't in good conscience turn a blind eye to the scoundrel's behavior. It was not a stretch to say the vicar was a rapist.

"I should think so. I will definitely recommend it."

Pen nodded. Her tongue slipped out to moisten her lips. She suddenly seemed nervous. "Then, do you suppose . . . would it be possible . . . could you suggest . . ."

"Just spit it out, will you?"

That annoyed her—and got her to say her piece.

Unfortunately.

"Could you ask the duke to consider replacing Godfrey with a respectable, unmarried man? One that's not too young, but not too old, either."

"Why would you care about the vicar's age or marital state?" He was afraid he knew the answer.

"I'm, er,"—she looked away—"hoping to marry him."

The words lodged like an arrow in his heart. He grunted—it was all he could manage when he was howling in pain inside.

"I know you say you'll be part of Harriet's life, Harry—"

That freed his tongue. "I don't just say it. I swear it."

Pen nodded, but didn't meet his eyes. "Yes. I know. I believe you, truly I do, but I still think Harriet would benefit from having a father."

"*I'm* her father."

"I know. I know. I meant a man who could *act* as her father. Who would be my, er, husband and so give us a real home." Her cheeks were flushed. "That's why I approached Godfrey—I wanted a home for Harriet."

She met his gaze. "Harriet saw through him at once, you know. She has your shrewd ability to size up people." She shook her head. "I should have listened to her."

She shook her head again, a bit harder, as if to dispel the thought. "I'll do better next time. Next time you can be sure I *will* listen to Harriet." And then she smiled. "So, do you think you can persuade the duke to send us a nice, marriageable man?"

He was not going to act as Pen's matchmaker—the notion was revolting.

"Grainger would laugh at me—or suggest I look for a comfortable bed in Bedlam—if I did anything so peculiar. He has no reason to listen to my advice with regard to vicars. I know next to nothing about procuring one."

Pen's shoulders slumped. "But you can mention my situation, can't you? It can't hurt."

It hurt far too much. "What about love, Pen? Didn't you just tell me I shouldn't marry Lady Susan if I don't love her?"

"Yes, but that's different."

"How?"

She looked at him as if he were a complete noddy. "You're a man. An earl! You just said yourself you are wealthy and powerful. You have far more control over your destiny than I do over mine."

She bit her lip, clearly frustrated. "If it weren't for Harriet, I wouldn't be husband hunting, Harry. But I've concluded if I marry now, by the time Harriet is of age to wed, people will have forgotten that she's your bastard."

Rage and pain roared through him at her words.

He was quite proud of himself. He didn't shout or curse. He just stood.

"I think it's time we left."

Chapter Fourteen

Pen walked along the path by the stream, Harriet's hand in hers.

Harriet's other hand was in Harry's, and she was chatting away at him, hopping and skipping and telling him everything the ducks had done while he and Pen had been talking. And he was telling her about the ducks—and other animals—he'd seen in Lisbon and Paris and Vienna.

He was charming and funny and Harriet was enchanted.

Pen was, too.

She'd wanted to plead work and flee back to the hopyard after their disastrous conversation. Harry would have welcomed her departure. Talk about looking daggers at someone! By rights she should be stretched out on the ground, pierced in so many places she looked like a pincushion.

But she couldn't do that to Harriet. Yes, it was getting very near the harvest. Yes, she had to keep a close eye out for bugs and blight. But she'd checked the plants before she'd gone down to the cottage this morning, and she would check them again when she and Harriet got back to the Home.

Harriet needed tending, too. She'd waited so patiently by the pond while Pen and Harry talked. And she was so obviously delighted to have both her parents together. Pen could afford these few hours to make her happy.

And, to be brutally honest, make herself happy. *She* wanted to be with Harry. She wanted to gather memories— the warmth in his eyes when he looked at Harriet, his smile, the sound of his voice—to store away for the long winter when he was gone, married to Lady Susan and doting on his heir. He'd only be here another day or two, after all.

And then perhaps fate would smile on her and the duke would send the village a vicar that was willing to take on a nine-year-old girl, a man who wasn't looking for a grand passion but just a comfortable, accommodating female to marry.

She looked at Harry and her heart cramped. He was smiling at Harriet as he listened intently to her convoluted story about Farmer Smith's piglets and Bessie the cow. The sad truth—the thing Pen hadn't admitted to him by the pond—was that she was very much afraid she'd never love another man, at least not the way she'd loved Harry—*still* loved him. She might respect someone else, value him, grow fond of him, perhaps even enjoy her marital duties. But feel the deep, consuming love she felt for Harry?

No.

Perhaps it was just as well. Maybe such a fierce emotion was destined to burn itself out. If she could have Harry forever, she might grow to hate him as passionately as she loved him now.

It was better to choose a diet of ale and mutton than to try to live on champagne and comfits.

"Why, if it isn't Lord Darrow. Look, Letitia. We've finally run him to ground."

Pen happened to be looking at Harry when he heard those words, so she saw him stiffen, shock freezing his features. But then, in a blink, he was relaxed and smiling, though this smile was formal and cold—very different from the one he'd just been sharing with Harriet.

"Lady Susan. Letitia. How"—he paused significantly—"*odd* to see you here."

And then Pen looked at the women—two exquisitely gowned females who were as out of place on this country path as Harry's Ajax was in the stall next to Bumblebee.

"Who are they, Papa?" Harriet's young voice was clear as a bell.

Surprise and, at least in Lady Susan's case, distaste twisted the women's expressions when they heard "Papa," though they must have discerned the situation the moment they'd seen Harry holding Harriet's hand—or, more to the point, when they'd seen Harriet's hair. After carrying crab apples, her bonnet had been relegated to the picnic basket.

Pen's hackles rose. If either woman said even one unkind word to Harriet, she would regret it—*deeply* regret it.

Is Harry going to claim Harriet? If he doesn't—

That would be a good thing. If Harry disavowed their daughter, Pen would be completely cured of her feelings for him.

But Harriet would be crushed. She couldn't let that happen.

She forced a smile and leaped into the conversational breach.

"Welcome to Little Puddledon." She let go of Harriet's hand and stepped forward to shield her from the women. "I'm Penelope Barnes, and this is my daughter, Harriet."

Letitia's face had gone carefully blank. Ah. Right. Her husband's proclivity for extramarital affairs must have caused her to be surprised by silver-blazed bastards all too often.

Lady Susan's face, on the other hand, was *not* blank. Her nose wrinkled in distaste. From her expression, one would think the woman had encountered a talking dunghill.

"And my daughter, too," Harry said from over Pen's shoulder, amusement in his voice.

Make that a talking dung *mountain*.

"Pen, as I'm sure you've guessed, this is my sister-in-law, Lady Darrow." Harry gestured to the shorter, plumper woman on the right. "I don't know if you ever encountered her when you lived on the estate."

She would kill with kindness. "I don't believe so, but I do remember when you married the previous earl, Lady Darrow. Everyone celebrated for days."

To her shock, Letitia looked at her and smiled—and Pen noticed the sadness in her eyes.

Oh. How could she have forgotten that Walter died just a little over a year ago? Letitia must have only recently put off mourning.

Perhaps they were not so unalike. They'd both lost the men in their lives suddenly, though of course Letitia's loss was far greater. And although Letitia wouldn't ever have to rely on her wits to survive the way Pen had—Harry would see that his sister-in-law and nieces were well taken care of—she must feel uncertain about her place in the world now. She was the Countess of Darrow, the mistress of a large estate, but the moment Harry married there'd be a new countess. Letitia would have to leave the homes she'd managed for years and make a life somewhere else.

Worse, her daughters would have to leave the only homes they'd ever known.

Letitia might be of the nobility, but she was also a mother. Like Pen.

"I'm very sorry for your loss," Pen said sincerely.

Letitia's eyes brightened. "Thank you."

"Lady Darrow!" Lady Susan said in shocked tones. "I can't believe you are talking to That Person."

"And this," Harry said, an edge to his voice, "is Lady Susan Palmer."

The witch—that is, the *woman* Harry was going to marry.
Remember—kill with kindness. "It's a pleasure to meet
you, Lady Susan." A barefaced, but polite, lie.

Lady Susan never even looked Pen's way. Instead, she
scowled at Harry and said, "I cannot believe you just introduced me to your wh—"

"Heavens, look at the time!" Pen said loudly. Thank God
she'd anticipated something like this might happen.

She kept talking, her words coming so fast no one, especially the deplorable Lady Susan, could get a word in edge-
wise. "I'm so sorry, ladies, Lord Darrow, but I'm afraid I
must get back to work. Here, give me the basket, my lord.
Come along, Harriet. Pardon us."

While she spoke, she grabbed the picnic basket from
Harry, took Harriet's hand, and stepped around the two
women.

Fortunately, Harriet didn't dig in her heels and argue.

Unfortunately, Harriet's compliance was probably because she sensed Lady Susan was about to insult them
further. Harriet *was* a good judge of character, after all.

Pen walked briskly—as quickly as she could and not be
running—down the path, her goal to get Harriet out of earshot
as fast as possible. Harriet had to trot to keep up.

"Is that the lady Papa is going to marry?" Harriet asked
in a small voice once Pen finally slowed down.

"Yes." How could Harry bear to spend one minute with
that shrew, let alone a lifetime?

"I don't like her."

Pen snorted. "I don't like her either."

"Why does Papa want to marry her?"

"She's very pretty."

"So are you!"

Pen smiled. "I think you may be slightly prejudiced,
Harriet. But Lady Susan is also an earl's daughter. She'll
know how to manage his household. It makes perfect sense."

Harriet scowled. "I don't think so. She's mean. She was going to call you a"—Harriet's voice faltered—"a wh-whore, wasn't she, Mama?"

"Yes." She'd heard that word more in the last few days than she had in her entire life.

"And she looked at me like I was a . . . a *slug*, ugly and slimy and d-dirty. Like I didn't belong here. Like I didn't belong anywhere."

Anger so intense it took Pen's breath away surged through her. How *dare* that woman make Harriet feel the smallest moment of discomfort! She wanted to go back, grab Lady Susan by the throat, and squeeze until the she-devil's face turned blue.

Instead she dropped the basket and pulled her daughter into her arms.

Harriet gasped and sniffed, fighting off tears. "Everyone will look at me that way, won't they, Mama? Because I'm a b-bastard."

"No. Not here in Little Puddledon." *Elsewhere, though . . .*

She wouldn't worry about that now. Harriet wasn't going anywhere. *They* weren't going anywhere.

"You are none of those things, Harriet. Of course you aren't."

"But people will say it. People will *think* it."

Yes, they might. Some probably will . . . Definitely will.

Despair threatened to swamp her. Hopelessness—

No. I can't give in to that. I can't give up. I have Harriet to take care of.

When she'd created her fictional husband years ago, it had been to protect Harriet, but the story had also protected her. As the years had gone by, she'd been lulled into a false sense of respectability. She'd come to care what people thought of her.

But I'm not *respectable. I can never be. I gave that up forever when I loved Harry.*

So what? Was she—and Harriet—supposed to crawl into a hole somewhere so respectable people needn't encounter them?

Being with Harry again had reminded her that once upon a time for a short while she'd been fearless. It was time to be fearless again—

But I'm a mother. I have to protect Harriet.

She looked down at the top of her daughter's head and her heart swelled. Perhaps teaching Harriet to be strong and fearless and independent was better than protecting her. If Harriet learned those skills, she could protect herself.

Pen held her daughter away from her and looked into her eyes. "Harriet, Lady Susan can call us whatever she wants. We don't have to care what she—what *anyone*—thinks of us."

Harriet did not look convinced.

"To some people—well, most people—I am not a proper person. When I chose to love your father without the Church's blessing, I broke one of society's biggest rules. I knew it and I knew what the consequences were, but I did it anyway. I loved your father that much."

Harriet frowned. "But Papa did it, too, and no one calls him a whore."

That made Pen laugh. "True. But the rules are different for men, especially noblemen."

"That's not fair!"

Good. Some of Harriet's spirit was coming back. Pen smiled. Nothing could keep her daughter down.

"Many things in life aren't fair, Harriet." Though in this situation, the inequality was grounded in some hard truth. If a woman's misbehavior resulted in a child, she was the one literally left holding the baby—Harriet, in Pen's case.

But if I hadn't misbehaved with Harry . . .

"I told you before that I'm sorry you weren't born in a

marriage, but I am *not* sorry at all that you *were* born. If I hadn't broken the rules with your papa, I wouldn't have you."

She hugged Harriet so tightly then, Harriet might have trouble breathing—but Harriet hugged her back just as tightly.

Lord, if I hadn't had Harriet, what would have become of me?

Likely I'd be some farmer's wife, living a boring, dependent, loveless existence.

Ugh.

"You know what, Harriet? I'd do it all over again. Every minute of it." It was true. She'd not trade her life here, with all its . . . complications and challenges for anything. "So if the Lady Susans of the world want to judge me for loving your father or you for being your father's daughter, they are free to do so. We will thumb our noses at them." And she suited her actions to her words.

Harriet giggled, and they started walking again, but in companionable silence this time. They were almost at the Home before Harriet spoke once more.

"You and Papa didn't seem very happy this morning. I thought when you got back so late last night, it would be like our picnic at the orchard, but it wasn't."

Lud! She'd thought she'd come in quietly enough that she hadn't wakened Harriet. "No, it wasn't."

"Did he ask you to be his mistress?"

"Yes."

"And you told him no, didn't you?"

Harriet sounded more disappointed than angry.

"Yes. I'm sorry. I know you wanted to live close to him. And having a house to ourselves would be nice. But . . ."

Perhaps meeting Lady Susan, as painful as it had been, had been good. Now Harriet must understand better how Society worked.

It was one thing to be defiant about a fact you couldn't change. It was quite another to ask for more abuse.

"You don't want to be anywhere near Lady Susan, do you?"

Harriet shook her head vehemently—and then her eyes filled with tears again. "So is Papa going to leave and never come back? Will I not see him again?"

Pen put her arm around Harriet's shoulders. "Oh, Harriet, no. He'll be back. He told me so this morning very clearly. He said that no matter how many children he might have in his marriage, you will always be his firstborn. He won't abandon you."

Harriet blinked away her tears, but she still didn't look happy.

"I wish he'd marry *you*."

Lord! Pen's heart fluttered with—what? Longing?

No point in encouraging *that* fantasy—either hers or Harriet's. "The earl's not going to marry me. I've told you that before."

Harriet scowled. "You'd make a much better wife than that mean Lady Susan."

Pen forced herself to laugh. "No, I wouldn't. I wouldn't have the first idea how to manage his houses, and I certainly wouldn't know how to go on in his social circle. Can you imagine me at a London ball?"

"Yes."

Harriet must have a very vivid imagination. Pen couldn't picture it.

Well, that wasn't completely true. She *could* picture it— and it was a nightmare. The thought of attending a Society event made her blood run cold. She wouldn't know how to behave, how to dress, what to say. She wouldn't even know the steps to the dances. And that wasn't taking into account the way all the noble lords and ladies would sneer at her. Lady Susan's contempt had been just a small taste of what would be in store for her if she *did* try to rub elbows with the *ton*.

She'd be miserable, and Harry would be mortified. She never wanted to put herself—and him—in that position.

"I would be very much a fish out of water, Harriet. I've never been to London—or to any city at all."

"Then we could stay at Darrow when Papa went to London."

Harriet was not going to let this go easily.

Of course she wasn't—she wanted it too badly.

"Your father is an earl, Harriet. He has to spend weeks in London when Parliament is in session. I think he'll want his wife to come with him, don't you?"

Harriet frowned and shrugged.

"And staying at Darrow wouldn't answer anyway. I suspect the people there would be even more displeased to have me installed as countess than to have me living in the village as your father's mistress." She gently smoothed a stray hair back from Harriet's face. "I'm sorry, Harriet. Sometimes the thing we most want is impossible."

"It's *not* impossible," Harriet said, stomping her foot. Then she turned and ran off toward the house.

Pen just stood where she was. She knew brangling with Harriet, especially now, wouldn't help matters, but that wasn't what kept her rooted to the spot. No, it was something far worse.

She'd known she couldn't marry Harry. She'd listed all the reasons why. But apparently, she hadn't truly convinced herself, not deep in her heart.

Now, after seeing Lady Susan's disdainful face and explaining matters to Harriet, it finally—*finally*—hit home.

The one thing she most wanted—to be Harry's wife and be a family with him and Harriet—was completely, absolutely, beyond her reach.

* * *

Pure, unadulterated rage roared through Harry as he watched Pen hustle Harriet away. He couldn't even look at Lady Susan or Letitia for fear he'd explode. What the *hell* were they doing in Little Puddledon?

There was only one explanation he could think of—they'd managed to discover his whereabouts from someone in Grainger's household and had come after him.

Had Grainger himself betrayed him? If he had, Harry would have a word with him when next he saw him—or, even better, go a few bouts with him at Gentleman Jackson's. Grainger was reputed to be an excellent fighter, but so was Harry. He might take a few hits, but he'd land some blows himself.

The thought was intensely satisfying.

And then Lady Susan sniffed, and his eyes reflexively looked her way. Her mouth was pinched, her nose in the air as if she'd caught a whiff of something vile.

His rage went from hot to ice cold. Lady Susan was going to be very, very sorry she'd had the temerity to pursue him to Little Puddledon.

"I cannot believe you just introduced me to your whore and your bastard, Lord Darrow," she said in outraged tones.

He clenched his jaw to keep from treating the spoiled spawn of Lord Langley to a long and vivid string of curses. If looks could kill, she'd be stretched out lifeless in the dirt.

Lady Susan is a female. I must remain civil.

Letitia didn't know him well, but she could recognize cold fury when she saw it.

"Er, Lady Susan. Perhaps we should return to the inn. Lord Darrow's mother and Lord Muddlegate must be wondering where we are."

Good Lord! Mama's here, too?

He turned his glare to Letitia, who had the grace to shrug apologetically.

Lady Susan plowed ahead. Apparently, the dolt thought his silence meant he was suitably penitent rather than literally speechless with rage.

"I don't mean to object to the liaison itself, you understand," she said haughtily. "Of course not. I know the ways of the world. You are free to have as many whores and bastards as you like. Do not, however, make the mistake of introducing them to me *ever* again. You must know how demeaning that is."

He found his voice. "Yes. You are correct. Very demeaning. You can rest assured I'll apologize to Mrs. Barnes when next I see her."

Lady Susan had been smiling—well, smirking—until he'd mentioned Pen.

"Apologize to Mrs. Barnes? Whatever for?"

"Lady Susan, we really ought to go," Letitia said.

Neither Lady Susan nor he paid any attention to Letitia's feeble attempt to avert disaster.

Except it wasn't disaster, at least for him. It was a blessing in disguise.

Well, hardly disguised. He'd known in his gut that marrying Lady Susan was a bad idea. Why else had he put off offering for her again and again? His conversations with Pen had forced him to face the fact that not only did he not love Lady Susan, he didn't like her. And now, seeing how she'd treated Pen and Harriet . . .

There wasn't a word strong enough to describe how much he loathed her.

And yes, he'd acknowledge she had some grounds for complaint. The general rule in Society was that a man should see to it that his mistress and his wife never met. But Pen and Lady Susan *had* met, quite by accident. Pen had behaved with generosity and poise while Lord Langley's spoiled daughter had acted precisely like the small-minded harpy she was.

Bloody hell, Pen was a *person*. She deserved to be treated with basic respect, no matter what her station in life. And Harriet was an innocent child.

"For introducing you to her, of course," he said, keeping his voice level. "Though I do believe, now that I think of it, she introduced herself."

What other woman would have had the presence of mind to do what Pen had done—to take control of an awkward situation and protect their daughter from insult?

Lady Susan looked momentarily confused by his choice of pronouns, but then latched on to his second sentence. "Yes, I believe you are correct. She did introduce herself. Such a bold piece! Once we are married—"

"Pardon me?" Aha! The jade had given him precisely the opening he wanted.

"Lady Susan," Letitia said, still trying to avoid the disaster she saw barreling toward them. "I *really* do think we should go back to the inn and let the earl continue on his walk by himself."

Lady Susan might as well have been deaf, so completely did she ignore Letitia. She kept her eyes—her *glare*—on him, while swatting her hand in Letitia's direction as if his sister-in-law was nothing more than an annoying, buzzing insect.

"I said, once we are married—"

He cut her off. "That's what I thought you said. Wherever did you get the daft notion we are going to wed?"

Lady Susan's mouth dropped open.

"Lady Susan, please." Letitia went so far as to tug on the woman's arm. "It's time we returned. Clearly Lord Darrow is eager to continue his walk. Let's give him the solitude he needs to consider . . . matters." She looked at Harry.

He gave her a small smile. It was all the icy fury currently coursing through his veins would allow. But he did sincerely appreciate her effort to remove the harridan before he did or said something he would regret.

Letitia blinked, gave him a wobbly smile in return, and then looked worriedly at Lady Susan—who angrily shook off her hold.

Zeus! Lord Langley's daughter was like a terrier with a rat, he being the rat. Her brows had snapped down into a deep scowl, and she flashed her teeth in what was more a snarl than a smile as she, well, growled, "I am perfect for you. I'm young enough to give you an heir, I'm attractive, and I'm an earl's daughter. *And* I've said I'll turn a blind eye to your little"—she flicked her fingers in the direction Pen had gone—"peccadillos."

He hadn't thought he could get any angrier, but— surprise!—he could.

If Lady Susan were male, he could vent some of his fury with his fists.

If she were male, they would not be having this "discussion."

"Of course, we are going to be married," she said. "Everyone expects it."

He raised both brows in feigned surprise and said, with a precisely calculated edge of disdain, "They do? How . . . odd."

"There is nothing odd about it." Lady Susan stomped one slippered foot on the path. "*I* expect it. Why else do you think I wasted my time at the Duke of Grainger's house party? You were the only eligible male there—at least the only one shopping for a wife. My father spent the entire party waiting for you to ask for my hand."

"And I never did, did I?"

Lady Susan stomped her foot again. Letitia had—wisely— given up and stepped back out of the fray, clasping her hands in front of her, likely to keep from wrapping them around his or Lady Susan's neck.

To be honest, he probably should apologize for raising Lady Susan's hopes. She did have some basis for complaint—he'd shown a marked interest in her—

No, to be fair, she was right. He *had* intended to offer for her. He'd just changed his mind.

Thank God.

He drew in a breath to beg her pardon, but the woman spoke first, throwing her hands up in the air.

"I cannot believe this!" She was stiff with anger, her words coming in short, sharp bursts. "I wasted the entire Season on you. The *entire* Season." She jabbed her finger at him with each word. "I could have got any number of lords—Arronder or Whatenly or Neardorn—to come up to scratch if I'd exerted the slightest effort to do so, you know."

That was no great surprise. The three lords she'd mentioned still needed to get an heir, but none could be considered a catch. Arronder was in his fifties. Whatenly wasn't much younger and had already buried two wives. Neardorn was Harry's age, but had long been rumored to prefer men to women.

"My father told me I'd played my cards wrong when the Season's last ball came and went and you *still* hadn't offered. But your mama said—and your sister-in-law, too—" She glared at Letitia.

Letitia glared back and opened her mouth to respond, but Lady Susan swept on.

"—told me not to give up hope, that you'd promised to find a bride this year and would keep your word. That I was the only one you were courting. And then I got invited to the duke's house party. So of course, I thought you would finally—*finally*—pop the question there. But no. Instead, you ran off."

That assessment wasn't far from the truth, unfortunately.

But he was glad he'd turned craven. If he'd stayed—hell, if that rainstorm hadn't come in right when it had—he'd have sentenced himself to a life of misery with the dreadful Lady Susan.

Grainger had done him an enormous favor. "The duke asked me to attend to a matter for him."

Lady Susan sniffed derisively. "That's what I was able to wheedle out of the stableboy as well, but now I see what you were really up to." She shrugged. "As I said, you are welcome to have as many whores as you like. In fact, I'd much rather you take your animal lusts out on those common females who can better withstand such attentions. As an earl's daughter, I expect constraint and courtesy in the marital bed."

Now didn't *that* sound jolly. Thank *God* he hadn't offered for this earl's daughter. And yes, this was precisely what he'd thought she wanted—what he'd told Pen she wanted. But hearing her actually say the words—

His stomach twisted.

No, he could not live with such a cold fish—and he certainly couldn't bed one. If he tried, he'd likely find himself unable to perform for the first time in his life.

And hot—very hot—on the heels of *that* thought came the memory of what he'd done with Pen in the cottage last night.

"You have no experience, Lady Susan," Letitia said quietly. "You might find your marital duties not so very objectionable once you know more precisely what they entail."

Oh, Lord. Could this conversation get any more awkward? He didn't want to know anything about his brother's marriage.

Lady Susan, of course, had no compunction about wading into matters that did not concern her. "I am not an idiot. Nor an infant. I've heard what men do to their wives and it sounds very uncomfortable." She gave Letitia a hard look. "And don't tell me you liked it. I believe you banned the late earl from your bed, did you not?"

Letitia turned red and her entire body seemed to droop. "I did, but only because the doctor told me I would die if I conceived another child so soon after I'd lost the last one."

Lord! His mother had told him about the miscarriages, but she hadn't shared that last bit. "I'm sorry, Letitia," he said, reaching out to clasp his sister-in-law's shoulder.

She smiled wanly back at him.

And then Lady Susan barged into their moment of rapport.

"See? It is just as I said. Gently bred ladies are too delicate for"—her nose wrinkled in disgust—"male lust. Wed me, Lord Darrow, to get your heir and then have your *fun*"—she waved her hand distastefully in the direction Pen had gone—"with your bit of muslin." She laughed. "I mean, it's not as if you can marry her, right?"

He stared at her.

Why can't *I marry Pen?*

He was a bloody earl, for God's sake. If he couldn't do as he wished, who could?

He felt himself start to grin.

"Thank you for your *generous* offer, Lady Susan, but I must decline."

Chapter Fifteen

Of course, Lady Susan didn't accept that.

"What do you mean, you must decline? You can't decline. You need an heir, don't you? You even promised your mother you'd find a wife this Season, and the Season is over. I've said I'm willing to marry you and look the other way when you engage in your extramarital escapades." Lady Susan snorted. "What is the problem? Of course, you'll marry me."

Anger and disgust jostled with each other in his breast, but the emotion that prevailed was relief. Zeus, he'd had a narrow escape.

He tried to remain polite. "Yes, I need an heir. And yes, I promised my mother I'd find a wife this Season. But no, I won't marry you."

Lady Susan put her hands on her hips. "Oh? So, then who are you going to marry?"

He probably shouldn't tell her, but if his suit was successful, she'd find out soon enough. And, much as it reflected badly on him, he couldn't resist throwing his decision in her supercilious face.

"I hope Mrs. Barnes will agree to marry me."

Lady Susan's reaction was all he could have hoped for.

Shock widened her eyes and caused her jaw to drop, and then anger swept in to tighten her features.

Followed, unfortunately, by corrosive spite, something he should have anticipated.

"You're going to marry your *whore?* Good God! Are you *mad?* I'm sure the woman doesn't know the first thing about running an earl's household. More, I'd be shocked if any of your servants wish to be ordered about by the creature. Do you think they will like having one of their own put above them? Not to mention the *ton* will never accept such a common, low-born woman. Every door will be shut against her. You'll be the laughingstock of London."

And you will still be on the shelf. Everyone will speculate about what fatal flaw kept the Earl of Darrow from offering for you.

He thought the words, but managed to keep from saying them. He was very proud of his self-control. "Are you quite finished?"

"No!"

Her hand flashed up, but his reflexes were excellent. He blocked her arm before her palm connected with his face—and then he blocked her other arm.

"I will tolerate your vituperation this one time, madam," he said, leaning toward her, holding her gaze with his—and keeping a loose grasp on her wrists so she couldn't try once more to slap him. "But do not think to repeat this scene ever again. And if I catch the faintest whisper that you said or did anything to impugn Mrs. Barnes's character, I will let it be known *exactly* what I think of you."

He saw a flicker of fear in her eyes and felt a faint brush of pity. It could not be easy being an older woman still languishing on the Marriage Mart—

And if Lady Susan wasn't such an annoying, whining, grasping female, she'd not be in that position.

In any event, the fear was gone, replaced by temper.

"Are you threatening me?" she spat at him.

"No," he said coldly. "I'm *promising* you."

Her eyes widened, and then she pulled back. He let her go.

"You, sirrah, are no gentleman."

He shrugged. There was no point in prolonging this encounter.

She looked at Letitia. "I should never have listened to you when you suggested this"—she threw him a dark scowl—"*person* was interested in marriage."

"And I should never have mentioned the possibility. Clearly you two will not suit." Letitia's tone was flat.

Lady Susan glared at her as if she expected her to say something more, but Letitia held her tongue.

"Well! I am going back to that horrible inn now," Lady Susan finally said, waspishly. "I would insist on returning to London today if we hadn't just arrived, but the roads in and out of this pitiful village are so dreadful I'm sure the coachman would not agree to travel them again so soon."

And then she raised her chin and focused on Harry. "So, you are in luck, my lord. You have a few hours to reconsider your foolish decision. If you come to your senses before the morning, you *might* be able to persuade me to have you after all."

Years of good manners turned the laugh her words had surprised out of him into a cough. He didn't trust himself to speak though—he was certain to say something cutting—so he just bowed wordlessly.

She frowned at him, and then she frowned at Letitia. "Are you coming?"

Letitia shook her head no.

"Well!" Lady Susan looked at Harry again. "Well!" Then she turned on her heel and stormed off down the path.

"She's right, you know," Letitia said as soon as Lady Susan was safely out of earshot.

"About what?" He was afraid he knew all too well.

"The *ton* will never accept Mrs. Barnes."

No. That couldn't be true. He wouldn't let it be true. He'd—

First things first.

He sighed. "I hope you are wrong, but that is not my most pressing problem at the moment."

"Oh? What is?"

"Getting Mrs. Barnes—Pen—to accept me."

Letitia's eyes widened. "What? Surely she'll jump at the chance to be a countess."

"Not Pen." She *should* jump at it. It would solve all her problems—and his and Harriet's as well. But one never knew with Pen, she was so bloody independent and strong-willed.

Letitia looked doubtful, but nodded nonetheless, apparently willing to accept his view of the matter. "She seemed poised and self-assured. Is her birth really dreadful?"

He rubbed the back of his neck. "I'm afraid so. Her father was a tenant farmer—an often drunk one."

"Oh, dear. And her mother?"

"Died long ago. I don't think Pen remembers her. But I'm confident she wasn't of the gentry, either."

Letitia shook her head. "Then I think you'd better wait until next Season and try your luck again on the Marriage Mart. I know you promised to marry this year, but it's very unlikely a few more months will make any difference."

He snorted. "So, you're not going to urge me to go groveling to Lady Susan?"

Letitia laughed and then wrinkled her noise in disgust. "Definitely not. I do apologize for putting her in your way. I had no idea she was so dreadful."

"Well, to be fair, neither did I." He'd known he didn't love her, but who expected love in a *ton* marriage? And she didn't love him, so he wouldn't be breaking her heart—if she had a heart to break.

"She wanted to be a countess, and I needed an heir. I thought we'd rub along together well enough." He shuddered. "I almost offered for her at Grainger's, you know. Lord, that would have been a disaster."

"Yes, indeed." Letitia smiled. "Chalk it up to a lesson learned. You'll be more discerning next time."

Next time . . .

God, he didn't want there to be a next time. He couldn't face any more balls and soirees, all the false gaiety, the batted eyelashes and coy looks. None of the women he'd met in London had cared a farthing about *him*—they just cared how many farthings he had in his bank account.

"I'm done with the Marriage Mart."

"Harry—"

"I'm serious. I'm determined to ask Pen if she'll have me."

His sister-in-law frowned, but he went on before she could present the arguments she'd clearly marshalled. "I love her, Letitia. I think I always have."

Letitia rolled her eyes.

He'd seen her daughters do that, but never her.

"Love? Pshaw!" she said dismissively. "I suspect it is far more likely you are in lust with Mrs. Barnes."

"Letitia!" Yes, lust was part of what he felt—a large part—but it certainly wasn't the entire story . . . was it?

Can I be sure?

Of course, he could. He'd had plenty of experience with lust. This was different.

"Think, Harry. You've just met her again—and discovered you have a daughter. Of course, your emotions are disordered. Give it time. It will pass."

"No. You're wrong." What Letitia said made sense. It was reasonable, even wise—in other circumstances.

She didn't know how deep his feelings ran.

She was shaking her head. "Love—romantic love—is a fleeting thing. You may think it will last forever, but trust me on this. It will be worn away, day after day, by every careless word, every slight, every broken promise until you feel nothing at all, not even anger or hurt."

Ah. "I'm sorry."

Being married to Walter must have been hell.

She waved away his sympathy. "I—your brother wasn't the easiest husband." She grimaced. "He had a roving eye—I knew that when I met him—and I let it bother me. My mistake."

He put a hand on her shoulder. "No, Walter's mistake."

She shook her head as she fished her handkerchief out of her pocket. "For a while I thought if only I were prettier or wittier or more . . . demonstrative, he'd be satisfied. But he never was." She blew her nose. "I was a fool."

"No, you weren't. Walter was very . . . charming. You weren't the only woman to, er, fall in love with him."

She snorted—and then blew her nose again. "Clearly. I don't even know how many mistresses he had. He tried to be discreet in the beginning, but after I couldn't—"

She pressed her lips together while she struggled for control.

"After I had to turn him away from my bed, he didn't bother to hide his liaisons." Her shoulders drooped. "If I'd been able to give him a son, perhaps then . . ."

He squeezed her shoulder. "No. Don't think that way."

What should he say? Wading into the swirling eddies of someone's marriage was fraught with danger—one could be pulled under by hidden currents at any moment.

"Walter was hopping from bed to bed long before he met you, Letitia. You know that. Look how many children there are with the Graham streak scattered all over Darrow. I've always understood that my mother, at least, hoped marriage would settle him."

"It didn't," Letitia said bitterly. "Maybe if he'd married someone else—"

He stopped her. Yes, he supposed that might be true, but there was no point in speculating about the unknowable. "Maybe, but I think it wouldn't have made any difference. They say a leopard can't change its spots, don't they?"

"Y-yes."

"You gave Walter three lovely daughters. My brother was a fool not to value them—and you—properly."

Her chin came up. "The girls *are* very dear, are they not?"

"Yes, they are." *Perhaps this is the way to win Letitia over.* "I'm a father now, Letitia. That's another reason I want to marry Pen. I want to have my daughter in my household."

Letitia didn't smile and agree as he'd hoped she would. Instead a deep line appeared between her brows.

"That's laudable, Harry, but think carefully about this. It's not just Mrs. Barnes who won't be accepted. Your daughter may be ostracized as well."

Anger flared in his gut. "No one will hurt Harriet. I'll see to that."

She gave him a long look. "Children can be very cruel. You won't—you can't—hover over Harriet every moment of every day. It wouldn't be good for her even if you could."

She touched his arm. "And it's not only the children, of course. It's their mothers and fathers. It's the servants—you must know Lady Susan was right about that. People will not be happy about you putting one of their own above them, especially as they must all know Mrs. Barnes's family history."

He scowled. "I'll let go anyone who is rude to my wife and child."

"But will you even know whom to blame? These things can be very insidious. A comment here, a whisper there. If everyone is offended by your choice of wife, the entire atmosphere can be poisoned in no time."

Letitia was wrong—she had to be.

"And the situation will be even worse in London. You might—*might*—be able to get the people on your estate to accept Mrs. Barnes and Harriet. Ultimately, your servants and tenants don't have much choice, do they? They depend on you for everything. But London and the *ton*—" Letitia shook her head. "That's a completely different matter."

Harry's jaws were clenched so tightly, he thought they might shatter. "I don't care about the *ton*. It doesn't matter to me—and I can't believe it will matter to Pen—if Society shuts its doors to us. I don't want tickets to Almack's."

But how would *Pen feel being shunned and excluded? Would she be angry? Hurt?*

He could protect her . . . couldn't he?

"Harry, the problem is bigger than that."

I can't give Pen up. I deserve some *happiness.*

Letitia put her hand gently on his arm again. "I know you say you love Mrs. Barnes. I understand that you want to marry her, but please consider what you are asking of *her*. To make her your countess . . ." Her fingers tightened, and she shook his arm a little. "It would be like throwing a kitten into a lion's den. She'd be torn apart. The kinder thing might be to set her up in a house of her own—here, perhaps—and visit her whenever you can."

"I suggested that, but Pen wanted no part of it." And the notion no longer appealed to him, either.

"Oh? What was her objection?"

"That I'd be breaking my marriage vows."

Letitia's eyes widened—and she swallowed a giggle. "How . . . quaint." She shrugged. "I'm sure you can persuade her."

"No, I can't." And his gut told him it would be wrong to try.

Letitia gave him a cautious look as if he might be a trifle demented, and then she sighed. "Then perhaps you just need to let her go, Harry."

No! I can't do that. I need *Pen. And I need Harriet, too.*

"You saw how Pen behaved just now, Letitia. She was far more the lady than Lady Susan was." There might have been a touch of desperation in his voice.

Letitia just shook her head. "This is England, Harry. Birth means more than behavior. Far more."

It shouldn't. Some of the men he'd trusted with his life on the Continent had been the sons of farmers and shopkeepers. They'd been smarter and braver than many of the noblemen he'd encountered, those who'd never had to struggle for anything in their lives.

"Not to me. I was never meant to be earl—you know that better than anyone, Letitia. I'm not used to nor do I particularly enjoy the trappings of the peerage. I'll go to London to take my place in Parliament, and I'll try to manage my estates well, but I need Pen."

"Harry . . ."

"Please say you'll accept her, if I can get her to marry me." This time he was the one who touched *her* arm. "I think it will help my cause with her if I can tell her my family approves—" That might be asking too much. "Well, or at least that you don't *disapprove* of our marriage."

She let out a long breath. "But Harry, even setting aside Mrs. Barnes's birth, she is just not qualified to be countess. I can't imagine she knows the first thing about running your household."

"I don't know about that. She helps operate the Home."

Letitia blinked at him. "The Home?"

Right. Neither she nor Mama would know about the Home.

"The Benevolent Home for the Maintenance and Support of Spinsters, Widows, and Abandoned Women and their Unfortunate Children."

Letitia blinked again. It *was* a mouthful.

"Lord Havenridge's widow established the place, and the Duke of Grainger helps support it." Or he was sure Grainger *would* support it once he knew what it was. "Pen is in charge of the agricultural side of the enterprise—she knows far more about crops and growing things than I do."

"Hmm." Letitia nodded slowly. "Well, I suppose that's good. And being associated with Lady Havenridge can't hurt, even though she's not been a part of Society for years. My brother ran in the same circles as her husband. Havenridge was a notorious gambler, but also a good-natured sort who was well liked. It caused a scandal when he killed himself, but that was long ago."

He hadn't thought about the Lady Havenridge connection. What about . . . no. He wouldn't mention Miss Anderson, since he knew nothing about her background.

"Pen's very capable, though I'm sure there *will* be many things she'll have to learn." If he managed to get Pen to agree to have him, it wouldn't hurt—and would likely help a great deal—if Letitia would give her some guidance.

"Would you be willing to stay on for a while at the dower house with Mama and show Pen how to go on?"

Letitia flushed and seemed gratified to be asked to help. "Yes, I suppose I could if Mrs. Barnes—"

"*Pen*. You will, I hope, be her sister-in-law, Letitia."

Letitia nodded. "Pen, then. I'll help, if Pen wishes it."

"Splendid. And having your girls there will give Harriet someone to play with."

"Ah . . ." Letitia frowned as if this was something she needed to mull over.

Zeus! Letitia couldn't mean to keep her girls away from Harriet, could she? That would be disastrous, far worse than the problems Harriet was facing at the Home. This would be *family* rejecting her.

He struggled to control his temper. Nothing would be helped by ripping up at his sister-in-law.

"She's my daughter, Letitia. The girls' cousin. And while my marrying Pen won't make Harriet legitimate, acknowledging her as my daughter will go far to smoothing her way. I suspect her birth won't matter to any but the highest sticklers as the years pass."

Letitia finally nodded. "You're probably right about that." She let out a long breath. "Very well. Harriet seemed well-behaved. I can't promise until I know her and her mother better, but I will go into the situation with an open mind." She smiled a little ruefully. "I have to protect my daughters, too."

"Of course. I'm not expecting any of this to be easy." He just hoped it didn't prove impossible.

They started walking back toward the inn.

"And will you have a word with my mother, Letitia? I'll speak to her myself soon, but not now when I might encounter Lady Susan. I've exhausted my ability to be polite to that woman." He scowled at his sister-in-law. "What did you mean, helping her track me down? She couldn't have come here without you and Mama and Muddlegate accompanying her."

Letitia looked properly abashed. "I *am* sorry about that. I should have listened to the whispers about her, but I'm afraid I took them as sour grapes. I'd never seen her be as horrid as she was here." She flushed. "I'd thought she'd be an amiable sister-in-law, and"—her flush deepened—"I suppose I also thought she'd wish to stay in London, letting me continue on at Darrow as if nothing had changed."

He gripped her shoulder in what he hoped was a bracing way. "I know this has been hard on you and the girls, Letitia. Don't worry. No matter what happens, I'll look out for you. I'm the head of the family now." He grinned. "And as to setting Lady Susan on me? Do your best to help Pen and all will be forgiven."

"Pen!"

Pen glanced up from checking her hop plants—and then straightened. Caro looked a bit windblown and . . . unsettled. "What is it? Did something happen at the brewhouse?"

Caro shook her head. "No. I'm not coming from there. I was up at the main house, passing the front parlor, when Jo stepped out and asked me to fetch you. She has a woman who wants to see you."

"Oh. A new resident?" Perhaps the woman had some agricultural experience. That would be very good news. She should start training someone to manage the hops in case things worked out for her with the new vicar. She'd still be in the village, of course, so could lend a hand, but she'd not be able to keep as close an eye on the hop plants as they needed.

"No. I don't think so. I only got a glimpse, but she looked finely dressed and quite self-assured."

"Oh." While they occasionally got women dressed well—servants often got their mistresses' castoffs—most, if not all, came with their will and pride and independence in tatters. So who could it—

Lud! Can Lady Susan have come to complain about me?

Well, so be it. If the woman was expecting her to bow and scrape and apologize, she was going to be very disappointed.

"Very well. I'll go at once." She wouldn't even take time to wash her hands or comb her hair. She was a working woman, after all, and this unscheduled visit was an interruption.

Caro stopped her. "Does everything still look good for the harvest?"

Pen grinned. All was well with the world if Caro could maintain her single-mindedness. "Yes. I think the hops will be ready to pick in about a week."

"Excellent!"

Fortunately, Caro stayed behind to have a look at the plants herself. Pen didn't feel like talking. She was too busy rehearsing exactly what she'd say to Lady Susan. Not that she'd have the courage to tell her *everything* she wanted to—

She paused in the middle of the yard, remembering far too clearly the expression of loathing and superiority that had twisted the woman's features when she'd encountered her and Harriet on the path by the stream.

She started walking again, new determination in her stride. Perhaps she *would* be able to tell Lady Susan *precisely* what she thought of her.

She hurried up the steps to the house and through the entry, pulled open the door to the parlor—and froze.

"Pen. It's lovely to see you again."

Lady Darrow—Harry's mother—sat in the yellow brocade chair by the front window.

"Mama!"

Pen's heart jumped and she inhaled sharply. Her focus had narrowed so much to Lady Darrow, she hadn't noticed Harriet, sitting on the worn, red chair just on the other side of the end table.

What has Harry's mother said to her?

"Grandmamma is here!" Harriet slid off the chair and came over, giving her little hop skip across the carpet. She was positively glowing.

Nothing bad . . . yet.

"Yes. I see that," Pen said evenly as her eyes swung back to Lady Darrow. Her heart started to pound, and her palms grew damp. *How am I going to protect Harriet?*

Lady Darrow smiled rather kindly. "I was very happy to make Harriet's acquaintance." She looked with what appeared to be real warmth at Pen's—and Harry's—daughter. "You should run along now, dear, and let me talk to your mother alone."

Harriet looked at Pen, and Pen nodded, relieved—and thankful—that Harriet wouldn't hear whatever Lady Darrow had to say—and what Pen would say in response.

She didn't know if she was going to curse or cry.

Harriet looked back at Lady Darrow. "You won't leave without saying good-bye will you, Grandmamma?"

"Of course not." Lady Darrow smiled again and nodded at Pen. "As long as your mother doesn't object."

Which sent Harriet's wide, pleading eyes back to Pen. "You *won't* object, will you, Mama?"

"I don't think I will, Harriet, but I don't know for certain." She gave Harry's mother a long, level gaze.

"But, Mama . . ."

"Your mother is just watching out for you, Harriet," Lady Darrow said gently. "Go along now. It will be all right."

Harriet hesitated—and then she nodded, gave her grandmother and Pen one last look, and left.

Pen closed the door and turned to face Harry's mother.

"Come sit down, Pen." Lady Darrow gestured to the chair Harriet had vacated.

Pen stayed where she was. She didn't want to be rude, but she also didn't want to get too close to Harry's mother until she knew what was going on. "Why are you here?"

Someone knocked on the door.

Pen spun around, thinking Harriet must have returned, and said, as she opened it, "I told you—oh."

It wasn't Harriet. It was Jo with tea and cake.

"Oh, good. Caro found you," Jo said as she came in and set down her tray. She poured two cups of tea and put them, along with a plate of sliced seedcake, on the table between Lady Darrow and the empty chair. "There you go.

Now do have a comfortable coze. I'm sure you have much to discuss." She smiled at them both and headed for the door.

"Jo." Something that felt very much like panic closed Pen's throat, stopping her from saying more. She had to clench her hands in her skirt to keep from grabbing Jo's arm.

"Just listen to what Lady Darrow has to say, Pen," Jo said quietly. "It can't hurt, can it?" And then she slipped out and shut the door behind her.

Pen stared at the closed door and tried to swallow her panic. It *could* hurt. Whatever Lady Darrow had to say could *kill* her.

Nonsense. She was a grown woman now with a child and important work to do, not the little girl who had gazed in awe at Harry's beautiful, elegant mother sitting in the Darrow family pew nor the older girl who had loved the countess's son so thoroughly.

Harry. Oh, God.

She finally turned to face her visitor. Lady Darrow gestured to the empty chair again.

Pen still stayed by the door. "Why are you here? Did Harry send you?" She tried to keep her voice level. She didn't want Lady Darrow to discern how upset she was.

Why in the world would Harry send his mother to speak to me? Surely, he doesn't expect her *to try to persuade me to become his mistress.*

She took a deep breath and tried to calm down. Did Harry even know his mother was in the village? He'd seemed surprised when they'd encountered Lady Susan and Letitia by the stream. He hadn't mentioned his mother.

"No, he didn't send me. He doesn't know I'm here. Please do sit down, Pen. I truly don't think I'm going to say anything to upset you." Lady Darrow smiled. "On the contrary, I hope we can join forces to help ensure my son's happiness."

So somehow, Harry's mother *did* know. "You don't have

to worry, Lady Darrow. I've already told him I won't be his mistress."

Perhaps that was being too blunt, but there was no point in prevaricating. Lady Darrow had met Harriet. She knew now if she hadn't then that Pen and Harry had been lovers. It would be reasonable for her to conclude Harry was here to revive that relationship.

A far-too-detailed memory of what she'd done with Harry in the cottage last night popped into her thoughts.

She pushed it firmly out again.

Lady Darrow smiled. "Good."

Good, indeed. Now perhaps the woman would take her leave and Pen could—

"I do hope I can convince you to be his wife, however."

Pen stared at Lady Darrow for several heartbeats while Harry's mother looked calmly back at her.

She can't have said what I think she said.

She tottered over to sit in the empty chair before her knees gave out.

"Pardon me. I . . ." She swallowed. "That is . . ." She looked intently at Lady Darrow. "Did you just say you wanted me to *marry* Harry?"

Lady Darrow's smile widened and she nodded. "Yes, that is precisely what I said."

Pen blinked. "But . . ." She scoured her brain. She couldn't come up with a single plausible reason. "Why?"

Lady Darrow shifted a bit on her seat as if she wasn't quite comfortable. "Perhaps you'll understand better if I begin at the beginning. You see, I knew about Harriet before she was born, but I thought she was Walter's child."

"*What?!*" If Lady Darrow had thought Harriet was Walter's, then, obviously, she'd also thought Pen had had carnal relations with the man.

The notion was revolting. And insulting.

"Why did you think that?"

A small frown formed between Lady Darrow's brows. "I'm not certain. I might just have assumed it. Irate fathers were always coming to see the earl about Walter's, er, wild oats. He had so many illegitimate children, people even had a name for them."

Pen nodded. "Walter's whelps."

Lady Darrow flinched.

Oh, blast. She should have bitten her tongue.

"Yes, Walter's whelps. So, when I heard your father had come to speak to the earl, I thought he was just the next in a long, depressing line."

"But *Walter* and *me*?"

Lady Darrow smiled. "You must remember, I didn't know you, except by sight. And if I'd been at the estate that summer, I might have noticed you and Harry were together frequently, but I was in London until just before Harry left for the Continent."

That's right. Now Pen remembered. Lady Darrow had stayed at Darrow House, so Letitia, who'd been pregnant with Bianca and having a very hard time of it, could be closer to her physician.

Walter, however, not being one to, er, *hover* over his wife, had been in the country, busily hopping in and out of any bed he could. But not *her* bed.

Though she could see how Lady Darrow might have assumed otherwise.

Harry's mother tapped her teacup against her lip. "You know, now that I think about it, I believe the servants told me your father said the baby was Walter's."

Pen stiffened. "No, he wouldn't—"

She stopped, mouth ajar. Of course, that was *exactly* what her father would have done, and without a moment's hesitation. He'd likely have assumed he'd have less of an argument if he claimed Walter, the well-known philanderer, as her baby's father. As Lady Darrow said, everyone expected Walter to scatter his bastards over the countryside. And perhaps he'd also thought he'd get a better deal by accusing the heir.

Oh, hell.

She'd thought she was done being hurt by her father.

Chapter Sixteen

"I'll confess I put the matter out of my mind," Lady Darrow was saying. "Does that sound callous?"

She sighed, suddenly looking all of her fifty-some years. "Perhaps it is. But I had a new granddaughter to dote on, and, well, when faced with the same pain over and over again, I long ago learned I had to take steps to protect my heart or it would shatter."

Lady Darrow put down her teacup with a clink. "I have at least a dozen grandchildren on the estate whom I can't claim, Pen, and who I didn't know about until the Graham streak finally appeared in their hair when they were two or three years old—or even older. Before Walter died, I used to wonder at every christening in the parish church—is this baby one of mine?"

She rubbed her hand over her face. "But of course they can never be mine. Even once the streak appears and it's clear they are Walter's, everyone pretends they belong to whichever farmer the earl was able to pawn Walter's pregnant paramour off on."

Her expression grew sadder. "And it doesn't help Letitia's spirits that eight of those children are boys."

Pen nodded. She'd never looked at the situation from

Lady Darrow's point of view before, but now that she did . . .
Yes, she could see it would be painful.

"As you must know—or will discover soon enough—a
mother's job is difficult, frustrating, and sometimes, if one
is especially unlucky, extremely disheartening—even heart-
breaking. I couldn't keep Walter from fornicating with any
willing female he wished to. I just thanked God he only
fornicated with willing women." Her face froze. "At least,
as far as I know. I don't believe anyone ever accused him
of rape."

Lady Darrow looked at Pen, the unspoken question in
her eyes.

Pen hastened to reassure her. "I never heard even a whisper of Walter forcing himself on anyone, Lady Darrow. He
didn't have to. Women—not me, of course, but many, many
women—were anxious to, er, entertain him. He had a reputation for being very—" She probably shouldn't tell Walter's
mother the glowing reviews Walter's amatory skills had
received. "—pleasant."

A little of the tightness left Lady Darrow's face. "That's
good. I-I did wonder from time to time, but the thought of
Walter . . ." She shook her head. "No, it was too horrible to
contemplate."

"I would think if Walter had forced himself on anyone,"
Pen said in what she hoped was a reassuring tone, "his
victim's father would have come storming up to the house to
tell the earl."

Lady Darrow nodded. "That's what I've always told
myself."

"Didn't you ask Lord Darrow?" Pen frowned. Lady
Darrow had said the *servants* told her Pen's father had
claimed Harriet was Walter's child. Odd. She would have
thought the earl would have shared that information with his
wife directly.

Lady Darrow shook her head. "No. Darrow and I didn't

discuss such things. Well, we didn't discuss anything. We had a typical marriage of convenience, I'm afraid. Once I'd given him his heir and spare, I went my way and he went his. There were times when weeks would pass without us exchanging a single word. It was very . . . lonely."

Oh. Suddenly Pen wondered if the composed, ethereal beauty she'd always admired in Lady Darrow had really been hard-won detachment.

"Harry told me he expected to have a marriage of convenience with Lady Susan." The words tumbled out before she could stop them.

Stupid! It's none of my concern. Lady Darrow will— rightly—put me in my place.

Still, she hated the thought of Harry condemned to such a sterile union, especially now that she'd met Lady Susan.

It's the way of the world—of his world.

Pen frowned.

And mine, too?

Wasn't she looking for something similar—an amiable union built on respect and courtesy?

Likely it was only in fairy tales that a man and a woman married for love and lived happily ever after.

To her surprise, Lady Darrow did not take her to task for her impudence. Instead, she nodded.

"Yes, I think that is precisely what he *would* have done, which is why it would be much, much better for him to marry you."

And just like that, they were back at the preposterous notion they'd begun with.

"I don't understand." She *must* be missing some crucial piece of information. "Harry told me you were, er, *urging* him to find a bride from the *ton* during the London Season." Badgering, more like.

"I'm sorry to say I was." Lady Darrow sighed. "I wasn't thinking clearly. You see, when Walter d-died—"

Suddenly her eyes filled with tears. She sniffed a few

times, and then pulled out her handkerchief and blew her nose. When she spoke again, her voice was halting.

"As I'm sure you can imagine, b-burying a child is one of the most p-painful things a mother can endure. Walter had many sins, but he was still my son. And he was only thirty-five. Strong and healthy. His d-death was a terrible, terrible shock."

Pen put a comforting hand on Lady Darrow's arm. She *could* imagine—all too well. If anything were to happen to Harriet . . .

Dear God, I'd want to die.

Lady Darrow blew her nose again and took a sustaining sip of tea. "And Letitia and the girls were distraught, of course. It was a horrible time. Just horrible. I-I think I went a little mad."

She shook her head as if that would dispel the memory. "I let myself be consumed by the need for an heir, Pen. It was all I could think about." She frowned. "And it was so . . . silly. I've suspected for years, ever since Letitia's last mis-carriage, that Harry would inherit the title, and yet I never felt the need to write and tell him to come home and marry. But when Walter died—"

She pressed her lips together and swallowed several times.

"Harry *had* to come home then. He was the earl. He had to take up his new responsibilities—and one of those was to marry and get an heir. *He* doesn't have a brother to follow after him. If he dies without a son, everything goes to a distant cousin, a man I've never met or even corresponded with. And if that happens, I don't know what will become of me and Letitia and the girls."

Pen understood all too well the desperation she heard in Lady Darrow's voice. She'd felt it, too, when she'd left Darrow and then again when Aunt Margaret died.

"So, yes, I made him promise to find a bride this Season.

I thought I was right to do so, especially after the first ball when he complained how young all the girls were. They were only going to seem younger the older he got."

Pen nodded. Harry had said as much.

"He went to almost all the Season's events, danced with any number of girls—and he chose Lady Susan. I knew he didn't love her, but, as I know all too well, love isn't necessary to get an heir. Just a bit of respect. Some courtesy."

Exactly what Pen had thought to look for.

"It was what I'd had with his father. It wasn't . . . wonderful, but it wasn't *dreadful*, and it got the job done."

Lady Darrow blew out a long breath. "I admit I was annoyed with him when he didn't offer for Lady Susan before the Season was over—he'd told me he would—but when we were all invited to the Duke of Grainger's party, I thought Grainger was going to help with the matter."

She laughed. "Which he did, though not in the way I was expecting. I was very, ah, *displeased* with the duke when I got up Saturday morning to discover Harry had vanished. He was suspiciously vague as to where Harry had gone, but then Lady Susan was able discover Harry's whereabouts from a stableboy, so we set off—Lady Susan, Letitia, and I in the traveling coach and my friend, Lord Muddlegate, on his horse. Lady Susan's father washed his hands of the matter and went back to Langley."

Lady Darrow wrinkled her nose. "I now know why— Lady Susan is a *very* unpleasant traveling companion. I was heartily sick of her long before we reached Little Puddledon. And then, when she got back from that walk a little while ago . . ." Harry's mother grimaced.

Pen could well imagine how incensed Lady Susan must have been.

"There wasn't much we could have done to avoid her, Lady Darrow. It wasn't as if we could cross a street or duck into a shop. We were walking by the stream when we

encountered her and Letitia." Pen frowned, remembering
that awful moment. "I know it's not considered good form
for someone like me to address people like Lady Susan
and Letitia, but my first—my only—concern was to protect
Harriet. They knew she was Harry's daughter. I couldn't
risk them hurting her feelings or embarrassing her in
any way."

Lady Darrow was nodding as if she agreed with her.
"Yes. Quite right. You did exactly as you should have."

Had Pen heard correctly? "But I'm . . ." She wouldn't say
the word. "I'm not married to the father of my child."

"You're the mother of my grandchild."

True, but beside the point. Didn't the woman understand?

"Lady Darrow, Lady Susan was going to call me a . . ."
Oh, just say it. "She was going to call me a whore. I got
Harriet away before she did, but Harriet's very bright. She
knew what Lady Susan was going to say."

Pen leaned forward a little and held Lady Darrow's eyes
with hers. It was very important the woman understand.

"I want you to know that I am not . . . That is, Harry is the
only man I have ever been with. I loved him and I showed
him that love, even though I knew I was breaking the rules.
I don't regret it, and I don't regret Harriet. I work hard to
support us and to see she has everything she needs. She can
read and write, add and subtract. When she is older, I will
help her find a trade or a craft or some way to support herself and be independent. I can and I will take care of her."

"I know you will," Lady Darrow said, patting Pen's arm,
"but she still needs a father."

"Yes, she does." Pen gripped her hands tightly together.
"I hope to find her one soon. The village will be getting a
new vicar. I—"

Lady Darrow cut her off. "Balderdash! There's no need
to go looking at vicars. Harriet *has* a father."

"Well, yes, of course. But, as you know—"

"Marry Harry."

And there it was again.

Pen gaped at the woman for several seconds before she found her voice. "Lady Darrow, please! You and I both know I cannot do that."

"And why not?" Lady Darrow helped herself to a slice of seedcake. "Oh, this is very good."

Pen was happy for the distraction. "Yes. Avis, the girl who does all our baking, is quite gifted. Our main business now is brewing, but we still sell some of Avis's baked goods."

"I do believe this seedcake is as good as any I've had, even in London." Lady Darrow took another bite, savored it, and then washed it down with some tea. "You might be able to find a market for it in Town, if you wished." She smiled. "But you were telling me why you can't marry Harry."

Sadly, they were back to that. Of course, they were. Pen could see she wasn't getting out of this room without discussing the matter to Lady Darrow's satisfaction. She thought briefly about walking out, but she'd really missed her best opportunity to do that—and she wouldn't put it past Lady Darrow to follow her.

"There are too many reasons to list them all."

Harry's maddening mother raised her brows. "Try."

Very well, she'd play this game for a little while. "My birth. I'm only a farmer's daughter—a *drunken* farmer's daughter."

Lady Darrow nodded. "True. I suppose we all began as farmers or hunters or traders or . . . soldiers. A lot of men earned their titles by killing people for the king."

"Er . . ." Pen blinked, her mouth half open. She supposed there was some truth to that.

"Oh, I'm not advocating that we go the way of the Americans or, worse, the French," Lady Darrow said, "but I do sometimes wonder if we put too much emphasis on a person's birth. I mean, just look at Lady Susan. She's an earl's daughter, but she's also crass, selfish, and exceedingly annoying."

"Mmm." Pen agreed wholeheartedly.

"And your father didn't take to drinking in excess until after your mother died. I always thought he was drowning his sorrows."

"W-What?" Pen stared at Lady Darrow. "You knew my mother?"

Lady Darrow nodded slowly, a frown appearing between her brows. "Yes. She was my abigail. She came with me when I married the earl. I quite depended on her at first, while I was getting used to Darrow"—Lady Darrow smiled—"both the place and the man. Perhaps that's why I tried to convince her not to wed your father. But she would not be dissuaded. She thought him handsome and fun and exciting." Lady Darrow shook her head. "She was besotted."

Pen wished she could remember her mother. She wanted to ask Lady Darrow—

No. That would prolong this exceedingly awkward conversation.

Lady Darrow sighed. "I've always thought I should have kept more of an eye out for you, but I'm afraid I got distracted by my own problems. And then when I believed Walter had—" She shook her head. "I thought I would see you married to a local farmer, and I'd have yet another grandchild in the village that I couldn't claim."

She took a sip of tea and looked at Pen over the rim of the cup. "Why didn't you marry a local man?"

"The only one available—or at least the one the earl offered Papa—was the blacksmith's son." Pen couldn't keep the revulsion from her voice.

Lady Darrow inhaled sharply. "*Felix?!* You would have been miserable."

She would have been miserable married to anyone but Harry, but with Felix she'd have been . . .

She couldn't think of a word strong enough to adequately convey the horror she'd have endured as Felix's wife.

"Yes. I refused to consider the match. My father, however, did not agree with my decision. We, er, *argued* about it. That's why I left."

Lady Darrow nodded. "Ah. I was so busy with Letitia and the new baby, I didn't miss you right away. When I finally asked the vicar's wife where you were, she said you'd gone to your aunt's and were much better off. So I let the matter drop."

She looked a bit . . . remorseful before glancing down to dust a few crumbs off her lap. When she looked back up, there was steely determination in her eyes.

Oh, Lord.

"Now that we've dispensed with your birth, what's the next reason you think you can't marry my son?"

They had not dispensed with her birth, but there was clearly no point in belaboring that, especially as Pen had, unfortunately, a mountain of other deficiencies.

"I had a child out of wedlock."

"Harry's child." Lady Darrow swept her fingers through the air as if that took care of reason number two.

Pen frowned. She wasn't a complete chawbacon. She knew the woman was making too light of the situation. "It's not that simple."

"But it is. I grant you, Harriet's birth *would* be an issue if she were a boy—she couldn't inherit—but since she's a girl"—Lady Darrow brushed her hands together as if disposing of some dirt, which perhaps she was—"no problem. You merely anticipated your vows."

"By almost ten years."

Lady Darrow shrugged. "Who's counting?"

"Everyone!"

Harry's mother laughed. "No, they're not. It's only fun to count when it's months you're counting. For some reason people enjoy trying to determine if a child born in a couple's first year of marriage was conceived before the wedding."

Well, perhaps Lady Darrow was right about that, but the issue was more complicated.

"People will care when it comes time for Harriet to think about marrying."

Lady Darrow still seemed unconcerned. "I suppose it's possible some high sticklers could balk at her birth, but I see that as a good thing. It will serve to weed out the disagreeable fellows, the male versions of Lady Susan, if you will."

If Pen was willing to step into the fantasy world Lady Darrow was constructing, she supposed she could agree on that point.

"She's the Earl of Darrow's daughter, Pen. Nothing can change that. She'll have Harry's love and support—and I'm sure the love and support of her brother, the future earl." Lady Darrow grinned. "At least I hope she has a brother or two and some sisters as well."

Harriet would like a few siblings. And I wager Harry would be very good with babies—

Stop! You can't let yourself get lulled into believing Lady Darrow's fiction.

"I predict she'll be the most sought after girl the year she makes her debut." Lady Darrow smiled. "Besides being an earl's daughter, she's lovely, bright, independent, and strong-minded."

A warm burst of pride swelled Pen's chest. "She is, isn't she?"

And she is also illegitimate.

It was time to be clear-eyed and acknowledge cold, hard facts. Pen opened her mouth—

Isn't it a fact that it would be better to be an earl's acknowledged daughter than a vicar's adopted one?

She took refuge in a slice of seedcake.

Could Lady Darrow be correct? She'd always believed Harriet's birth to be an insurmountable barrier. But legitimacy was only a legal tie. She hadn't considered how blood would connect Harriet to Harry and Lady Darrow.

But Harriet's birth wasn't the only issue. There was also Pen's unsuitability.

"I don't know anything about Society, Lady Darrow. I have no idea how to be a countess—or even what that position entails." *Besides frolicking in bed with Harry.*

Good Lord! She could not think such things, especially in front of the hawkeyed Lady Darrow.

Pen hurried on. "I've never been to a ball or a soiree or"—she tried to think of the other exotic entertainments she'd read about in the newspapers—"a rout or masquerade or, well, anything. I don't know how to dance or ride."

There. Surely *that* would convince the woman.

It did not.

"I'll teach you how to go on, or Letitia or Harry will. I imagine it will be exhausting in the beginning for all of us, but you don't have to learn everything at once."

How could Lady Darrow be so blasé? What she described . . . It was like expecting a barely crawling baby to suddenly be able to . . . to discuss Thomas Coke's theories on crop rotation.

Which she actually knew a bit about.

"I don't know how to manage a household like the earl's."

"Letitia and I can certainly help you with that, but to be honest, Mrs. Marsh—you might remember her, she's been housekeeper at Darrow for ages—will be just as happy if you defer to her in everything." Lady Darrow smiled a bit conspiratorially. "Though you do need to object once in a while, if for no other reason than to keep her on her toes."

"Oh." Pen could feel her resistance beginning to weaken,

but she feared she was being worn down rather than truly persuaded by Lady Darrow's arguments.

"You stood up to your father," Lady Darrow said, "found a refuge for you and your daughter—*twice*, and somehow developed a marketable skill. *And* Lady Havenridge told me earlier that you not only grow hops and other things central to the Home's businesses, you help her and Miss Anderson run the entire operation. I'd say you definitely have the backbone and determination and skills to succeed as Countess of Darrow."

Perhaps Lady Darrow was right. . . .

No, she wasn't. She—and Pen—were overlooking the most important issue.

"Lady Darrow, even if you are correct, there is one major problem with my marrying your son."

"Oh, and what might that be?"

"He hasn't asked!" She stopped herself. The truth was quite a bit worse than that. "Actually, he *has* asked—but not to be his wife. The position he wishes me to fill is that of mistress."

Lady Darrow looked positively gleeful, going so far as to give a little bounce in her chair. "That's the best part! After you left Harry, Letitia, and Lady Susan on the path by the stream, Lady Susan tore into Harry. At least that's how she described it. I haven't seen Harry or Letitia yet to get their side of the story. I came up here to find you as soon as I could get free of that harpy."

"Oh."

"Oh, yes. She stalked into the Dancing Duck in high dudgeon. Lord Muddlegate and I were in the common room, having a cup of tea—well, I was having tea. Muddles was having a large glass of Widow's Brew—which he liked very much, by the way. Said it was one of the best ales he's ever tasted. And he's a bit of a connoisseur when it comes to such things. Belongs to the Ancient Association of Ale

Aficionados." Lady Darrow laughed. "They came up with that name a month or two ago to make their regular drinking bouts sound more impressive. They meet at a London tavern twice a month to argue about ale, among many other things."

Ah, a safe topic. Pen grabbed on to it like a drowning woman would grab on to a passing log.

"I'm certain Caro—Miss Anderson, our brewster—would be delighted to send a few bottles of Widow's Brew back to Town with him. She's been wanting to get our ale into a London public house for some time. Have you met Caro? I can introduce you, if you like."

Lady Darrow shook her head. "Thank you, but Lady Havenridge has offered to show me around when you and I have finished our discussion." She grinned. "I hope you'll have more important matters to attend to than giving me a tour. Now, where was I?"

Better to just get this over with. "You said you were at the Dancing Duck."

"Oh, right. So there Muddles and I sat, drinking our respective beverages, when Lady Susan threw open the door." Lady Darrow shook her head again and shuddered. "To think I wanted Harry to marry that woman! I will have to get down on my knees tonight and thank God the Duke of Grainger meddled in the matter. I was very annoyed with him for spoiling my plans when I left his estate, but now I realize he saved me from a life of torment. Saved Harry, too, which I suppose was his main goal." She laughed. "He does not like Lady Susan."

Lady Darrow took another slice of seedcake. "Do consider expanding your distribution of this. It's quite extraordinary."

"I will mention it to Jo." Was Lady Darrow ever going to get to the point?

Do I really wish her to?

Lady Darrow swallowed her seedcake with some tea. "So,

Lady Susan immediately caught sight of me. Not surprising. It's not a large room, and Muddles and I happened to be the only patrons there—fortunately as Lady Susan didn't bother to keep her voice down." Lady Darrow frowned. "I'm sure if you ask Bess, the innkeeper, she can recount the whole tale for your edification—and likely the edification of the entire village when people gather there this evening."

Oh, Lord. Lady Darrow was correct. Bess was certain to gossip—it was the main reason she'd taken on the job of innkeeper. She loved being at the center of things, and the inn was the best spot in the village for that, what with the tavern and the—admittedly few—travelers coming and going.

"Lady Susan went on at great length about how very of-fended she was to be forced to endure an introduction to you and Harriet. Well!" Lady Darrow scowled. "You can imagine what I felt then."

Actually, Pen couldn't, but she needn't be concerned. Lady Darrow proceeded to tell her.

"Here was this . . . this *shrew* yammering at me, in a *most* unpleasant way, about Harry and suddenly she's telling me— in terms I won't repeat—that I have a granddaughter nearby, and she is *Harry's* child!"

Lady Darrow beamed at Pen, and Pen grinned back. She couldn't help herself, the woman's joy was infectious.

And she felt . . . amazed, too. Could it be that she and Harriet had a family that wanted them?

Slow down. Wait until you know the full story. Until you know what Harry *wants.*

"Up until that moment, I had no idea Harry was a father and that you and his daughter were here. The instant I sorted it out, you can be certain I interrupted Lady Susan's ha-rangue to demand she tell me where I could find you. When she said she didn't know or care, I got up—rudely, I sup-pose, not that *I* cared at that point—and left her with poor Muddles while I asked the innkeeper your direction. And then I grabbed my bonnet and hurried up here, leaving Muddles to deal with Lady Susan."

Lady Darrow refreshed herself with some tea. "I'm sorry for abandoning Muddles, but he's a calm, good-natured sort. He'll just let Lady Susan's nasty words blow past him like the empty wind they are until she gets tired of spewing them."

"I see. Well, I'm very happy you came, and I'm certain Harriet is delighted, too, but I'm afraid I still don't see why you think Harry wishes me to be anything other than his mistress."

Lady Darrow stared at her—and then laughed. "Oh, dear! Did I forget that part?"

"Which part?" Pen asked cautiously.

"The part where Lady Susan told Muddles and me in the most affronted tone you can imagine that Harry told her himself that he hoped you would marry him!"

"Ah." Pen gaped at Harry's mother. She must have misunderstood. "Harry wants to marry me?"

"Yes!" Lady Darrow put her teacup down with a decided clink and stood. "Now go find my son so he can propose. I'm eager to have you—and my granddaughter—move to Darrow as soon as may be."

Chapter Seventeen

Harry climbed out of the water and picked up his towel. When he'd got back from walking with Letitia, he'd decided to take a quick bath in the pool by the waterfall before getting dressed and heading up to the Home to try his luck with Pen.

He rubbed his hair briskly.

Poor Letitia.

Now that his sister-in-law was no longer pushing Lady Susan at him, he felt as if an invisible wall had fallen. He no longer had to keep his guard up around her, and that had allowed him to really listen to her and understand how worried she'd been for herself and her daughters.

I should have paid more attention to her when I first got home. I should have addressed her concerns then.

He hoped he'd been able to put them to rest now.

He used the towel on his back.

She hadn't said it in so many words, but he thought the reason she'd joined forces with Mama to get him married was to put an end to the uncertainty. She didn't care about the succession. She just wanted matters settled so she knew what she had to do to take care of her girls.

She could have relied on him to see to things.

She hadn't known that. She didn't know *him*. He'd been hardly more than a boy when he'd left England. And she'd certainly never been able to rely on Walter for anything.

He dried off his legs.

Well, time healed all wounds. As the days and months passed, Letitia should feel more confident.

It might help her if she could bring herself to help Pen—

Assuming he could convince Pen to marry him.

Pen.

He grinned at the waterfall.

Just thinking of marrying her made him feel better than he'd felt since he'd learned of Walter's death. Calmer. Happier.

As if he'd been wandering lost in the woods and had finally found the path home. . . .

He paused.

God, I've felt lost ever since I left Darrow as a boy. Ever since I left Pen.

Perhaps there were some wounds that time couldn't heal.

He closed his eyes, thought back . . .

Could it be that Pen had been his anchor, his touchstone, all these years, always in the back of his thoughts and deep in his heart, so deep he hadn't realized it until now?

I have *to persuade her to marry me. If I can't—*

He ran the towel over his chest. He couldn't think about that. He'd just have to present his, er, case as best he could—hence the bath. He'd choose his best clothes, too—well, the best ones he had on hand. He hadn't packed with a marriage proposal in mind.

What if she refuses?

He wouldn't—*couldn't*—contemplate that. Pen loved him. She'd said as much. She would *want* to be persuaded.

Persuaded, not seduced. Convinced, not overwhelmed. He'd need to win her head as well as her heart and her body.

He'd have to have a counterargument for every argument she threw at him.

At least I can tell her Letitia will support her—

Well, Letitia hadn't committed to that, but he thought she was leaning that way. And Mama might be willing to help, too. From what Letitia had said, they'd both come to loathe Lady Susan.

He picked up his breeches, shook them out—

Oh, why bother getting dressed just to get redressed in a few minutes? The cottage wasn't far. He'd just wrap his towel around his middle. The jays and squirrels wouldn't be offended by his near nudity.

He gathered the rest of his clothing and started back down the path to the cottage.

Letitia had said—in a very cautious, tentative voice—that she might like to marry again. She was lonely—had, he suspected, been lonely even when Walter was alive—and wished for companionship.

Having her marry would certainly make things tidier. Once Pen was comfortable with her duties, Letitia wouldn't have much to do, especially as she'd be sharing the dower house with Mama.

Unless Mama was planning to remarry as well. Now that he thought about it, he'd been stumbling over Muddlegate a lot recently. That would be . . . odd, but he shouldn't begrudge her some happiness, either. His father had been gone for several years, not that he'd been especially attentive when he was alive.

Harry snorted. His parents had had a classic marriage of convenience. He should have taken their relationship as the perfect example of what he *didn't* want, and yet he'd been on the verge of making the same mistake. If he—

"Fuc—!" He managed to bite off the profanity before the word offended . . . the jays and squirrels. He must be entertaining them immensely by hopping about on one foot.

He picked up the acorn he'd unwittingly stepped on and flung it into the woods. Perhaps he should have put on his boots at least. Too late to bother now—he was almost at the cottage. He'd just be more careful.

He kept his eyes trained on the path for any more hazards, heaving a sigh of relief once he was safely on the cottage's smooth, acorn-free floor. He started up the stairs to the bedroom.

Hmm. I really don't have much to wear and nothing I haven't worn before.

Oh, well. He'd just give everything the sniff test and choose whatever was least objectionable. He grinned. He hoped he'd not be wearing clothes for very long. Once—*if*—he got Pen to agree to marry him, they could come back here to finish their *discussion* in bed.

He ducked to navigate the doorway—

"Hul-lo."

That low, artificially sultry voice wasn't Pen's.

He snapped his head up—and crashed it into the lintel.

"Uhh!" He braced himself against the doorjamb, grabbing his head and clenching his teeth to withstand the pain and keep the string of curses that had lined up on his tongue unsaid.

Who was in his room? Surely not . . .

His vision cleared.

Bloody, bloody, *bloody* hell, it *was* Lady Susan, and worse, she was sitting on the bed, stark naked.

"Take me!" She threw open her arms, flopped back, and spread her legs.

He stared at her in horror—and then his instinct for self-preservation kicked in. He turned and fled down the stairs, realizing, a moment too late, that he'd dropped his clothes when he'd hit his head. At least he'd managed to keep hold of his towel.

He paused in the living area, looked around wildly—

There was no place to hide. He'd have to head for the woods. Blast! If only he'd thought to put on his boots. But there was nothing for it now. Better bruised and bloody feet than—

"Got you!" Two female arms wrapped around his waist.

Zeus, the woman could move quickly when she wanted to. He hadn't even heard her feet on the stairs, but that was likely because of the blood pounding in his ears.

He twisted in her grasp, slipped free, and put as much space between them as he could.

Unfortunately, his towel did not accompany him. It now dangled from Lady Susan's fingers.

She dropped it on the floor as her eyes dropped to examine his cock. Normally that organ swelled with pride and enthusiasm under feminine attention, but this time it shrank, as if trying to hide.

"That really is quite ugly."

It shrank a bit more. He pulled one of the chairs out from the table and stepped behind it.

"Madam, I insist you leave immediately. It is extremely improper for you to be here, especially dressed—or, rather, not dressed—as you are."

She spread her arms wide and rotated slowly, giving him a far-too-complete view of her body. "Like what you see?"

Normally he'd be kind—or at least tactful.

The time for such niceties was long past. "No."

And, to his surprise, it was true. It wasn't that Lady Susan's body was unattractive. It wasn't. It had all the requisite parts. They were even nicely shaped. But it wasn't Pen's body.

He looked down to confirm that *his* body agreed with that assessment.

It did. His cock was as small and limp as if he'd just got out of ice water.

Good God, if Pen doesn't marry me, I'll have to join a monastery.

If he'd worried for even an instant that he'd wounded Lady Susan's feelings, he needn't have. She apparently had no feelings.

She put her hands on her naked hips, arms akimbo. "What's the matter with you? I thought men were driven wild by the sight of a naked woman."

He scowled at her, insulted on behalf of his gender. "Men are not mindless beasts, madam."

She looked at him skeptically and then shrugged. "Well, that's good, then. You won't be bothering me once I've done my duty." Her lips pulled into a very unpleasant smile. "And if you do have any of those needs"—she looked down at his cock which was now shielded from her inspection by the chair—"you can take care of them with your whore."

Fury at her using that horrid word to describe Pen threatened to blind him, but he beat it back. He had to focus on his goal—getting the obnoxious woman into her clothes and out of the cottage as quickly as possible.

And to cure her of her daft notion they were going to wed.

"Madam, you seem to be laboring under a misconception. I. Am. Not. Marrying. You." He said each word slowly and distinctly so she could not miss his meaning.

"Oh, yes, you are."

Was the woman insane? He'd thought her boring, annoying, and rude, but he hadn't added Bedlamite to that list . . . yet.

"No, I'm not."

"Yes, you are."

"No. I. Am. Not." This was ridiculous. He felt like he was back at Eton, arguing with another child. "Now please get your clothing on and go back to the inn."

She crossed her arms defiantly. "You *have* to marry me. You've compromised me."

"No, I haven't." Perhaps the woman was worried she'd gone too far to draw back. He would set her fears to rest. "If you will just get dressed and leave now, no one need know any of this occurred."

He should have saved his breath.

The witch grinned at him. "You *have* compromised me— or it will look like you have, which is all that matters. There's a nice red spot on the sheet upstairs where you took my virginity—I got some pig's blood from the butcher in the village—and I left a note for Letitia to come find me here if I wasn't back in half an hour."

She smirked. "As you can tell, I don't have my watch with me at the moment, but I think we probably have less than ten minutes until she arrives."

Hot panic flooded him, speeding up his heart and breathing. How was he to save himself?

And then years of experience at getting out of difficult situations took over. He pushed aside the anxious, fearful thoughts to focus solely on the problem at hand.

Yes, he was in a bad position—he could see that. Ha! A blind man could see that. But he must remember: he was innocent. No one could force him to marry this woman. Not marrying her might cause a huge scandal—of *course* it would cause a huge scandal—but a scandal was far better than being condemned to a life sentence with this harpy. *That* was what he must keep in mind. Focusing on that truth would see him through this mess.

It might help if he could discover what was driving Lady Susan's behavior.

"Why are you doing this? Why would you want to marry a man who doesn't want you?"

She flinched a little at that, but her voice was steady and determined when she answered.

"Because I need a husband. My father told me if I did not find one this Season, he was shipping me off to my aunt in the wilds of Northumberland." Her expression hardened. "I refuse to go up there. It's cold and dark and there are more sheep than people. And I'd never see London again."

"Ah. I'm sorry." And he was. It was too bad that women didn't have more control over their destinies.

But then he thought of Pen. She'd been in a terrible position—one far worse than Lady Susan's—and yet she'd managed to chart her own course.

Still, he'd admit his indecisiveness was somewhat to blame for Lady Susan's situation. If he'd nipped things in the bud immediately, she might be betrothed to Arronder or Whately or Neardorn now.

"Would it help if I had a word with your father?"

"Only if the word is to request my hand in marriage."

The blasted woman was not going to give up.

"Madam, for the last time: I am not going to marry you."

"Yes, you are. The scandal will be enormous if you don't."

"For you. Think. If word of this"—he gestured at her nakedness and then toward the stairs and around the room—"gets out, you'll never find a husband."

She jabbed her finger at him. "I'll never find one if I'm shuttled off to Northumberland, either. And the scandal will be enormous for you, too. Earls are not supposed to ruin other earl's daughters." She sniffed derisively. "*I* am not a farmer's brat."

His anger flared again. "Careful. That 'farmer's brat' is going to be the next Countess of Darrow." *I hope.* "I can't imagine you wish to alienate her—and me." Though if Lady Susan was indeed relegated to Northumberland, he supposed it wouldn't matter.

"If word gets out you've ruined me, you won't be able to show your face in London with or without your commoner bride."

"Then I'll stay in the country. And I *haven't* ruined you. How many times do I have to say it? If any ruining's been done, you've done it to yourself."

They glared at each other in silence—a silence suddenly broken by a loud knock.

They both jumped.

Bloody hell. Harry's eyes flew to the door and then back to his towel, lying in a heap too close to Lady Susan and too far from him to reach.

Lady Susan's face lit with excitement. "Come in!" she said, and then she darted toward him.

Reflexes, honed from years of living by his wits, took over. He vaulted over the table just as the door opened.

"Letiti . . ." he said.

It wasn't Letitia. It was Pen.

Pen stood gaping on the threshold. She'd done what Harry's mother had told her to do. She'd come down to the cottage so Harry could propose. But Harry was naked and chasing a naked Lady Susan around . . .

No. That is, yes, Harry was naked and Lady Susan was naked, but it looked as if Harry was the one being chased.

"Harriet isn't with you, is she?" Harry asked, leaping behind a chair to shield his male-est bit from view.

"No." Pen closed the door behind her. The fewer people who saw this . . . whatever it was, the better.

"What are *you* doing here?" Lady Susan asked in an oddly accusatory tone for a woman standing in a man's quarters without a stitch of clothing on.

"Er." What *was* she doing there? She couldn't very well say she'd come down in the hope Harry would propose, especially given the attire—or lack thereof—of the other people in the room. Had she interrupted a tryst?

From Harry's expression, she thought not. So, what in the world *was* going on?

"Thank *God* you're here." Harry dashed over, putting his hands on her shoulders and holding her in front of him, literally hiding behind her skirts. "This woman is trying to make it look like I compromised her."

"He *did* compromise me! He took me in the room upstairs. You can see my blood upon his sheets!"

"It's pig's blood," Harry said by her ear. "Or at least, that's what she told me. She said she got it from the butcher."

"Oh." Pen tried to focus on Lady Susan's face rather than the vast expanse of skin below it. "Did you tell Mr. Sanders what you needed the pig's blood for?"

"Of course, I didn't. I—" Lady Susan's face froze as she realized she was confirming Harry's story.

Harry's hands tightened on Pen's shoulders in a quick, surreptitious hug.

Lady Susan's brows slammed down. "That is, I never spoke to any butcher. The blood is my own." She pointed at Harry. "Lord Darrow took my virginity, and now he must marry me."

Pen felt Harry stiffen and inhale as if to defend himself, so she spoke first.

"Ah. Well, that's good then. If you *had* got some pig's blood from Mr. Sanders, the story would be all over the village by now. Mr. Sanders *does* like to talk. And, of course, he'd wonder what in the world a fancy London lady like you would need pig's blood for. It would become quite the topic of speculation, as I'm sure you can imagine."

Pen would wager Lady Susan was imagining it all too well. Her face had turned a rather interesting shade of greenish white.

"When one of the women at the Home was getting ready

to marry the haberdasher in the next village over," Pen said, "she found herself in a similar predicament. She had somehow neglected to tell her husband-to-be that she *wasn't* a virgin, and felt it too, er, complicated to mention the matter at such a late date. So, she needed some blood, as well. Only, she knew better than to get it from Mr. Sanders."

Pen smiled and said in what she tried to make sound like a helpful tone, "I believe she ended up just pricking her finger and smearing it on the sheets. You might consider that the next time you try to trap a man into marriage."

She heard Harry chuckle—well, *felt* him chuckle, since he'd now wrapped his arms around her and pulled her tightly back against him.

"Zeus, I love you, Pen," he murmured, stirring her hair and tickling her ear.

She grinned. Perhaps his mother was right. Perhaps he *was* going to propose—as soon as she could get rid of the annoying Lady Susan.

The woman was scowling now, her mouth opening and closing like a fish's.

"You should get dressed, you know," Pen said. "It's really not the thing to stand around naked like that."

"Oh!" Lady Susan was almost spitting. "You . . . you . . ."

Heavens! Was she going to suffer an apoplexy right before Pen's eyes?

Evil satisfaction tinged with genuine alarm filled her chest—followed by a touch of guilt.

I should be better than this—

"You *worm*!"

Or perhaps not.

"You baseborn whore." Spittle did indeed fly from Lady Susan's lips. "You aren't fit to empty my chamber pot."

Pen heard—and felt—Harry make a low growling sound.

She rubbed her hands up and down his bare arms to soothe and distract him. To her surprise, she wasn't the slightest bit wounded by Lady Susan's words—likely because she had Harry's naked body pressed against her back.

If this was some sort of contest, Pen had already won the prize.

"No one in London will accept you. The *ton* will turn its back on you. They'll slam their doors in your face. You'll be a laughingstock."

"Pen," Harry said in a tight voice, "you don't have to listen to this woman's vile words."

"I know," she said quietly, "but as long as she's just shouting, I think we should let her blather on." She patted one of his naked forearms. "The only alternative is to leave, and you aren't precisely dressed to go out."

She felt him chuckle. "True."

Lady Susan was full-out shrieking now. "Even Lord Darrow's mother and sister-in-law will shun you. They want *me* to marry him. *Me,* do you hear?"

"I expect they can hear you all the way in the village," said another voice.

"Letitia?" Pen and Harry said in unison.

Harry shuffled around so Pen shielded him from his sister-in-law as well as Lady Susan.

Letitia stepped inside, shutting the door carefully behind her and addressing it instead of turning to face the people in the room.

"Sorry," she said. "I tried knocking but no one seemed to hear me. Do you suppose you could get dressed, Harry? And you, too, Lady Susan?"

"Letitia, thank God you are here," Lady Susan said, ignoring her request. "Your brother-in-law raped me—"

Pen felt Harry stiffen.

"I did not!"

"—and is now refusing to marry me."

"Because I didn't rape you," Harry said heatedly. "I didn't touch you."

"So why are you naked, Harry?" Letitia asked the door.

Pen would like to hear the answer to that question as well. She wished she could see Harry's expression, but he was still using her as a shield.

"He's naked because he was having his wicked way with me!" Lady Susan said dramatically.

"I'm naked because I'd just come back from bathing in the pond when I discovered Lady Susan sitting on my bed. My towel's over there on the floor. It was around my waist until she grabbed it away from me."

Pen hadn't noticed the towel before.

Lady Susan stepped forward, putting her body in the way as if to block Pen's view. If she'd been wearing a dress, she'd have been successful. As it was, she just gave Pen a closer look at her hairy shins and thick ankles.

"He came down to get some"—Lady Susan glanced around and saw the decanter on the mantel—"brandy to ply me with alcohol."

"It's empty," Harry said.

Lady Susan ignored him. "His clothes are upstairs—"

"Where I was going to get clean ones."

"—by the bed where he dropped them."

"By the door where I hit my head when you ambushed me. Pen knows how low that ceiling is."

Pen nodded. "Yes. It's a very, very small room with a very low ceiling."

"I was just stepping over the threshold when I discovered Lady Susan lying—er, well, sitting—in wait. She startled me, and I whacked my head. As soon as I recovered my senses—and saw her flop back on the bed—I fled." Pen felt Harry's body move as if he was shrugging. "Though to be honest, I'm not certain where I would have fled to, dressed only in a towel. I was *very* happy when Pen arrived."

Lady Susan had her hands on her hips. Now she jabbed a

finger in their direction. Pen had to marvel at how she could stand there naked and carry on as if she were dressed for tea.

Perhaps she's clothed in desperation.

"Do not believe him, Letitia. My blood is on his sheets."

"It's pig's blood," Harry said. "She admitted as much to me."

"It will be easy enough to find out about the blood," Pen offered. "Just ask the butcher."

Letitia finally turned away from the door, but directed her gaze at the ceiling to avoid all the nakedness.

"No need. When I got your note, Lady Susan, I asked Bess if she'd seen you—I thought you might have come back and I'd missed you. She said she hadn't and then asked what you wanted the vial of pig's blood for." Letitia sighed. "Well, actually, she'd guessed what you wanted it for. She was just interested in whether I thought you'd be successful in trapping the earl into marriage."

That surprised a laugh out of Pen. Trust Bess to get to the heart of the matter. "Bess lived up at the Home before she took over at the inn. She knows all the tricks."

Lady Susan's face—well, her entire body—flushed with anger. She stomped her foot on the floor, but since it was as naked as the rest of her, it didn't make much sound.

"Get dressed, madam," Harry said. "It's past time for you to leave."

"Yes." Letitia nodded. "Please. You are embarrassing— and not just because you insist on displaying every inch of skin God gave you."

Lady Susan glared at Letitia, and then she glared at Pen and Harry, and then she finally—*finally*—turned and went upstairs.

Letitia walked over to pick the towel off the floor and bring it to Harry, all the while keeping her eyes averted.

"I'm sorry, Letitia." Harry let go of Pen to wrap the towel around his middle—and Pen immediately missed the warmth of his body. "I assume you and Mama will have to share the traveling coach with that shrew all the way back to London."

"Yes." Letitia grimaced. "She was a terrible companion on the way here. Now . . ." She shrugged. "I can only hope she'll sulk in a corner for the entire journey. If she doesn't, I suppose I shall offer it up as penance for having been daft enough to think she'd make you a suitable wife."

And then Letitia smiled at Pen. "Lord Muddlegate was with Bess in the tavern. He's become quite a fan of your Widow's Brew."

Pen nodded. "So Lady Darrow told me."

Harry's brows rose. "You were talking to my mother?"

"Yes. She came up to the Home to meet Harriet." She was not going to say more about that visit until she and Harry were alone.

"How did she know you were there?"

"Lady Susan told her."

Harry's brows rose higher.

"While you and I were talking," Letitia said, "Lady Susan went back to the inn. Muddles told me he and your mother were sitting in the tavern when she confronted them."

Letitia turned to Pen. "He also said Lady Darrow was very excited to discover you were here, Pen. She'd known you'd had a child—"

"Wait." Harry's voice suddenly was tight with anger. "Mama knew Pen was increasing and never told me?"

"She thought the child was Walter's," Pen said.

"Oh." Harry frowned. "Why?"

"Because Walter was the one who was notorious for sowing wild oats." Letitia's voice was dry and bitter.

"But Pen and *Walter?*" Harry asked. "How could Mama have thought that? Pen would never—"

Harry stopped abruptly, his mouth still open, perhaps finally realizing that he was wading into dangerous waters.

He cleared his throat. "That is, I would have thought Mama would have noticed that Pen and I, er . . ."

Pen touched Harry's arm. "Remember? Your mother spent that summer at Darrow House."

"When I was pregnant with Bianca," Letitia said, "and right after she was born."

"Oh. Right. Yes. I do remember now."

"In any event," Letitia moved on from that awkward topic, "Lady Darrow set off at once for the Home, leaving Muddles at the inn with his tankard and instructions to tell me where she'd gone."

At that point, Lady Susan stomped down the stairs—now that she had her shoes on, she could express her anger more effectively—and over to glare at them again.

Well, no. She focused all her ire on Pen. "Think carefully before you agree to marry the earl," she said in a low, furious voice. "The *ton* will never accept a farmer's brat as Countess of Darrow."

"That's enough, Lady Susan," Harry said.

The woman kept her eyes on Pen. "It's for her own good. She probably doesn't realize how completely she'll be shunned."

True, Pen had never been to London, but she wasn't about to accept Lady Susan's belittling comment in silence.

"I've met you, haven't I?" Pen said. "I think I have a very good idea how shallow and mean the *ton* can be." Brave words said in what she hoped was a firm voice to mask the fact that she was shaking like a leaf inside. Yes, Harry's mother had said she'd support her, and she assumed Letitia would as well, but ... .

But she was getting ahead of herself. Nothing was settled between her and Harry yet.

"If I hear the faintest whisper you've uttered one word against Mrs. Barnes," Harry said in a cold, hard voice, "I will feel compelled to share the details of today's antics.

I'm sure the men at White's will be greatly entertained by the story of your unsuccessful, *naked* attempt to trap me into marrying you."

That got Lady Susan to look away from Pen.

"You wouldn't do that," she said, frowning at Harry. But her face had grown very pale and her voice lacked conviction.

"Oh, yes, I would. I give you my word. Breathe one syllable against Mrs. Barnes, and you will very much regret it." His smile was as cold as his voice. "Even in the wilds of Northumberland."

"Come along, Lady Susan," Letitia said, opening the door. "It's past time for us to go."

Lady Susan glared at Harry and then at Pen, and then she followed Letitia out the door, leaving Pen alone with Harry.

Finally.

Chapter Eighteen

It was very, very quiet once the door closed. Harry looked at Pen.

She was looking at the floor. Hell.

This was not going to be easy.

It *should* be easy. With any other woman, he'd be certain of an immediate *yes* and a quick retreat to the bed upstairs. After all, he was going to offer to make Pen his *wife*, not his mistress. It would mean wealth and prestige, but likely more important to her, security for her and Harriet.

And love. She must know it would mean love.

Good God, she'd been willing to marry the vicar—the current one or his replacement—to provide for their daughter. Surely, this was a better bargain.

But this was Pen. There was no telling how she would react.

"I'm sorry about Lady Susan," he said. Start at the edges of an issue, the non-threatening, less important parts. Find agreement—and then build on that. That strategy had worked well for him in diplomatic situations. He hoped it would work here, too, in the most important negotiation of his life.

She looked up. A smile wavered across her lips. "That was very odd."

He laughed. "Odd? It was beyond bizarre." At the time, he'd felt like he was caught in a nightmare, but now that it was over, he could see its comedic aspects.

He touched his head gingerly. "I thought I was going to pass out, I hit the lintel so hard. I have quite a lump."

Was she going to offer to kiss it and make it better?

Of course not.

"I'm very glad you are not going to marry her."

"So am I." He'd had a close escape there. Now that he was free, he had to wonder why he'd considered allying himself with the harpy in the first place. Had he been mad?

No. You knew if you couldn't have Pen, it didn't matter whom you married.

"She would have made your life miserable."

"Yes." Why hadn't he realized it sooner? It seemed so obvious now. It *wasn't* a person's birth that mattered. It was their character.

An uneasy silence settled over the room again.

He needed to tell Pen he loved her. He needed to ask— *beg*—her to marry him.

He couldn't form the words.

Damnation. He'd calmly faced down any number of men who wanted to kill or maim him and had matched wits with some of the brightest men and women in Britain and on the Continent. Why was he so hesitant to come to the point and say what he wanted—what he *needed*—to say?

Not hesitant. Afraid.

No, make that *terrified*. There was no non-threatening, less important part to this negotiation. It wasn't, in fact, a negotiation at all. It was a point of hard decision. A turning point. If he offered and Pen declined, he'd lose everything: his heart, his happiness, his hope. He'd be an empty husk, moving through life as a soulless automaton.

His brain told him he was being melodramatic. His heart told him he was, if anything, understating the case.

Pen took a deep breath as if she'd come to some decision—some unpleasant decision he'd guess from the way she squared her shoulders.

Oh, what the bloody hell. Better to be brave and go out in a beautiful, bright explosion than be a coward and slither through the dirt to vanish into a narrow crevice.

"I love you," he said, before she could speak.

She paused. "And I love you, too, Harry, but—"

He stepped close to her and laid one finger on her lips. "Marry me, Pen. Please? I promise you won't regret it. I'll strive every day, every minute, to see that you don't."

He hadn't meant to grovel, but once he let the words free, that was where they went.

Pen's eyes smiled at him as she gently pushed his finger aside. Did she think he was fooling?

He tried to grasp her hand, but it slipped away—just as he felt *her* slipping away.

Panic rose in his throat, but he swallowed it down . . . for now.

"I don't know, Harry."

Well, that was better than no. "What can I say—or do—to convince you?"

She laughed at that. "No *doing,* Harry." She looked at him—and looked away. "And put some clothes on."

He was not leaving her until this was finished. He was too afraid if he went upstairs now, he'd come down to find her gone and he would lose her forever.

It wasn't a sensible, rational thought, but he wasn't feeling very sensible or rational at the moment.

"Only if you'll come upstairs with me."

Pen shook her head. "Oh, no. I know better than to do that."

Oh? His cock stirred. Could he seduce Pen into marrying him?

Perhaps, but that would not be the honorable thing to do, unfortunately. Nor would it get him what he really wanted—Pen's enthusiastic, unconditional agreement. A yes now would mean nothing if she wished later she'd said no.

"Harry, I came down here with the thought that I *would* marry you. Your mother was very persuasive. She made light of my birth, my history, my ignorance—she brushed it all aside and made me think I could indeed become the Countess of Darrow."

"And you can!"

Pen shook her head slowly. Sadly. "No, I can't. Lady Susan brought that truth firmly home to me just now. She's right. The *ton* won't accept a farmer's brat. They'll shun me—and they'll shun Harriet." Her voice grew thin. She took a deep, shuddery breath. "My lowly origins will burden any legitimate children we might have and likely cause people to look askance at you as well. I can't let that happen."

She put a hand on his arm—and then snatched it back as if the touch of his warm flesh had burned her. "It's better this way."

"No, it's not. I *love* you."

"Now. But think, Harry. Would you still love me after years of watching your friends snub me? After seeing your children laughed at—or, worse, ostracized—because of their mother's birth? Or would your love erode, bit by bit, day by day, with each new insult?" She shook her head and looked away from him. "Love isn't everything, and it doesn't exist in a vacuum."

Letitia said much the same . . .

But Letitia's love had died because of Walter. Death had come from within the marriage, not from outside it. Hell, he doubted Walter had been capable of love. He certainly hadn't been able to manage fidelity.

His love was real. He would stand with Pen. They would face every trial together.

She started for the door. "You've had a hard year with the death of Walter and all the changes it brought—all your new responsibilities. And then having your mother and sister-in-law push you to marry—it's been too much. I'm sure next Season, after you've given yourself time to settle into things—and if your relatives don't badger you—you'll have more luck finding a proper bride."

His control snapped. *"Stop!"*

He walked over to stand an inch from Pen. He couldn't touch her. He didn't trust himself.

"Yes, the last year has been hell. Bloody hell." He wasn't shouting, but the words came out hard and sharp like blows. He saw Pen flinch, and he was sorry for it, but she'd called this out of him, and he thought she was strong enough to take it.

"You know why it's been so hellish?" He didn't expect her to answer—he swept on without giving her time to say anything. At this point he couldn't stop the flow of words. If he tried, he'd explode.

"It was hellish because I was alone. No one understood *me*. I wasn't Harry anymore, I was the Earl of Darrow. Can you understand that? The person I've become over all the years of my life"—he opened the fingers on both hands, stretching them wide—"gone like a puff of smoke. People wanted to meet the earl, talk to the earl, marry the earl. In some horribly strange way I'd become Walter and my father."

"I'm sor—"

The words wouldn't stop for apologies.

"You don't know how to be a countess? Well, I don't know how to be a bloody earl. I wasn't raised to be one—that was Walter's job. I was going to find my own way. I *did* find my own way. And then Walter died and I had to give it all up."

He ran his hands through his hair, remembering how desperate he'd felt—*still* felt.

"I mourned Walter, but you know we were never close. I felt badly that a man was cut down in his prime, leaving my sister-in-law a widow and my nieces without a father, but I was angry, too. Walter had been careless, bloody irresponsible, and now I and everyone else had to pay the price."

He felt Pen's hand on his arm, stroking, soothing, but still he couldn't stop.

"I am not a child, Pen. I've lived as many—more—years on this earth than you have. I haven't spent the last decade prancing around in starched linen and dancing shoes. Don't you patronize me and pat me on the head and tell me all will be well next year because it *fucking* won't."

"Harry." Pen wrapped her arms around him.

He clutched her to him as if she was the one thing keeping him from slipping under—or being pulled under by his dark feelings.

She probably was.

"Don't tell me how I'm going to feel, Pen. Don't tell me love isn't important. I know life is hard and sometimes people die and sometimes bad things happen. And I know—or I can see—that love isn't everything. But it's a lot. It's more than anything else I know. I don't want to give it up. I don't want to live a nice, proper life with a nice, proper, pedigreed wife. I'd rather stand against the whole fucking *ton* with you than dance in their bloody ballrooms with someone else."

Harry was holding her too tightly. She could barely breathe.

Well, and she was holding him tightly, too. And crying. That didn't make breathing any easier.

Finally, he let her go. He stepped away without looking at her, turned his back, and kept it turned as he sniffed several times.

She pulled out her handkerchief and handed it to him.

He took it and turned away again, blowing his nose. "Pardon me. I apologize for . . ." He paused as if searching for the proper word.

For baring his soul? For letting down his defenses?

"For such an unseemly lack of control."

He was back to being the Earl of Darrow. Though even the Harry she'd known years ago had never been as open as he'd been just now.

Not that they'd spent much time talking that summer.

She went over and wrapped her arms around him again, pressing her cheek against his warm back.

"I'm sorry, Harry."

He stiffened and then broke her hold, stepping away again, still not looking at her. "Yes. I understand. I should go . . ."

His voice trailed off. He must have realized that he was the one staying here. If anyone was to leave, it would be her.

She wasn't leaving.

"I'm sorry I didn't understand. I . . ." He'd been honest. She should be, too. "I'm afraid."

That got him to turn toward her. "Of what?" And then he saw that she'd been crying, too. "Oh, Pen."

He opened his arms. It might have been—likely was—an involuntary movement, but she took it as an invitation. It was going to be easier to say what she had to say against his chest than looking him in the eye.

Oh! She was enveloped in his comforting scent. Even breathing through a stuffy nose, she could smell it—the mix of cologne and soap and Harry.

"My whole life, I've had no one to rely on but myself, Harry. I had no mother, and my father—" The less said about her father, the better.

Harry's arms, which had held her loosely when she'd first pressed herself against him, tightened.

"I know, Pen. You were always so brave."

She shook her head. "On the outside perhaps. On the inside I was terrified. And when I discovered I was pregnant—" Lord, the fear she'd felt then had almost paralyzed her.

Perhaps it had been fortuitous that the earl had offered Felix as her only marital option. If he'd suggested *anyone* else, she might be—likely would be—long married now.

"I'm so sorry I wasn't there with you," he said, tightening his hold further. "I'm sorry you had to face that all alone."

What would have happened if he *had* been there? She couldn't see an eighteen-year-old Harry marrying her—or, perhaps more to the point, his father allowing such a thing.

"I had my aunt to go to." Thank God Aunt Margaret had taken her in. If she hadn't—no, she refused to let her thoughts go down that dark path again.

"But then she died and I was on my own once more, with Harriet to take care of. I *had* to be strong." She tilted her head back to look up at him. "I would do anything for Harriet, Harry. Anything. I'd give my life for her."

"I know."

What she hadn't fully realized until just now was that, to be strong, she'd built such thick walls around herself that she'd kept everyone—even Jo and Caro—out. Everyone but Harriet.

And Harry?

Perhaps even Harry. Oh, the memory of the hope and strength he'd given her when she was young was firmly in her heart. But . . .

Was she afraid to let him be more than a memory, to let him be her life as much as Harriet was?

No. *More* than Harriet. Harriet would grow up and leave her.

Her daughter was bound to her by blood. Harry would be linked only by choice. By love.

Do I have the courage to trust in love?

"I could have married Godfrey—well, no, now that I know how vile he is, I couldn't have. But before I knew that, I thought I could marry him because I'd be giving him only my body. Not my heart. He'd never have touched my h-heart. But if I marry you—"

She swallowed, pushing her panic down. Harry waited, one hand rubbing her back, comforting her.

"If I marry you, I risk everything."

"I won't hurt you, Pen. I swear I won't."

"I know you wouldn't mean to, but think, Harry." She snuffled several times, wiped her nose on her sleeve, and stepped back so she could look him in the face without craning her neck.

"Lady Susan was right. The *ton* won't accept me, and while you say that doesn't matter to you now, it might matter later. And then, if you turned away from me, if you took lovers like Walter did—" She drew in a deep, shuddery breath. "I think it would kill me." She tried to laugh, but it came out more as a gurgle. "Or I'd kill you."

That made him smile. He put his hands on her shoulders. "Pen, none of us can predict the future, but I hope you know me better than that. Do you *really* believe I'm that shallow? That fickle?"

"N-no." She'd thought him perfect when she was young. But she must be honest, no matter how painful it was to say the words. "But you were a boy when you left Darrow. You've been away for years. You've changed. We've both changed." She wiped her nose on her sleeve again. Too bad she'd given him her handkerchief. "I can't let what I *want* blind me to what *is,* especially since I have Harriet to consider."

The responsibility of a child did tend to focus one's thoughts.

Harry was frowning. "But you can't let fear blind you

either. To have changed that much, I'd have to be a different person."

"But *haven't* you changed, Harry? Just this morning you were planning to marry Lady Susan and wanted me to be your mistress." A bitter feeling of disillusionment gnawed at her. "Or were you always that way and I never saw it?" Perhaps she was blinder than she knew.

"No." Harry frowned. "I admit I was wrong—in so many ways—about marriage, but in my defense, I didn't know any better. A marriage of convenience is what my parents had and my brother. It's the normal arrangement in the *ton*. It's what Lady Susan wanted. She said as much to me just now."

He pushed Pen's hair back from her face. "But my heart knew, Pen. I just had to listen to it."

He shook his head. "I stalled all Season. I kept putting the matter off. I *knew* I was on the wrong path, headed toward a cliff, but I thought I had no other option. It took seeing you again—and discovering I had a daughter—to make me realize I could choose a different way—no, to realize I *wanted* a different way."

She wanted to believe him, but . . .

"You saw me and met Harriet two days ago and yet still this morning you planned to marry Lady Susan."

He grinned. "I'm not always the most nimble-witted, apparently." And then his expression turned serious again. "No, actually, I do need to thank Lady Susan for that. She was so shrewish and, well, *evil* to you and Harriet by the stream that she tore the scales from my eyes."

He cupped her jaw with his hands. "I don't want a marriage of convenience, Pen." He pulled a face. "What a misnomer! There would be nothing at all convenient about yoking myself to Lady Susan or any of her ilk."

He shook his head. "No, I want a *real* marriage, a marriage where I can share life's burdens and joys"—he grinned, waggling his brows, which made her giggle—"*and* have my 'animal needs' attended to. I think that would be *much* more convenient, don't you?"

She felt her resistance—and other things—begin to melt. It was very hard to withstand Harry when he smiled like that—especially when he was dressed in nothing more than a towel. His naked chest was *extremely* distracting.

He must have sensed that she was wavering, because his voice took on a cajoling tone.

"I *need* you, Pen. I think you've always been my compass, my North Star, even when you were here and I was on the Continent. You know *me*—Harry. You'll keep me from losing myself in the Earl of Darrow."

"Well . . ." It was true. She felt as if she knew him—and he knew her.

"My mother and Letitia think we should marry."

"Yes, but . . ." Surely, having Harry's mother and sister-in-law in favor of their union would help her face Society . . .

I did tell Harriet I'd thumb my nose at the ton.

"And you don't have to worry about Lady Susan. She's on the fringes of Polite Society—and, if what she told me is true, will soon be even farther removed. Leagues away—literally—in the wilds of Northumberland." He shrugged. "Pardon me for saying it but a lot of people will be delighted by her absence."

Pen would admit without the slightest hesitation that *she* would be delighted.

"I came to Little Puddledon as much to escape her as to help Grainger, you know." Harry smiled as his fingers played with an errant strand of her hair. "I really must thank the duke for that. He wanted me away from Lady Susan. Told me he'd have to cut our connection if I married her."

"Really?" Pen frowned. It was very hard to think when

Harry was touching her like this. She should step back out of his reach.

She didn't want to. "But that doesn't mean he'll prefer me."

"Oh, I can guarantee you he will—you don't chatter constantly about nothing like she does."

A little bubble of happiness grew in her chest. Perhaps she *could* marry Harry. "I have been known to go on and on about greenflies and mildew, though."

"I shall warn him, though he *is* a landowner. Perhaps he is interested in such things."

"And I do know something about agricultural theory."

"Ah." Harry's brow arched up, his eyes laughing. "The men will be shoving me aside to listen to you on that subject, I am sure."

And then his smile slid away. "So, will you marry me, Pen, and be my wife and the mother of my children? You have my solemn word that I will love and cherish you all the days of my life—even when you speak of greenflies." His lips quirked up at the edges. "Though I do not promise to listen to you on that subject."

She laughed. "I have some very interesting things to say about greenflies, you know."

"Mmm." He was starting to take the pins out of her hair. "I'm sure you do."

His fingers felt wonderful—but then he pulled his hands back so he was no longer touching her.

"*Will* you marry me, Pen? Because if you won't, we should stop this, and I should go upstairs—alone—and get dressed."

She looked at him. "Are you quite, *quite* certain, Harry? Farmers' daughters aren't supposed to marry earls."

"*This* farmer's daughter is supposed to marry *this* earl." He grinned. "I feel quite, *quite* certain of it." His grin widened. "Just think of me as another farmer, only one with a bigger farm."

She wanted so badly to say yes. "I'm used to working, you know."

"You'll have plenty to keep you busy." He leered at her, but then said, "And if you have extra time, I'm sure you can start a hopyard at Darrow."

She hadn't thought of that. "Do you have a brewhouse?"

"I believe so, but don't ask me for the details—and don't tell Miss Anderson."

Pen laughed. "She's got her hands full here. She might be interested in seeing if the village tavern at Darrow would care to sell Widow's Brew, though."

"I will leave those negotiations to you as my wife." He raised his brow. "Assuming you *are* my wife. *Will* you have me, Pen?"

She wanted to say yes, but . . .

"People will talk."

"People will always talk. People love to talk. I find I really don't care much what people say. The people who matter will support us—my mother and sister-in-law, Grainger and my true friends. As for the others?" He snapped his fingers. "Just think of them as greenflies on your hop plants. We will pick them out of our lives like the annoying bugs they are."

That made her laugh.

"Say yes, Pen. Please. My life isn't complete without you."

And hers wasn't complete without him. She'd thought Harriet was enough, that she'd spent all her love on her daughter, but she'd been wrong. She had more love—a different sort of love—for Harry.

She'd swear she felt her heart expand then. Now that she'd taken down her walls, there was room for it to grow.

She'd thought the walls had protected her, but perhaps they'd just imprisoned her.

But he's an earl—

Right. An exalted sort of farmer.

She looked into his handsome and oh, so, precious and familiar face.

Be fearless . . .

Harry made her fearless.

She *was* going to marry him. It might be mad, but she was going to do it.

"Very well. Yes. I accept your offer."

His grin was blinding.

Her grin must be equally blinding . . . and then she frowned. "But I can't leave the Home until after we harvest the hops, you know." Regrettable, but true.

"When will that be?" His fingers went back to work on her hair.

"A week or two. Maybe three."

He nodded, pulling the last pin free. "I'll talk to Grainger about replacing the vicar. If he can do it quickly, we can be married by license here."

He combed his fingers through her hair. It felt wonderful.

And then he bent his head to whisper by her ear, "I hope you don't mean to make me wait until then." His lips touched her skin and she shivered.

She couldn't wait.

We should tell Harriet . . .

Harriet was with her grandmother. They could tell her— and Harry's mother and Letitia—soon enough. They had something more important to attend to first.

She put her hands on his chest—his warm, bare chest. "Let's go upstairs."